ENDANGERED

A KATE REID NOVEL
BOOK 5

ROBIN MAHLE

HARP HOUSE PUBLISHING, LLC.

Published by HARP House Publishing
July, 2016 (1st edition)

1

The flight attendant waited until the crosscheck was complete before opening the door of the craft. One by one, passengers were freed from the confines of the flying tin can that packed them in with increasing density. Among them was Special Agent Nick Scarborough and, as he deplaned, the steamy air proved stifling from the moment he stepped onto the gangway. Virginia was in the midst of an early summer heatwave and Nick had spent the past week in Maine. The dramatic change in temperature was a jolt to his system.

An amendment to his original itinerary had come by way of a phone call from an old friend and now he found himself arriving days earlier than intended and standing in the middle of Ronald Reagan Airport, ready to drive to the heart of Fairfax County. It was a call he'd wished he had never received, and as he made his way through the terminal and toward the parking garage, Nick recalled their last meeting. It had been at a bar, toasting Nick's recent appointment to SSA status. *Has it been that long?* he thought.

An old buddy from Nick's early days at the Bureau, Jake Talbot, summoned him because his son had been missing for the past twenty-four hours. They'd kept in touch over the years from their first meeting while Jake worked in data analysis, though he'd since moved on to the private sector. However, he knew his friend had risen in the ranks of the FBI and was desperate for his guidance. The twelve-year-old boy hadn't returned home after baseball practice only half a mile away. Jake and his wife, Rachel, had been working late, leaving their eldest son in charge, who called his parents after being unable to reach his brother, Colton. When both parents arrived home, the boy was still missing.

The frantic call reached Nick's ears late yesterday afternoon while still attending the conference in Bangor on new forensics techniques. He left early and was now on his way to the Talbot home.

The air conditioner in his SUV was cranked to full blast and was beginning to cool the sweltering car. Nick's suit jacket, which he was still wearing, seemed counterintuitive and he quickly shed the coat, tossing it onto the passenger seat.

Fairfax County Police was already on the case, but Jake called upon his friend, knowing where Nick's expertise lay and praying he might offer assistance to the local authorities.

By mid-morning, Nick reached the Talbot home; a newly constructed two-story in the suburbs recently acquired by the two-income family. He was not the first to arrive, however, and he spotted the unmarked car that undoubtedly belonged to the detective assigned to the case. The last thing he wanted to do was to step on anyone's toes, so he would sit back and listen until he could offer something useful.

Nick locked up the car and made his way to the front door. His arrival had been noticed and Jake now stood on the front porch. The man had sallow cheeks and dark circles under his eyes; it wasn't a stretch to assume he'd had little to no sleep since this horrific new reality surfaced. The two were relatively close in age and it startled Nick to see his friend looking so much older than he. It had been a few years since they'd seen each other, but given Nick's choice of career, he should have been the one appearing more aged by comparison. However, Nick didn't have any children, and perhaps that made all the difference.

"Jake, buddy." Nick offered his hand on approach and pulled the man into an embrace. After a brief pat on the back, he stepped away. "Any news?"

Jake shook his head. "Come in. Rachel's anxious to see you." He led the way inside where his wife sat at the kitchen table across from a woman he could only assume was the detective. "Rachel, Nick's here." His hoarse voice barely carried across the room.

Rachel had been a stunner from what Nick could recall, but right now, she appeared lost, saddened, and heartbroken, and it was difficult to see any beauty beyond that. "Rachel, it's good to see you." He bowed to kiss her cheek.

"You too, Nick. You're looking well."

Any response on his part would be trivial and so he merely shrugged his shoulders. He turned his attention to the woman next to her. "And you must be the detective assigned to the investigation?"

"Detective Andrea Mason, Major Crimes Unit."

Her firm grip left the impression that this was her jurisdiction, in case he was mistaken. In fact, it wasn't his intention to be anything more than a sounding board for his friend. "Special Agent Nick Scarborough. BAU, Washington Field Office. I'm just here as a family friend, Detective Mason, so please—continue." He took a seat at the end of the table.

"Can I get you anything, Nick?" Jake asked.

"Water would be great, thank you."

"As I was saying, Mrs. Talbot, we'd like to continue enlisting the help of volunteers for the search party in hopes of broadening our area."

"Here you go." Jake placed a glass of water on the table and walked toward his wife to sit next to her. "How many do we have so far?" he asked the detective.

"Thirty. Along with fifteen of our officers, we'll be able to cover a large area from the baseball field, south toward the Walmart, and north toward the gas station. I figure about half a mile wide. It'll take two shifts, but we can cover that area by tomorrow morning. Officer Newsome is on site now, organizing the search."

"Then what are we waiting for?" Rachel looked at Jake. "We need to get out there."

"Okay." Detective Mason rose from the table. "Agent Scarborough, will you be joining us?"

Nick waited for Jake's confirmation. "Of course."

THE SEARCH HAD BEGUN to unfold and several volunteers were making headway. "I can't thank you enough for coming out here with us, Nick. I know you must have your hands full." Jake moved a large stick back and forth in front of him, taking caution with each step through the overgrown lots behind the baseball field.

"Nothing else needs my attention more than this right now." He was silent for a moment, recognizing a scene he'd witnessed many times before. "So, when did you last hear from Colton?"

"Right after school, before he started practice. He sent me a text message just letting me know where he was."

"He sent me the same text," Rachel began. The three had each been separated by ten feet and so she had to raise her voice over the sound of others walking alongside them. "We were both still at work. It was about three o'clock."

"And you said Scott tried to reach him around five when he should've already made it home?"

"Yes," Jake began. "He was already home from school and knew what time Colton finished up. He called me around 5:30, when I was on my way home, to let me know Colton hadn't made it back and wasn't answering his cell. That's when I tried him. It just went to voicemail."

"Straight to voicemail, like it had been turned off," Rachel added.

Jake acknowledged his wife and continued. "I got home shortly after six. The three of us jumped in my car and we drove around looking for him. We called his friends. No one had seen him since practice."

"We searched for about three hours before deciding to call the police," Rachel said. "I guess we thought he was just out messing around or something and lost track of time. But it was well past dark and he knew better."

The blistering sun was making its way higher in the blue sky right along with the heat. Nick considered the story as they moved carefully through the brush, wiping the sweat from his brow. He wished they hadn't waited so long to make the initial call to the police. The first hours were critical in any missing persons case, although he understood why they assumed the boy was probably elsewhere with friends. Parents don't believe their kid will be the one to go missing until it happens. "Where's Scott now?" Nick asked.

"He's with Rachel's parents. I didn't think it was a good idea to have him out here. I mean, Christ, he's only fifteen. He doesn't need to see..." Jake trailed off after noticing Rachel's eyes redden again.

Several feet ahead and to the west, they heard someone shouting.

"Over here! Over here!" the man said.

"Oh God!" Rachel sprinted in the direction of the cries.

"Oh hell." Jake followed a few steps behind her.

Nick feared the worst as he made his way toward the growing crowd huddled around something they'd found. He spotted Detective Mason just feet in front of him. "Do we know what's going on up there?"

"One of my officers radioed me. Said someone found a cell phone."

He felt relief wash over him because at least it wasn't the boy's body. Although this find wasn't much better. It would only confirm the theory that he had been abducted.

"Is that his phone?" Rachel clung to Jake as they neared the item.

Detective Mason raced to catch up to them. "Just hang on a

second. Don't touch anything." She pushed through the crowd and spotted a cell phone. It was face up, but the screen was broken.

"That's his phone." Rachel stepped closer. "That's his phone." She covered her mouth and tears streamed down her face. "Oh God." She turned away and screamed toward the open grounds. "Colton! Colton!"

Jake pulled her close. "Rachel, honey. Calm down, baby. We don't know anything yet."

"We need to bag this," Detective Mason said to one of her officers. "You're sure it's Colton's?" she asked the parents, who were still huddled together.

"Yes," Jake said. "His screen wasn't broken, but it has the same blue cover."

"We'll get this to Forensics ASAP." Turning to the crowd, she continued, "Let's keep at it, people. We're burning daylight."

Kate's cell phone flashed and began to buzz on her nightstand. She turned to answer it, noting that it was one o'clock in the morning. The call was from Nick. She glanced at Mike, who was lying next to her, sound asleep, and raised, quietly padding into the living room.

"Nick? What's going on? Where are you?" Kate tried to keep her voice down so as not to wake Mike, but she hadn't heard from him since yesterday when he landed and had begun to worry.

"I'm still in Springfield. We found a cell phone and the

parents confirmed it was their son's, but I need to be here for a few days. Just until we can get a handle on what's going on."

"Does Dwight know?"

"Yes. I called him just before you. I asked him to let Campbell know what happened. I don't think it'll be a problem unless anything comes up."

"Dwight and I will have it covered until you return. I'm still assisting him with the Ackerman case."

"What's left to do there? I thought the federal prosecutor had everything he needed."

"I guess there are a few loose ends, but we should have it wrapped up by week's end. Don't worry about us. You just take care of what you got going on right now." Kate heard footsteps and, from the shadowed hall, Mike emerged. She smiled.

"What's up?" he whispered.

Kate put her hand over the speaker. "It's Nick. I'll just be a minute."

Mike nodded and made his way into the kitchen, grabbing a bottle of water from the fridge.

"Who's that?" Nick asked.

"Oh, sorry. That's just Mike. Listen, let us know if you need anything at all. If we can help, you know we will."

"I know. I'd better let you get back to bed. I'll touch base again soon. Goodnight, Kate." Nick ended the call and leaned against the large oak that encompassed much of the backyard of the Talbot home. Gazing at the vivid stars that rested against a black sky, he worried for this family and what it would do to them if they lost their boy. It was a circumstance he'd faced many times, but this was different; these people were his friends.

Nick had gone outside, unable to sleep after the long day, and imagined Jake and Rachel were probably staring at their bedroom ceiling right about now. He pressed Kate's contact information again just to look at her picture. Her face was comforting. Months had passed since Georgia was transferred from the WFO and while he'd come to terms with the end of that relationship, he had yet to come to terms with his newly acknowledged feelings for Kate. She knew nothing of them and would never know as far as Nick was concerned. Her relationship with Deputy Mike Burgess had blossomed and they seemed to spend all of their spare time together now. Nick believed it was only a matter of time before Burgess pulled up roots and moved in with her.

So, as far as Kate knew, Nick was still her closest friend, probably best friend, only ahead of Dwight by a marginal amount. He would not ruin the happiness she seemed to have finally grasped, even at the expense of his own.

"You couldn't sleep either?" Jake meandered onto the deck outside into the still-warm night air. With a cigarette between his lips, he flicked the lighter and its tiny flame underscored his dispirited expression.

Nick pushed off the tree and began walking in his direction until he perched himself on the edge of the deck. "Na. So you're smoking again, huh?"

Jake examined the vice he'd once relied upon, watching a thin trail of white smoke waft above him. "I guess so."

"How's Rachel holding up?"

"It doesn't matter what I say or do, she thinks this is her fault."

"This isn't the fault of either one of you."

"I know that, but she's a mom. She thinks she should've been at his practice like she usually was. Rachel's hardly ever missed any of them, but she had a late conference call. Hell, I hardly make his practices. I'm always so goddam busy with work." He wiped his pooling eyes with the back of his hand. "God damn it, Nick. Where's my boy, huh? Where's my son?"

Nick laid his arm over Jake's shoulders. "We'll find him, brother."

"Sorry to wake you." Kate made her way into the kitchen and held out her hand. "Mind if I have a sip?"

"Go right ahead." He handed her the water. "Why was he calling so late?"

"He's been out helping them search for that boy and I think this was the only time he'd had to spare."

"Still no luck?"

She shook her head. "I guess they found the boy's cell phone."

"That's not a good sign."

"Not really, no. I'm sure Nick hasn't had any sleep and he figured I'd answer. I always do."

Mike placed his hand against her cheek. "That's why I love you, Kate. You're always there for your friends—and for me." He pressed his lips to hers, kissing her so that any question of his love would vanish if it was ever there at all.

A smile masked her face, knowing how she felt about him too, and recognized the end of a long journey that culminated in this moment. He had taken the extra steps, gone the extra mile each and every time they were together. It wasn't often enough as far as he was concerned and she was coming around to his way of thinking. Still, he'd made mention of taking the next step, but something in the back of Kate's mind caused her to remain hesitant.

They'd been traveling back and forth, mostly him visiting her, but when work allowed, she went to see him too. It was a relationship she hadn't really believed would last, but it had—almost six months now and here he was, standing in front of her now, looking at her like she believed no man would ever look again.

"Come on. Let's go back to bed. You've got an early flight." She took his hand and led him down the hall.

"I wish you hadn't reminded me." He lifted her from her feet, her bare legs dangling as she was in his solid arms. "Well, I guess you'll just have to help me take my mind off of it again."

2

Forty-eight hours and still no sign of Colton Talbot. The community searched, the police talked to everyone who'd seen him the day he disappeared, and the only clue they had was the boy's cell phone. Nick had helped in the search efforts and had assisted the detective in every way he could, but ineptitude began to erode his confidence. This wasn't an official BAU investigation; in fact, it wasn't even in the FBI's jurisdiction, and Nick thought that maybe if it was, perhaps he could do more.

ASAC Campbell, however, was growing anxious to have his SSA back in Washington. While Kate and Dwight continued, in their best efforts, to cover for him, Nick knew he would have to return soon. Tensions between the two had only recently begun to ease and pulling at that thread was a bad idea.

Rachel walked into the kitchen and spotted Nick scrolling through his cell phone while he sipped on a cup of coffee. "Morning." The energy to speak more than a few words was beyond her capacity. What had been a dim light of hope at the discovery of Colton's cell phone was diminishing with each passing hour and Rachel simply had no desire to make any efforts at conversation.

"Good morning." Nick had also grown uncomfortable as time dragged on. They both looked to him for answers and yet he had none. "Can I get you a coffee?" His offer was in vain as she'd already made her way to the coffee pot.

"Thanks, I got it."

He looked through the kitchen window into the front yard, imagining that the two Talbot boys probably often played catch with each other, as boys do. There had been times he envied those of his friends who'd had families and children. This was not one of them. He would not ask if Rachel slept; he knew she hadn't. He would not ask how she was doing, for it was obvious she was not doing well. Instead, the silence would fall over them, further extinguishing the optimism that had briefly filled this home.

Rachel's cell phone rang from its cradled position on the kitchen desk. She made her way over without haste. "Hello?"

Nick cast his eyes in her direction; waiting, listening.

She raised her head, a luster in her eyes flickered, and began to nod. "Thank you, detective. We'll be down as soon as possible." She ended the call and returned Nick's glance. The slightest hint of promise sounded in her voice. "That was Detective Mason. She said forensics came back on the phone and she wants us to come down as soon as we can."

"Okay. That's good. That's very good." Nick rose from the table. "Where's Jake?"

"He's in the shower. I'll go tell him."

"What about Scott?"

"I'd prefer if he stayed here with my mother."

"Of course." Nick watched Rachel make her way upstairs. He tempered his enthusiasm because any number of things could have shown up on that phone. The family had already given their prints to the police, so they'd be able to discount them. The detective had also already accessed the phone itself, with the help of the parents, who knew the passcode. Nothing out of the ordinary had been discovered, nor had they discovered anything on Colton's laptop in his room. They'd all but ruled out an internet predator. What concerned him was that the detective wanted the family to come down, meaning that something fairly significant was discovered. Perhaps they'd taken prints and had a hit. That would be the best-case scenario because at least they would have someone to go after. If they found foreign prints with no hits in the system, then they'd have to begin ruling out Colton's friends, teachers, and classmates. It would drag things out substantially and that was the worst possible outcome.

Their arrival at the Springfield District Police station was heralded by several local reporters. The story had drawn interest in the community, as they always did.

"Just go straight in; don't stop to talk to the press." Nick began to step out from the seat of his SUV. He stood guard while Rachel and Jake emerged, trying his best to block them from view. It was a futile effort.

"Mr. and Mrs. Talbot, do the police have any suspects?

When will you be issuing a statement?" one of the reporters asked.

Nick shook his head when Jake turned his attention to the man. Jake seemed to take heed and continued inside, his arm wrapped around Rachel.

Detective Mason stood just inside the entrance. "Sorry about that. Come on back." She led the way to her office. "I'd like you to consider making a statement in the near future, Mr. and Mrs. Talbot. At the very least, maybe Agent Scarborough can make one on your behalf."

"I think I'd like to have something to say to them regarding the status of the investigation, detective. What do you have on the phone? That's why we're here." Nick realized his tone was harsh and regretted it immediately. The detective was probably right, but his disdain for the media was no secret.

"Have a seat." Mason pointed toward a small table in her office. "I'd like to bring in the forensics technician who's working on this." She stepped away and made a brief call to summon the officer.

Moments later, the man appeared, tablet in hand. "Good morning, Mr. and Mrs. Talbot. I'm Officer Trombly." He shook their hands and looked at Nick. "You must be Agent Scarborough? I've heard a lot about you."

Nick returned the handshake and sat back down. "I'm a family friend, just here for support." He felt the need to acknowledge his place once again.

The officer returned his attention to Jake and Rachel. "I know Detective Mason informed you that we ran your son's phone for prints as well as any other organic material," he continued. "After excluding the family's prints and DNA that you submitted, we were able to find something of interest." He typed on his tablet for a moment and then placed it on the table for the parents to see. He then pointed to the screen. "While we didn't find any other prints, we did find a trace of saliva on the screen."

"Saliva?" Jake appeared confused. "What? Did someone lick his phone or something?"

"No," the detective began. "It appears to be a drop of spittle, maybe from proximity to whoever was holding it."

"You mean, someone who was talking or yelling or something?" Rachel asked. "Like the person spits when he talks?"

"Something like that, yes," the officer replied.

"Did you get any hits?" Nick was anxious for answers.

"Yes. We got a match to a man who was released from prison last year." She turned to Officer Trombly. "Please pull up his photo."

The officer slid his finger along the tablet. "This is Lyle Stroud. Thirty-two years old, released from Augusta Correctional in Augusta County, Virginia after serving six years for aggravated indecent assault against a minor."

Rachel clutched Jake's shoulder. "Oh my God. This is who took our son?" She looked to Detective Mason. "Why was this man released? For God's sake. How could someone like that be let out?"

"I understand how you must feel, Rachel, but Stroud served his time. He had no prior convictions and received just over the minimum sentence, which was a second-degree felony."

"Then he should be registered," Nick added. "We should know where he last resided."

"As soon as we got the hit, I reached out to the Department

of Justice. They said he was living in Winchester, about 70-odd miles from here. They've already informed Fredrick County police there and have sent someone to check on him."

"Well, he's clearly not going to be there, is he?" Jake directed his growing anger at the detective. "He took my son, so it seems pretty unlikely he would go back home."

Nick picked up on the rising tensions and needed to throw his friend a lifeline. "This is how they start looking for him, Jake. Someone had to have seen him leave or miss work or something along those lines. It's the best place for them to start."

"The important thing is that we have a name." Mason looked toward Rachel. "We'll track him down and we'll find your son."

When Kate arrived at her desk, she was greeted by stacks of paper—files from the Ackerman investigation, along with fifty or so emails and a few voicemails. So, a pretty typical day so far.

"Morning," she said to Agent Vasquez.

"Good morning. Hey, have you heard from Scarborough today?"

"No, but he's still in Springfield. I'm sure he'll touch base later." Kate looked over her shoulder. "Have you seen Jameson around?"

"He's here. I saw him earlier."

"I'll go see if he's heard from Scarborough yet." Kate headed down the hallway toward Dwight's office. She peeked inside. "Good morning."

Dwight cast his eyes upward from his desk. "Good morning. Come in."

"Have you heard from Nick? I talked to him the other night, but nothing since then." Her arms folded with concern as she walked in.

"He called me a short while ago, actually. They have a suspect now, but that's about all they have."

"Really? Who?"

"Some ex-con who was living in Winchester, or near there. Got out about a year ago and had kept a low profile, until this."

"I assume they have no idea where he is?"

"They got County PD checking out his home. I know Nick's going crazy over this. He wants to take the lead, but he can't and you know how he gets."

"Must be hard for him, especially since it's his friend's kid. Any word on when he's coming back?"

"Soon. There's really not much for him to do except offer a shoulder. His hands are tied. He's got Fairfax County and now Frederick County PD involved, but nothing that would make this a federal case."

"Well, you and I both know that's not going to stop him."

"I'm sure you're right. And you and I will be right beside him." Dwight smiled.

"I should be ready to hand off the Ackerman files by tomorrow. Anything else coming on board?"

"I have to head out to consult with Baltimore PD later today. But apart from that, finishing up the Ackerman files to hand off to the federal prosecutor is our priority."

"Okay. I'll get on it. Let me know when you hear from him again."

"Just give him a call. He'll answer."

"He's under a lot of pressure right now—I don't want to bother him. And, I don't know if you've noticed, but he hasn't been exactly chummy with me lately. He'll make the odd call to keep me updated, but that's about it. Very cut and dry."

"I think he's just trying to give you some space. Your probationary period will be up in less than six months. I think he wants to be sure Campbell sees that you no longer need to be under his wing. Especially considering how you were assigned here. He won't risk your position, not when you're this close to permanent status."

"Yeah, okay." Kate felt something else was there, whether Dwight would admit it or not. Nick had pulled away from her in recent months. Perhaps it had been because she no longer felt alone and stopped running to him for everything. She'd regained much of her independence and her former self. That was what he'd said he wanted for her all along, but she'd begun to think otherwise.

Kate returned to her desk and got to the task at hand, but it didn't stop her from thinking about Nick and what she could do to help. The parents must have been beside themselves. Her thoughts drifted just for a moment to the Davies' and what it had meant to them when Kate and Nick had returned Ashley's necklace. Because Kate didn't have children and was fairly certain she never would, she couldn't possibly put herself in their shoes and neither could Nick. But it didn't mean neither of them had compassion or empathy for them.

In a short time, the files on her desk had halved and email replies had been sent. Kate was nothing if not efficient. It was a quality Campbell would surely consider in her final assessment. The sound of her cell phone on the desk diverted her attention from Ackerman, a man who had murdered and mutilated six women over the course of a year. She was glad not to have been the field agent assigned to that case. As the Supervisory Special Agent, Nick assigned Vasquez and Dwight. Kate hadn't taken it well at first but realized that Nick's often preferential treatment could jeopardize her career, so the assignment went to Vasquez while Kate assisted with the forensics and research on the case.

She thought his ears must've been burning when she noticed the caller ID. "Nick. How are you? I was just asking Dwight about you."

"Listen, Kate, I was wondering if you could do me a favor?"

"Sure. What's going on?"

"Can you do some digging around for me on a Lyle Stroud? I'm emailing you now with the details."

"What do you want to know?"

"Everything. I have a suspicion that DOJ lost track of him and so I want to know where he's been for the past year. I want a background check, employment history, and any details you can find on his conviction. I want to know how this guy thinks and what he might be after."

"Sure. Local PD's working on this too, right?"

"Yes."

"So, if I start reaching out to these guys, what are they going to say?"

"Figure out a way to work around it. I know you can." The line was silent for a moment. "Kate, there could be a federal case here for us. I just need all my ducks in a row before I bring it up for consideration."

"I'll get started on it right away. Do you know when you're coming back?"

"Tonight. I know I need to get back to the office, and I told Jake I'd do what I could from there. In the meantime, the detective here, Mason, has got a good handle on things. I just think we can do more."

"Understood. I'll see you later, then."

"Thanks, Kate. And, just keep this quiet for now." Nick ended the call and turned to Jake.

"I'll get what I can. I've just put one of my agents on it."

The two began to walk out into the backyard while Rachel and her mother talked in the kitchen.

"Can you believe this shit, man?" Jake lit up yet again. "Some ex-con, in jail for sexual assault of a minor. Fucking figures." He puffed hard, nearly burning half the cigarette. "They aren't going to find him. He took my boy and now he's gone." He turned to Nick. "How the hell are we gonna get through this? Rachel's at her wit's end. I know she hasn't slept. I haven't slept. Scott sits in his room, playing video games or some shit. He thinks this is all his fault."

"I'll figure something out, Jake, I swear to you. And I'm not trying to dismiss the work Mason and her team are doing, but I can do more and I will." Nick thrust his hands in his pockets. "I'm sorry I have to leave, but I'm not far and if you need me, just call."

"I understand. You got a job to do, I get that. I'm just grateful you've been here, helping us get through this. I know we don't get a chance to see each other much anymore. Shit, you're a big-time federal agent and I'm some grunt computer engineer." Jake peered over his shoulder toward the kitchen window and regarded his wife. "But I wouldn't trade it for the world. I love my family, Nick. I love my kids. You just don't know what it's like." Jake trailed off, embarrassed by his remarks.

"You're right. I don't know what it's like to have a wife and kids to care for; to love. I envy you for that, I really do." It seemed only now to truly occur to Nick that he had desired a family of his own. For years, it just seemed impossible, given his chosen career. But as he looked into the eyes of his friend and the awful pain behind them, he realized what was at stake when you wore your heart on your sleeve. Nick had seen much suffering in his years as a federal agent, too much suffering. But this was different; worse somehow.

"I promise you, Jake, I'll do everything in my power to help you find Colton. And we'll catch the son of a bitch who took him."

3

No sooner had Nick returned to his office than ASAC Campbell appeared in his doorway, looking ready to jump down his throat for the time he'd been taken away from his usual duties. "You're back?"

Nick turned away from his computer. "Yes, sir."

"Good. How's the investigation going? They have anything yet?" Campbell's tone softened when he noticed Nick's haggard appearance.

"They have a suspect, an ex-con, but no leads as to his location yet."

"I'm sorry to hear that. I realize you want to jump in on this, and I don't have a problem with you offering guidance to the local authorities, but please remember that this isn't our territory. I know you wouldn't want to jeopardize their case, so be mindful to stay at arm's length."

"I understand and I know we've got a lot on our plates anyway. I won't let this deter me from my work here." The confirmation of his dedication was really just for Campbell's benefit. He wouldn't let anything interfere with his job, but he also knew that he was more than capable of handling both.

"Glad to have you back." Campbell turned on his heel. "I'll let you get to it."

Nick watched his boss walk away and felt that their relationship was on the mend. The trust they'd shared for so many years was returning and it was a good feeling. He would heed the warning and take care not to cross the jurisdictional line, at least, not enough that anyone would notice. But if they asked for help, that would be a different story. Jake was still his friend and Nick had access and resources to more than the Fairfax County police ever would. In fact, this brought to mind Kate. He raised the receiver of his desk phone and dialed Kate's extension. "Morning. You turn up anything on what we discussed yesterday?"

"Some; and if you've got a minute, we can go over it. I'll be right there."

"Great. Thanks." Nick had become hesitant to reach out to her as often as he used to. He attempted to cut the cord, as it were. Which was difficult because he'd grown accustomed to having her there whenever he needed her. And it had taken him a while to realize he was doing her a disservice.

Moments later, Kate arrived. "How you holding up?" She found her seat.

"A little tired, but that's nothing compared to what the Talbots are going through."

"I'm sure." She opened the folder in her hands. "To that end, I was able to retrieve some additional information that I'm not sure if the local police have received or not." She pulled out the background check. "Employment records show Lyle Stroud was mostly a seasonal worker, unable to really hold down anything permanent."

"It's pretty tough to get a good job with his type of background."

"Agreed. Anyway, his last place of employment was at a dairy farm from January through April of this year." She looked at Nick. "I guess that's a busy time for dairy farmers."

"So where's he been for the past month? According to Detective Mason, he never missed an appointment with his parole officer until a few weeks ago. What was he doing between the end of April and now, three weeks later?"

"Planning? Anyone check out the employer? See if there were any disciplinary problems with him?" Kate asked.

"I don't know, but I'll find out." Nick appeared to be considering an idea as he placed his thumb and forefinger beneath his clean-shaven chin.

"What is it?"

"I'm just racking my brain trying to figure out how we can justify turning this into a federal investigation."

"Well, he's obviously violated parole, but it wasn't a federal parole. And now he's suspected of kidnapping and he's presumably no longer at the residence where he was registered." Kate looked on in search of an answer.

"It's not a stretch to hand it over to us," Nick continued. "I can run it by the prosecutor. Problem is, I don't want to sidestep Detective Mason. She seems fairly protective of her territory, but maybe I can convince her she needs our help. We're all after the same thing—finding Colton Talbot."

"What about Campbell? What's he got to say about all this?" Kate asked.

"He made it clear earlier that this wasn't WFO material. Then again, he did say I could offer assistance if they asked."

"He's given you some leeway, then. Look, I'm finished with the Ackerman files. Maybe we can run it by Campbell first, but I think we need to make a trip to this dairy farm and talk to the owner. We need a sense of what this guy was doing or planning and what his behavior was like. It seems strange that he's been on parole for a year and all of a sudden drives eighty miles to kidnap a kid, or worse."

"I think that's a good idea. We'll get the okay and then talk to Detective Mason. She may want in on it while her team continues to vet other leads."

"I'll wait to hear from you." She started to leave.

"Thanks, Kate."

"For what?"

"For helping me see a path."

LYLE STROUD PULLED into the gas station. His ten-year-old Ford pickup truck was coasting in on fumes and with the kid in tow, he needed to avoid car trouble of any kind. He pulled alongside one of the pumps and peered over his shoulder. "I'm telling you now, you try anything at all and I'll kill you, you understand?"

Colton still shuddered with fear and nodded his agreement.

"Put the hat and sunglasses on now." Lyle stepped out and

walked around to the other side, opening Colton's door. "Let's get this over with."

The boy slowly pushed off the rear passenger seat of the extended cab, wearing the disguise, including a hoodie, which was unusual considering the heat.

Lyle walked beside Colton, squeezing his left arm enough so that he knew who was in charge.

The cashier behind the counter smiled. "Good evening."

"Twenty on pump 5." Lyle tossed a twenty-dollar bill onto the counter.

The cashier opened the register. "Can I get anything else for you?"

He peered behind the counter to the cigarettes and mini liquor bottles. "Three of those Jim Beams and a pack of Marlboros."

Colton stayed completely still and stared through the sunglasses at the cashier, but the man seemed unconcerned. He spotted the camera in the far back corner and raised his eyes to it.

Stroud noticed the gesture and glared at the boy, who immediately returned his gaze to the floor.

"That'll be thirty-five sixty, please." The cashier cast a glance at the boy. "How you doing, son?"

"Fine," Colton replied with fear in his voice he hoped would be perceived.

"Come on, son. Let's go." Stroud grabbed him by the arm again before any more exchanges between him and the clerk.

"You two have a nice night."

The clerk had been oblivious. The problem was that Colton looked like any other middle-schooler; sulky, indifferent, even wearing a hoodie in the middle of a heat spell. This was what Stroud had counted on.

They made it back out to the pumps and he opened the passenger door. "Get in." He slammed the door behind Colton and he began pumping gas.

This man had taken him three days ago. Colton was walking home, texting his friends as he walked from baseball practice. It was a clear day, but he remembered how sweaty he was and that he'd poured some of his water bottle over his head to cool him down. He remembered smiling at his friend's text reply to some lame joke when it happened. And now Colton began to feel as though he might never make it back home. He wondered where his parents were; where the police were. Why hadn't anyone found him yet?

Colton wasn't a big kid. In fact, he would probably be considered a little on the small side for his age. Lyle Stroud wasn't a big man either and Colton thought, on more than one occasion since this nightmare started, about trying to fight him. But he'd had a gun and kept him tied up most of the time. Sometimes Colton was forced to wear a gag. After the first two days of struggling, he realized wearing a gag was something he didn't want to do and so he quieted down since then.

As he peered through the passenger side view mirror, watching Stroud pump gas into the truck, he imagined killing him. Maybe if he could pry himself free in the night, he would murder him with his own gun. Every time the man touched him, he wanted to kill him. He was angry for being here. He was angry his parents hadn't found him. But in the end, Colton felt helpless to do anything but sit back and take it. He turned away from the mirror, looking now through the windshield at the empty, darkening road ahead. He blinked to clear his eyes of the tears that had welled. *I want to go home.*

"HEY." Dwight stood outside Nick's door. "Mind if I come in?"

Nick waved a welcoming hand.

"What's the word from Campbell? Is he going to loosen the reins a little?" Dwight took a seat.

"He doesn't want this to be an official BAU investigation, but he is willing to allow me to advise if I'm asked."

"And did you mention this to Detective Mason?"

"It won't change much. I've already been doing what I can for them. She wants to find Colton just as much as I do."

"Don't worry about things on our end. Kate and I can handle it. You should be turning your attention to where you're needed and right now, that's in Fairfax."

"I'd like us to do this as a team," Nick said.

"Whatever you need us to do here, we'll do."

"Earlier, in speaking with the detective, I asked if she'd reached out to Stroud's previous employer and his parole officer." Nick leaned back in his chair. "She'd already spoken to the parole officer and yesterday sent a forensics team to his house. But with almost seventy-two hours having passed, she's open to us talking to the dairy farmer, just to get it done sooner rather than later. So, how about we make a trip there this afternoon? Can you free up your schedule?"

"Absolutely. I'll see what Kate's got going on."

"Actually, I think it's best if you and I head over there by ourselves. I think she could be of more use here for the time being."

Dwight studied Nick with some concern. "That won't be a problem. Let me know when you're ready to head out." Dwight made his way back into the corridor and headed to Kate's desk.

He tapped her on the shoulder.

"Hey, Dwight. What's up?"

"Nick and I are going to drive out to talk to Stroud's employer this afternoon. I think he wants you to hang back and help out from here."

A vague sense of bewilderment flashed in her eyes. "You want me to stay here?" She turned back to her desk. "Okay, great."

"I'm sorry, Kate. Nick just thinks you'll be of more use from here. That's all."

"Sure, no, I get it. It's no problem at all." Kate's smile was forced and she knew Dwight would see through it, but he appeared to have nothing more to say on the matter.

"I'll let you know what we find." Dwight hesitated but soon continued. "See you soon."

First, it was the Ackerman case, and now this? Kate was beginning to feel slighted by Nick and while she knew that special treatment was out of the question, she thought that the three of them were still a team. Maybe she'd been wrong in that assumption. She was just a probie, after all.

Hadn't Nick just offered her thanks for helping him toward a solution this morning? Her reward was to be shut out of yet another investigation? Kate rose from her chair and marched to Nick's office. She'd already begun gathering information for him and now it felt like he was pulling the rug from beneath her. She needed to know why.

"Can I come in?" She walked inside his office without waiting for a reply.

He looked up from his computer. "What's up?"

"I was just wondering why I'm not coming with you and Dwight to talk to the farmer. I thought you wanted me to work on this?"

"I do, but I need you here right now. There's no point in all three of us going. I need you to keep Campbell happy and help with any research we'll need." He sat upright in his chair. "Are you pissed or something?"

"Well, yeah. I mean, I've been stuck in this office for the past few months. I've hardly been in the field at all and I just want to know why."

"Kate, have a seat."

"I'd prefer to stand, thanks." She folded her arms and realized she sounded like an insolent child. Then again, he seemed to be treating her like one.

"Okay. Look, this is an off-the-book investigation for a start and I need someone here to manage anything else that might come up. Campbell's allowing us to assist only and that's what I intend to do and I thought that's what you'd want to do as well."

"It is. It's just that I feel like I need to gain more field experience if I'm to be evaluated for full agent status. And besides that, I thought you would want me there, you know, to help out." Her reasoning had been sound up until that last remark, which she now regretted.

"I've been trying to let you spread your wings a little. You and I both know that I can't continue to hold your hand."

Her eyes widened with astonishment at this unjustified criticism.

"That's not what I mean. What I mean to say is that the more you handle on your own, out from under my shadow, the more Campbell will be willing to advance your position. Given our history, I can't risk him making a decision based on what *I've* done for you. He needs to see that you can stand on your own two feet."

Kate placed her hands on her hips, rejecting his logic. "I guess the Durham investigation meant nothing." While she still felt there were reasons beyond what he was sharing at the moment, her argument had been made. "I'll do what I can from here, then." She turned on her heel and walked away.

Nick cast his gaze toward the ceiling. Troubled by the conversation, he sighed heavily and closed his eyes. In the years he'd known Kate, he'd always stood by her; always. So it was no wonder why she was upset by this turn of events. Still, he had no choice but to consider her career, as he always had. And no matter what the voice in his head was whispering, he knew he was doing this for the right reasons and not for selfish ones. She would thank him for it in the end. Even if it meant they might grow apart as a result. It was probably better that way.

4

The aroma of the dairy farm wafted inside the air conditioning vents as the agents approached the massive facility. It was the fresh, runny odor of manure from cows fed on cheap corn silage and the only thing that could've made it worse was if it had been a humid day, which fortunately it wasn't. Rows of cow shelters, metal buildings, and a main office entrance were off to the left.

"Well, this is pleasant." Dwight stepped out of the car and onto the gravel parking lot. He crinkled his nose as he tossed a glance to Nick, who had also just stepped outside. "This is why I don't live in the country." He brushed the sleeves of his suit jacket as though that might lessen the stink. It didn't.

"Quit your belly-aching and let's get inside." Nick dusted up the gravel as he stepped toward the entrance. The sign on the glass door read "McMillan Dairy," and below that was a picture of a smiling cow with large, sagging udders. Nick turned to Dwight and plastered a cheesy grin on his face, mimicking the cow. Dwight chuckled.

Inside, the walls of the office were covered in wood paneling and lined with plaques of various awards from the dairy industry. They walked inside atop a creaking false floor toward the front desk.

"Good afternoon. I'm Special Agent Nick Scarborough and this is Special Agent Dwight Jameson. I phoned earlier?"

"Jameson, like the whiskey?" The leathery woman with platinum blonde helmet hair looked as though she'd had a close personal relationship with the brand and probably Joe Camel too.

"Yes, ma'am. We're here to see Mr. McMillan?" Nick replied.

"I'll buzz him up." She picked up the phone and announced their arrival. "He'll be right up. Please take a seat. Can I get you some water?"

"Thank you, no. We'll be fine." Nick sat down on the vinyl sofa.

Dwight soon followed.

Several minutes passed and Nick was growing suspicious. He furrowed his brow and discreetly tossed his palms upward toward Dwight. His partner shrugged in return.

"Ma'am, we're in a bit of a hurry," Nick began. "Would you mind finding out how much longer Mr. McMillan might be?"

"Of course. I do apologize." She raised the phone again. "Sir, the FBI is still up front waiting for you. Okay. Thank you."

"He's sorry for the delay and will be up momentarily."

"Thank you," Nick replied.

Moments later, a large man, rotund in appearance, emerged

from the back. "I'm so sorry." He offered his hand as the agents rose to their feet. "I got caught up on a call with one of my vendors. I do sincerely apologize."

"We understand." Nick returned the greeting. "I'm Agent Scarborough and this is Agent Jameson. We spoke on the phone earlier about a former employee?"

"Yes, of course. Please come back to my office." McMillan glanced at the woman. "Thank you, Bridget. Please hold my calls."

The agents followed him back to his office. The same decorator must have furnished his office as the lobby.

"Thank you for agreeing to meet." Nick sat down on one of the guest chairs opposite McMillan's desk. "I'd like to talk to you about Lyle Stroud."

"Yes, of course." He looked to Dwight and gestured toward the other chair. "Please, sir, have a seat." McMillan returned his attention to Nick. "Well, as I mentioned on the phone, he hasn't been to work in nearly a month. I asked around the first few days he didn't show up, because you know I have to let his parole officer know if there's a problem. And so anyways, I haven't seen nor heard from him since. Is he all right?"

"How much do you know about Stroud's history?"

"Enough, I suppose. He was in jail for assault and served some time for it. Look, Agent Scarborough, I believe in second chances and this man paid his dues so far as I'm concerned. Now what he did was despicable, but as I said, the man's done the time for his crime."

"He kidnapped a twelve-year-old boy three days ago and we're helping the local authorities track him down," Dwight added.

"I'm sorry; what?" McMillan leaned in, his belly spilling over onto his desk.

"He kidnapped a child in Fairfax County. We know it was him. He left behind DNA." Nick's face was masked in gravity.

"Cheese and rice, I don't believe it." McMillan shook his head. "He came to work on time every day, there were no problems from what I know. He did his job and went home. Good Lord." He rubbed his full cheeks.

"Yes, sir. It's hard to believe," Nick began. "Would you mind if we took a look around, particularly his workspace and maybe speak to a few of his co-workers?"

"I—I suppose that'd be all right. I want to cooperate, of course. I can call up his supervisor and have him take you back."

"We'd appreciate that, sir. Thank you," Nick replied.

The agents soon followed Stroud's supervisor, Travis Albright, to the milking stations where Stroud usually worked.

"His schedule was seven a.m. to noon on the line, then lunch, then one p.m. to five rotating between cleanup, feeding, and working in the pasteurization facility." Albright stopped at one of the milking stations.

"Did he have a locker? A desk?" Nick asked.

"A locker, yes. But there was no need for a desk."

"What about his co-workers? Anyone have trouble with him?" Dwight added.

"Well, let's find out." Albright approached a man running one of the stations. "Marco, you got a minute? These feds want to talk to you."

The man spun around, appearing nervous. He stood up and wiped his hands on his jeans. "Sure, I guess. What's this about?"

"Lyle Stroud," Albright said. "Guess he's in some kind of trouble. These gentlemen want to ask you about him."

"What do you want to know?" Marco looked at Nick.

"Did you notice anything suspicious about Stroud? Did he behave differently, particularly in the few days or weeks prior to him leaving?"

Marco's lips turned into a frown and his brow creased, as though he was thinking hard on the question. "Well, he'd tease the animals sometimes. But you know, not like a lot." He tossed a guilty look to his boss. "I suppose he kept to himself most of the time."

"You talking about Stroud?" Another man approached from farther down the line.

"You know him?" Dwight asked.

"He was a strange one, I'll tell you what."

"And you are?" Nick added.

"Chuck Lawrence." He extended his hand to Nick. "Pleasure. Stroud used to say some crazy shit—excuse me, stuff—about his time in prison. Oh, he made no secret of what he'd done in there. He didn't talk much about what he'd done to get himself locked up, but I know what he did. All of us do." Chuck looked at Albright and back to Nick. "Anyway, he wasn't right—up here." He tapped the side of his head with his index finger.

"Did he ever do or say anything to make you think he might—revert to his old ways?"

"Well, that depends on what old ways you're referring to. I think he had a few, uh, relationships in prison. He was careful not to say too much, though, 'cause that sort of behavior don't fly around here. But so far as I could tell, he didn't seem rehabilitated at all. I never said nothing to nobody, though. He never did nothing to any of us here, 'sept like Marco said, he'd get the cows riled up once in a while. Nothing worth losing his job over, I suppose."

"Did he say anything to either of you the day before he took off?" Nick paused for a moment to recall the exact date. "That would've been around the week of April 20th."

The men exchanged glances, and then Marco began, "Well, come to think of it, when I came in one morning around that time, I saw him stuffing his locker with, I guess, clothes, maybe? Like he was taking some kind of trip. I asked him what he had going on, but he never did answer and I just let it go."

"I see." Nick turned to Albright. "Can we have a look inside that locker?"

The agents followed the men to the changing area. Metal lockers lined the walls, stacked two high. There were a few benches in between and showers on the opposite end.

"That's his locker over there." Albright pointed to the locker in question.

"We'll need to get inside there." Nick turned to Albright. "You have a key?"

"It's a combination lock. Only the employee has access and we just haven't been bothered to try to get into it, I guess."

"Well, I'll need some bolt cutters, then."

Albright turned to Marco and nodded, seemingly instructing him to retrieve the requested item. Moments later, he returned.

"Thank you." Nick grabbed the tool, placed it on the five-dollar combination lock, and squeezed. The lock snapped with ease and he pulled off the remnants. The locker swung open.

Nick looked inside and quickly turned to Dwight, shaking his head. "Son of a bitch."

A TEXT CAME in on Kate's phone as she sat at her desk. A picture of a young girl, not more than ten, appeared and it came from Nick. Her phone rang immediately after.

"You get my text?"

"Yes. Who is this?"

"That's what I need you to find out. We found the picture inside Stroud's locker at the dairy farm. I need to know who she is and if she's been reported missing."

"I'll look into it right now and call you as soon as I find something."

"Thanks." Nick ended the call.

She pulled up the NCIC database, which housed twenty-one different files and over 13 million records. One such file was Missing Persons. Kate further narrowed her search by entering "EMJ," which lists missing juveniles, in the search parameters. This was where she would start. Once inside, she could continue to whittle down the field by entering "EME." That would classify a juvenile as endangered. Still, it would take some time to review the files, as they had no idea of where or if this girl was abducted. There were additional ways to narrow down the fields, including certain identifying markers. If she got a hit, the file would indicate the entering authority, thereby revealing where this girl was last seen. This was the most critical information.

Depending upon her findings, this case might no longer

merely be a sideline, but she couldn't look too far ahead right now. Nick was waiting on her and she had to work fast.

"Vasquez?" Kate peeked over her cubical wall. "Can you help me run a search? Scarborough's run into something new on the Stroud investigation and I could use the help."

"Yeah, of course. What do you have?"

Kate sent her a copy of the picture and they both went to work.

"Who's this girl?" Vasquez asked.

"Scarborough and Jameson need to ID her fast. They think she may be a victim of the same man who took Colton Talbot, his friend's son."

Vasquez began typing on her computer. The short partition between their desks allowed for easy conversation. "Did he find anything else of use?"

"Not that I'm aware of, but he didn't hang around on the line long enough for me to ask." Kate kept her eyes glued to the screen as the search parameters were entered. "Damn. There's a lot of files here."

"Same here," Vasquez replied. "What if we narrow it down to include the eastern region first? That'll cut down on a lot of this. If we don't get any hits, we can widen the search criteria."

"Good idea." Kate modified her search area. "How old do you think she is? Ten, eleven?"

"Probably. Let's enter nine, to be safe, up to thirteen. She can't be older than that."

"Unless she's been missing for a long time. But that would rule out Stroud, most likely." Kate considered another option. "We know he was still going to work every day prior to the 20th of April. What if we pair the dates down to January to the beginning of May?"

"It's hard to say," Vasquez began. "If she's one of his victims, she could have been taken long ago."

Kate understood Vasquez's point but had little time to sift through the thousands of records based on the image. She decided to use the dates and her instincts proved to be right. It took almost an hour, but the girl's face now stared back at her on the screen. Emily Aldrich, eleven years old, missing since April 23rd from her home near the community of Stephens City, not far from Winchester. "I found her."

Vasquez pushed her chair away from her desk and rolled over to Kate. "Who is she?"

"Emily Aldrich." Kate pointed to the screen. "No question; that's her."

"Definitely. Better get on the horn to Scarborough."

Before reaching for her cell, Kate emailed the file to him. That familiar zeal rose in her again. It was a feeling she hadn't experienced in the past few months; as though she'd been caged, her wings clipped. Exuberance at the idea that once again, she was a part of the team; that her involvement meant something and she could indeed contribute. Wasn't that the reason she was here after all?

"It's me." Her voice couldn't conceal her feelings. "Did you get the email?"

"I got it. Great work, Kate. We'll contact Fredrick County," Nick replied.

"What can I do from here?"

"Sit tight. We'll be back later and we can go over what we

have. With this potential second abduction, Campbell might be more willing to put this on the front burner."

Kate could hear Dwight in the background calling for Nick.

"I need to go. See you later."

On the one hand, Kate was deflated not to have another piece of the puzzle to work on, but on the other, if Campbell decided to prioritize this case for BAU, then they'd want the entire team on board. And that included her.

"What'd he say?" Vasquez peered over the top of the partition.

"They're due back later. He thinks Campbell will make it a BAU priority. But there's not much more we can do at this point. Thanks for helping me out on this."

"Any time."

Colton leaned toward the sliver of an opening between the wooden slats of the closet doors. He peered into the squalid hotel room. The man had bound his hands behind his back upon entering the cramped, dark closet that was filled with the acrid, ammonia-like smell of mothballs. He tried to garner the attention of the front desk attendant as they checked in but to no avail. The attendant couldn't have cared less about either the man, who undoubtedly appeared suspicious or the boy wearing a hoodie and looking forlorn.

His chances of escaping were becoming fewer and farther between and Colton fought off the sense that he would not get another chance and would die; maybe inside this closet. His parents would never find him and they would never know that they were in his thoughts every second until the last.

The man—who had a name, but Colton refused to think it, let alone speak it—sat on the edge of the bed. The old television, the likes Colton had never seen before, showed fuzzy images of a news broadcast. Maybe his picture would appear. He didn't know where or even when he was; only that days had passed. The man bore a resemblance to someone Colton had seen on television once, long ago. Although the actor was older than his abductor, he recalled the show because his parents watched it and he noticed it in passing because he wasn't allowed to watch it. The Sopranos. That's right. He remembered it now. This man looked like a younger, shorter version of the actor from the Sopranos, but hefty and slightly balding just the same. An old-school mobster, Colton thought.

He had a very good memory; eidetic, some people called it. His parents said it was because of his Autism, although Colton didn't understand what that meant exactly. He did well in school and had friends. He didn't feel any different from other kids. But his parents said he was on the spectrum, whatever that meant.

Colton shifted his weight and his shoe caught on the tracks of the closet door. The man must've heard him because he whipped his head sideways to look in his direction. Colton gasped and stepped back, stumbling on his own feet and falling against the back wall, but he managed to steady himself. He remained still, waiting for the man to open the door and grab him.

After a few moments, Colton realized he wasn't coming and

exhaled. He tried hard not to upset the man. Though he hadn't struck him in the face, he had put bruises on his arms from squeezing them. There were many reasons Colton didn't want to face his wrath, and frankly, the bruises on his arm were nothing compared to the rest of it.

5

The street was clearing and Nick glanced both ways before walking toward the driver's side of his SUV. "I know this is tough to hear, but I wanted it to come from me." Nick pressed the keyless entry; the lights flashed and the horn beeped. He stepped inside.

Dwight entered the passenger side and studied Nick while he spoke to Jake Talbot about this latest news.

"We just met with Fredrick County. They confirmed the girl's ID and are handling her family." He paused a moment and started the engine. "This puts us closer, Jake. We know where he's been and it won't be long before we find out where he's at or where he's going. What about Detective Mason? Anything from her? I haven't reached out to her yet with this."

Nick caught Dwight shaking his head out of the corner of his eye. He glanced over to see the troubled expression on his partner's face. That was pretty much how he felt right about now. Another kidnapping. He could only pray they would find both of those kids alive, even if the odds were stacked against them. "Good. Good. Let's keep them going on that front. I'll facilitate the coordination between the two districts. There'll be some overlap for sure. Listen, buddy, I got to go. We're on our way back to the shop. I'll stop by later tonight to check in on you two. Take care, man. Bye."

"This thing is starting to turn into a real shit-storm," Dwight began. "We know who we're after, but no one's found him; we've got two missing kids and God only knows if there are any more."

Nick blew through a yellow light, in a hurry to get back. "According to Jake, Detective Mason has received tips from people who say they've seen Stroud with a kid, but none have panned out yet. She's still in the middle of it, though."

"Someone has to have seen that son of a bitch," Dwight added. "What's our next move here?"

"We've got almost the entire Commonwealth of Virginia on the lookout for Stroud. It can't be long before he's found. But, as far as we're concerned, I'd like to work with Mason. She's established a timeline and has a location. I know she's already checked CCTV cameras in the area, but none of them captured Colton. He had to have been walking along neighborhood streets." Nick appeared frustrated. "I told Jake I'd stop by tonight. I think I just might head into Springfield to see Mason afterward. I'd like to find out who they've already talked to and get her thoughts on where she thinks Stroud's going to go. We're beyond forty-eight hours now. We need something."

"Nick, you know these guys got things covered. I think you showing up to see how Mason's doing might put her off accepting any more of our help. You said yourself she's protective of her territory. I understand your position here. Your friend's kid has gone missing. But second-guessing the work of the local police is only going to add tension to an already tense situation."

Nick lobbed a vexing glance toward his partner. "Well, what do you propose? That I sit here and do nothing?" His face was immediately masked in regret. "I'm sorry. I hear what you're saying, I do. But time is not on our side here and you know that. I can't go to Jake and tell him we did everything we could, but we were too late. I can't do that, man."

"Time is working against us. I fully agree with you. And it makes all the more sense to approach this from an angle local law enforcement isn't already handling."

"I'm listening." Nick continued through the thickening traffic. "God damn it! Why the hell is everyone going so God damn slow!" He slammed the steering wheel.

Dwight seemed to brush off Nick's growing frustration, accepting that it had nothing to do with traffic. "I'm saying we take what those guys have and expand on it."

"What do you mean?"

"Money, transportation, lodging. These are the three main things someone on the run is going to need. He doesn't know we're on to him yet. I'm sure he has no idea he left behind his DNA on that cell phone, so he's probably in his own vehicle still, which would've been included in the BOLO that went out with his picture as well as Colton Talbot's. So everyone's looking for a man in his thirties and a preteen boy in an old Ford pickup. What if we start by checking out hotels and motels within a hundred-mile radius of where he was abducted? He didn't go back home, so he had to go somewhere."

"You think he'd risk being seen checking into a hotel?"

"Who's going to give him a second glance? He would have no trouble blending. He had no friends; you said Mason had no luck with family, so where's he going to go? It would be a reasonable assumption that he doesn't have a great deal of money, nor would he consider staying in a city center or any highly populated area. This guy's going to be keeping off the grid as much as possible and finding hidden little motels that are cheap and where no one is likely to question him. He's going to stay on the move, Nick, because he has no other choice."

Nick considered the idea. "That could work. I mean, it's still going to be time-intensive, but like you said, he's got to be staying somewhere. He's on the run and unless he's saved every dime he's made over the past year since he left prison or robbed a bank, he's not going to be flush with a lot of cash."

"Okay. Let's get on that."

"We'll need to sit down with Campbell and get him up to speed and we can get Kate to help us out on this too. I think she's itching to do some field work again."

"I think it's time you let her." Dwight kept his eyes on the road ahead of them, purposely avoiding a rebuttal. "It knocked the wind out of you after the Durham incident. Everything you'd just gone through with Georgia and fighting like hell to keep your job. Hey, I don't blame you."

It seemed Dwight would get no argument from Nick on this occasion. "We'd better step it up. It's getting late."

Night settled over the WFO as Kate and a few other stragglers clung to what remained of the day. Kate had little reason to go home. The place would still be empty and she'd begun to appreciate the weekends when Mike would visit or vice versa. Kate had truly reestablished her life and it was so far removed from all she had known before, it seemed the Kate of years ago was a stranger to her. There were times, though, infrequent, but there nonetheless, when she would hold Mike and feel Marshall. That wound hadn't fully healed but was much less painful and she felt less guilty of her relationship with Mike with each passing day. She began to feel as though her transformation had been complete. And with only months left on her probation, her full status meant she could find a permanent place to call home. Buy a house, and buy a car, which she still hadn't yet felt comfortable doing. It was all within reach now. She'd even begun to come to terms with putting to use the money Marshall had left her. She'd accepted that he wanted her to have it and appreciated his putting that kind of faith in her.

But those ideas were for another time and, right now, she needed coffee. It was eight o'clock and she'd been there since seven a.m. Her team would arrive and want to meet with Campbell. And she was not wrong on either count. Minutes later, her two partners stepped off the elevator.

Kate waited for their approach, listening to their conversation behind her. She cast a look to Vasquez, who was also still working. Agent Vasquez—Alicia, although she preferred to be called by her last name—had become the closest thing Kate had to a sister since she lost Sam. It was a space, that while would never be completely filled, was at least partially occupied by this new relationship.

"Kate?" Dwight asked as he approached. "Come on back. We're going to meet with Campbell." He looked to Vasquez. "You too, if you've got a minute."

The two quickly parted from their seats, grabbed their laptops, and followed Dwight, who was several steps ahead. By the time they reached Campbell's office, Nick was already seated inside.

Campbell waved them in. "Take a seat and let's get started. It's late and I'd like to get home sometime before midnight." He turned to Nick. "What've you got for me?"

Nick retrieved the picture of the girl and tossed it on Campbell's desk. "This is Emily Aldrich, eleven years old, missing since April 23rd from a suburb of Fredrick County, not far from where our suspect lived. We found her picture inside of Stroud's locker at the dairy farm."

Campbell held the picture between his index finger and thumb, then eyed Nick. "Well, you got what you wanted." He set the picture back down and pushed it toward Nick. "This is your next case. Let's get on it."

The team continued to fill in ASAC Campbell and when he felt comfortable with the status of the investigation, he concluded the meeting. "Scarborough, I'll let you delegate as you see fit, but make sure you're working with Detective Mason. This multiple abduction case may now be federal, but I don't want the local authorities side-stepped." Campbell stood up and reached for his carrier bag, which hung over the back of his chair. "Now I need to get home and hopefully get a chance to say goodnight to my kids." He looked at the team with a fatherly gaze. "It wouldn't hurt for you all to do the same, although I suspect you won't."

Campbell was approaching his mid-forties and hardly old enough to act the surrogate dad to any of them. However, the team took their cue and left his office.

Kate caught up to Nick. "So, you're heading over to see the Talbots tonight?"

"I have to keep them up to speed. I know it's getting late, but trust me, neither of those parents is sleeping right now."

"I'm sure they aren't. Dwight mentioned the hotels. Should I get started on that?"

Nick stopped in the hall and turned to Kate. "You should go home, get some rest, and come in first thing in the morning. You'll need a fresh pair of eyes. It's a lot of information."

"I just don't feel right stopping. We have to find those kids." She followed Nick as he continued walking again.

"We aren't the only ones looking for them, or for Stroud. Mason's done a good job and we've just doubled our efforts. You'll be better off with some rest and will be less likely to make a mistake. We can't afford mistakes." Nick stopped in front of his office. "I'll see you in the morning. I'm going to head out."

"Goodnight." Kate knew he was right but felt thwarted nonetheless. However, the feeling loomed that neither of those kids would make it through the night if they even made it this far.

Shadow from the porch light cast down upon Nick's face as he knocked. His expression remained solemn but displayed resolve when his friend, Jake Talbot, opened the door of his home.

"You made it; come in." Jake stepped aside while Nick entered the quiet and sparsely lit home.

"I'm not disturbing you am I?"

"No. Scott's asleep, but Rachel's still up." Jake closed the door. "Can I get you a drink?" He already had one in hand.

"Absolutely." Nick followed him into the kitchen. "Evening, Rachel."

"Hey, Nick. Thanks for stopping by. I know it's late and you must be exhausted." Her appearance suggested she was the one who was suffering.

"I'm all right." Nick sat down at the table while Jake approached with a drink. "Thanks."

"Hope you don't mind gin." He took a seat next to his wife.

"Not at all." Nick sipped on the drink, then set it down and got to the business at hand. "So, as you know, I interviewed Stroud's co-workers this afternoon and shortly after that was when I phoned you about the picture I found."

"Emily something?" Jake added.

"Emily Aldrich."

"Did you find her?" Rachel's eyes suggested she didn't want to know the truth but felt compelled to ask.

"No. I'm afraid not. Not yet."

"So, everyone's looking for this piece of shit who's taken two kids, and he's been able to stay hidden." Jake tossed his drink back.

"Not for long, I promise you. We just got the okay to take this on—officially, as a federal investigation."

"What does that mean for us?" Rachel asked.

"That we'll be able to pool our resources with the other

jurisdictions and take a much more proactive approach, meaning we've just been put in charge."

"Well, I sure as hell hope you have a plan, my friend because it's been going on four days." Jake's eyes reddened as he reached for his wife's hand. "It's been too long."

"My team will be working with Detective Mason and her chief to coordinate our efforts. Our first task will be to supplement the detective's search by identifying the lodging Stroud would likely be housed in. A man on the run still needs a place to stay."

Rachel slowly rose from the table. "Whatever you need to do, please, Nick, just do it. Just find our son." She shuffled from the kitchen and up the stairs, leaving the men alone.

"I'd better let you get some rest." Nick stood up. "I'll keep you updated."

"I know you will. Thank you for coming by tonight. You didn't have to do that."

"Yes—I did."

KATE ARRIVED at the usual solitude of the small home she still rented from the old lady and her son. The time would come soon for her to again decide if she would stay. The son had already sent a couple of reminder emails stating that she needed to give them ninety days' notice if she was not intending to renew her lease. Well, that ninety days would be up next month. She still had no idea if she wanted to stay here and being so close to official permanent designation, she hesitated on a decision.

Her relationship with Mike further complicated the situation. He was a small-town guy who was happy being a small-town cop. But she also knew, mainly because he'd brought it up on more than one occasion, that he would move here to D.C. with her in a heartbeat. It was a decision she wasn't ready to make on that front either.

Right now, though, it was difficult to think about either of those major life-altering events. Her thoughts turned to Colton Talbot and Emily Aldrich; two kids who she desperately wanted to find before it was too late. And she knew all too well that "too late" may have already passed them by.

She walked out of her bedroom in an oversized t-shirt and gym shorts. The time showed eleven p.m. and she wondered if Nick had made it home yet. He had changed so much over the past few months. The likes of which she'd never seen in him before. His breakup with Georgia must have really taken its toll, but she suspected it was more than that too.

In the few years that they'd become close, she had learned to read him pretty well—and vice versa. And something in him changed after the Durham investigation ended. She recalled the change very early on. In fact, it was only days after her confrontation with Durham that she'd felt it. Distant, almost, but not quite, cold. Kate figured he just needed time to get over Georgia and get back on his feet after the struggles with ASAC Campbell. But it had gone on longer than she'd anticipated and her fears about him crept back up to the surface.

Maybe now she could help get things back to normal and stabilize their friendship once again because when they worked together, they were virtually unstoppable—feeding off one another's instincts. And this time would be different. This time, they would find those kids—alive. And rather than sit on her couch, absorbed by things that, in light of the current situation, seemed self-centered, she would do something useful. Sleep might eventually find her, but for now, she was reinvigorated and would not follow the advice of her superior.

Kate retrieved her computer and logged into the server. Nick wanted to search hotels and motels within a hundred-mile radius, and that was where she would start.

Two hours had passed and Kate finished the last drop of wine in her glass. She'd compiled an extensive list based on Nick's instructions. Lodging off the beaten path, cheap, and she narrowed it down further to include only those on a single level. Stroud wouldn't stay somewhere where he had to walk inside a lengthy corridor or ride an elevator with a kid who could draw attention. No, he would stay in a cheap motel, park his car right in front of the room, and take the kid inside, unseen by anyone.

Still, the list was large. She wanted to reach out to Nick, run it by him, and get his thoughts; bounce ideas on how to tackle the enormous task. But it was one a.m. and given his recent change in attitude toward her, perhaps it was best to wait until morning.

Kate looked at her cell phone, held it in her hands, and again considered it. "No. It'll have to wait." She set it down, uncurled her legs from the sofa, and took to her feet. "I've got to get some sleep."

6

The sunrise shone just ahead as Kate made her way into the office for an early start. Her excitement about the investigation fueled her brain for much of the night, and now coffee fueled it as she worked her way through downtown D.C.

A call rang through on her cell and she pressed the Bluetooth button to answer. "Hey there. Good morning. I wasn't expecting to hear from you so early."

"You're a tough lady to get a hold of, so I figured I'd give it a shot this morning. You busy?" Mike's voice sounded pleasant through the car's speakers.

"We had a meeting last night about a new case."

"Oh yeah?"

"Unfortunately, it's the one Nick's been working on for his friend. It wasn't really a BAU case. Well, it is now. Long story short, we're working to find a parolee who's responsible for not only taking the boy but also a girl not far from where he lived."

"Jesus." Mike's voice turned somber.

"So we're going to be running on this thing full bore."

"That probably means this weekend is out?"

Katie sensed his disappointment. "I'm afraid so, hon. I'll be buried in this for a while."

"I understand. No problem at all. Just keep me updated, okay?"

"I will. Thanks for this."

"For what?"

"For letting me do my job and not making me feel bad about it."

"Give me some credit, Kate. The important thing is that you guys find those kids. I'd better run and let you get to it. Talk later?"

"Definitely."

"Love you." Mike's words almost came across as a question.

"You too, babe. Bye." Kate ended the call just as she pulled into the parking garage. Minutes later, the elevator doors opened and she was back inside the bullpen. Seven a.m. on the dot. "Good morning."

"Morning." Agent Vasquez always went in early.

Kate logged into her email and retrieved the list she'd sent to herself late last night. "So I was checking into some things last night and I came up with a few places we should check out."

Vasquez rolled over to her. "Whatchya got?"

"Hotels and motels within a hundred-mile radius of where Colton Talbot was abducted. Scarborough figured he'd be staying somewhere off the beaten path, paying by cash and probably cheap places."

"Okay. So how many did you come up with?"

"Sixty-eight that fit the criteria, but if we don't get anywhere with that, we'll expand the search."

"Great. How about we divvy this up and get started?"

"Thanks." Kate felt someone approaching them from behind and when Vasquez turned back to see, her expression returned hardened.

"Can I see you for a minute?"

Dwight's face raised the hairs on Kate's neck. Something had happened. "Of course." She immediately followed him.

Nick sat behind his desk, staring at his computer screen. He noted their arrival. "Morning, go ahead and sit down." He swiveled his chair to face them. "I got a call around four a.m. from Detective Mason, who got a call from Frederick County Sheriff's office. Emily Aldrich's body was found in a park about thirty miles from her home."

Kate's heart sank. This was an expected outcome, given the length of time that had passed. Nonetheless, she maintained hope that it would not be the case this time. She was wrong. "What does this mean for our investigation?"

"We need to determine how and when she died," Dwight began. "We need to establish a timeline from when she was abducted to her death."

"This will help give us an idea as to roughly how much time we have to find Colton before he ends up dead too," Nick added.

He was nothing if not blunt and while Kate sometimes disliked that quality about him, he was almost always right. "I did some research last night." She half-expected a disapproving glare for disobeying his direct order to get some rest, but she would get no pushback today. "I found sixty-eight hotels that fit the criteria of where we think Stroud would have been likely to stay. Vasquez and I were about to get started on making some calls to see if any of the proprietors recognized Stroud or Colton."

"That's a big list. I'll pitch in. We need all hands on deck right now." Dwight looked at Nick. "Are you going to tell Colton's parents?"

Nick turned his gaze downward in search of an answer. "I'll have to. All right. Let's get on this hotel search."

As the two made their way out the door, Dwight pulled Kate aside in the hall.

"Thanks for jumping on that hotel thing. I think that's our best shot right now."

"This is really hard on him, isn't it?"

"It would be for anyone. I'm just afraid he's going to lose sight of things. Lose his perspective."

"I wouldn't blame him, just so long as it doesn't piss off Mason." Kate patted Dwight on his broad shoulder. "I'll get to work. Let me know if you need anything else. Otherwise, I'll keep you posted on my progress."

Detective Mason's urgent call shortly after his meeting prompted Nick to make the drive to Springfield. He entered the busy precinct and headed straight back to see the detective. The officer at the front desk called out to him and when Nick continued without answering, the officer sprinted to catch up to him, her hand resting on her gun; hackles raised by the security risk.

If Mason hadn't heard the commotion and stepped into the hall, Nick might've had a situation on his hands. "It's okay." Mason waved to her officer. "He's here for me." She turned to Nick. "Maybe next time, just check in up front first. Thanks for coming down."

Closing the door to her office, Mason walked around to her desk while Nick sat down and jumped right in. "Are you sure it's him?"

"A call came in just minutes before I phoned you about a sighting." Mason leaned in, her slender arms, bare from the sleeveless blouse, folded on her desk. "A man matching Stroud's description was seen with a boy matching Colton's at a rest stop along 95, heading north."

"Did they get a plate? Was it the same Ford truck?"

"Yes. We ran the plates and they're registered to Stroud."

Nick leaned back, lacing his fingers behind his head. "At least there's some God damn good news after learning about the girl. He doesn't realize we know who he is and what he drives. Do you have people heading in that direction? We don't have much time."

"I am well aware of that, Agent Scarborough, and yes, County Police and State Troopers are flooding the area. The call came in some time after he left the location because the caller had the good fortune to be listening to the Amber Alert and remembered the truck. I just don't know how much of a head start Stroud got."

"What about Emily Aldrich?"

"I spoke with the detective at Frederick County earlier. He said the ME should be able to determine the time of death relatively quickly. Possibly even by late today." Mason studied Nick with dark, inquiring eyes. "You didn't need to come all the way down here for this. I'm sure you all have your hands full. But I want you to know that we appreciate the help. We all want the same thing and that is to find Colton Talbot quickly."

Nick didn't need to drive the forty minutes for a conversation that could have happened over the phone. But he was who he was and despite what Dwight would say about it, he needed to be sure Mason and her team were doing everything in their power to find Colton. "Thank you. And you're probably right. It's just that sometimes, I prefer to be hands-on, you know?"

"Hands-on, like pulling the strings?" Mason smiled graciously, leaning back in her chair. Her thin, silk blouse revealed an outline of her satin bra.

She seemed to wield a power that triggered Nick to lower his defenses and he smiled, even chuckled at her comment. "Is it that obvious?" He ran his hand through his dark brown hair and hunched over, resting his elbows on his knees. "I'm sorry. It's just—well, it's my friend's kid, you know? Since all this started, I haven't felt quite useful enough."

"I get that. But now you guys have all the power. We're the ones who need to kowtow to you."

He raised back up, bothered by her remark. "Please don't think that's the case. Really. I've never been one to muscle any jurisdiction out of an investigation. If that's the way I've made it seem, please accept my apology."

Mason shooed away his words. "No, it's fine. We all get a little tense around here when the Feds get involved."

The sounds of the tires on the road made Colton want to sleep. He hadn't slept in days, save for a few hours here and there. The man made him lie down on the small bench seat in the extended cab of the truck and that was where he was now. His legs were too long as he'd hit a growth spurt over the winter and he was forced to curl them up to fit along the seat. His face clung to the tan vinyl both from tears and from sweat. Wherever they were headed, it was warm.

Colton only cried sometimes now, though. Only when he would think about how worried his parents must have been. He had reached the point that this was all there was left for him. He would not be found; at least, not alive.

The man had been in a hurry since this morning, but Colton didn't know why. He'd pulled him from the closet by his arm, dragging him across the stained carpet, and tossed him onto the bed.

"Eat!" he had demanded. "We're leaving in ten minutes." And then he tossed a dry bagel onto his lap.

Colton nearly choked on it and was allowed to wash it down with water from the bathroom sink. Still, it was food and a luxury.

The ten minutes must have flown by because he hadn't finished it before the man yanked him again by the arm and made him go outside to the truck. That was an hour ago.

He seemed to be slowing down and Colton felt the truck turn right and regain some speed, but not quite as fast as before. Maybe they were getting close to wherever it was he was being taken this time.

Soon, the truck rolled to a stop. The man turned back to him. "Stay here and don't you even think about moving."

When the man's footsteps had gone out of earshot, Colton positioned his arms for leverage and slowly pushed himself up, just until he could see over the extended cab door. He saw a rooftop of a house. The man was walking toward that house. He ducked down, fearing the man would turn back, but soon, he regained his courage and tried again. This time, Colton peered left, then right. Wherever they were, no one else seemed to be around. He spotted a house on the left, but it was very far away. On the right was nothing but fields, that he could see.

This squelched any hope of escape. It became clear that there was no place to run. The man would only have to jump back in the truck and chase after him. He was sure the punishment for such an act would be severe.

Someone opened the door where the man waited. An old woman. She smiled; she must have known him. The two talked and Colton wished he knew what they were saying. For a moment, the old woman's eyes shifted toward the truck and he dropped down. He froze, fearing she'd seen him. But maybe that wouldn't be a bad thing. He couldn't be sure, but it seemed her vision might have begun to fail her in her old age because no one came.

He assumed his previous position and waited. That was all he could do and all he had done for days or had it been weeks? Colton was losing track of time.

Moments later, the rear passenger door opened and the man towered over him. "Get up."

Colton wasted no time. Delays made the man angry. He scrambled to sit upright.

"Come with me and you'd better stay quiet. You understand?"

The man grabbed his arm and Colton winced as it had grown tender from the squeeze he kept on it. Colton was pulled to his feet and followed along beside him. They walked into the house. It was cool inside and sent a chill down Colton's overheated back. He didn't see the old woman and wondered where she could be. If he could just see her, maybe she would help him.

Instead, the man led him down the stairs into what appeared to be a basement. It looked like a living room to Colton. A television, a couch, and tables. Old stuff but looked clean. Cleaner than some of the hotels they'd been staying at. He wondered where he would stay. Where was the closet? Would it be dark inside or was there a light? He didn't ask.

"I don't want to hear a peep from you, boy. If I do, you'll sure as shit be sorry. You feel me?"

Colton nodded.

"Good." The man walked to a door and opened it. "Get in." He shoved Colton inside.

It was a bathroom; small and smelled like piss. Colton crinkled his nose.

The man closed the door and Colton turned on the light. There was no window and it would soon be hard to tell day from night. Based on the light of the sun when they were outside, Colton figured it had to be around noon, maybe one o'clock; a long time until dark. He didn't like the dark. Bad things happened then.

7

Kate burst into Nick's office without so much as a hello. "I got a match." She hurried to his desk and slid the sheet of paper toward him. "He was at the Sunrise Inn two nights ago. It's on the outskirts of Fredricksburg." She stood, hands on hips, nearly salivating at the find.

Nick was silent for a moment. He studied the information and looked at Kate. "I was with Mason earlier this morning and I followed up with her a short while ago. Someone called in a sighting. The location was north of Fredricksburg, but they haven't found him. Shit. Two days ago. Sounds like he might still be in the area." He began to rise. "Let's get down there; see if we can find anything that might help us pinpoint where he was headed. Go and find Dwight." As Nick was making his way toward the hall with Kate following, he stopped cold. "In fact. No. We'll hold off on talking to the local police unless we find something, then we'll get a forensics team in." Nick continued into the corridor.

Kate was only steps behind him but veered off to see Dwight. "A hotel manager thinks Stroud and Colton were there two nights ago. We're heading there now. Can you come?"

Dwight pushed up from his desk. "Let's go." He quickly joined Kate and they continued back toward the bullpen area.

"You guys heading out there?" Vasquez noted their hurried approach, already aware of Kate's discovery.

"I'll let you know what we find," Kate replied.

Nick appeared only moments later. "Okay. We're good to go." He took the lead as the three made their way into the parking garage and retrieved his keys. "I'll drive."

Dwight opened the passenger door. "Go ahead, Kate."

"Oh, no. It's fine. You've got longer legs than I do." He did, but not by much. The man was fit, but very broad and square. He always went out of his way to make Kate feel like an equal and she appreciated the gesture.

"All right." Dwight hopped in while Nick started the engine.

"It's roughly an hour's drive; assuming no traffic," Nick said. He sped out of the garage, tires squealing on the concrete.

"If we hadn't had the description of the truck, we might not have gotten far," Kate began as she buckled her seatbelt. "I don't think the manager paid much attention to the people who'd registered. He seemed more interested in what they were driving."

"In a place like that, it was probably to prevent someone from skipping out on extra room charges. I bet most of the patrons sign in under a false name or choose to pay cash. If the manager's got the plate number, it might cut down on those looking to get out of paying for something." Dwight chuckled. "Gotta love people."

Even in a moment like this, Dwight could find at least some fraction of humor. And in this job, it was a necessary quality.

"Or he was keeping track of the 'hourly folk' in case an angry spouse came looking," Kate replied.

"Let's just hope we get something signifying where they were headed afterward." Nick seemed unwilling to shed even the smallest bit of light on the situation.

Kate understood, of course, but this wasn't easy for any of them and this was how she and Dwight chose to handle it. "I guess we'll find out soon enough."

"We should let Detective Mason know about this." Dwight turned his attention to Nick. "Have you spoken with her yet?"

"Yes. She knows we're headed there now. I told her I'd keep her up to speed on our progress."

The rest of the journey remained uncomfortably quiet. Nick parked the car in front of the registration office and immediately stepped outside. The three soon approached the front desk. An older gentleman, appearing to lack any sense of urgency, hardly noted their arrival.

"Excuse me?" Nick retrieved his credentials. "I'm Special Agent Scarborough and this is my team. I believe Agent Reid spoke to you earlier."

The old man turned away from the small television that was broadcasting *Jeopardy* and eyed the agents, one by one. "I'll tell you the same thing I told her. I don't know where they was headed and I never saw the boy. I just saw the man and he said he wanted one night. I noted the vehicle as I always do and I gave her the plate number, make, and model. Ain't nothing else I can do, except let you all look in the room."

"Have you had any other guests in the room since that night?"

"No, sir. We ain't been that busy, but it was cleaned by the maid."

"Is the maid here today?" Nick pressed on.

"Yes. You can speak with her at your convenience. She'll let you in the room. It's number 24."

"Thank you for your cooperation, sir. Can you tell me where your employee is at the moment?"

"She's in room 18 last I checked." The man turned back to his game show.

They walked back outside into the late afternoon heat that reached a fever pitch as the early summer put a chokehold on spring. Nick removed his suit jacket, revealing his extreme discomfort both at the situation and at the rising temperature.

"I see it. It's just over here." Kate pointed in the direction of room 18. The door was propped open and a cleaning cart waited outside. "Looks like she's still in there." She took the lead while the others fell in line.

The room smelled of disinfectant. The sheets were huddled in a mass on the floor and all the lights were on. None of this, however, improved the underlying stale odor of the forty-year-old building that had likely seen its share of licentious humanity.

"Excuse me." Kate stepped over the threshold, noting the dour expression of the middle-aged woman.

She stood up straight, mop in hand, and standing just outside the bathroom door. "This room isn't ready yet."

"I'm actually here to see you. I was just in the office and your manager said you were in here."

"What do you need?" Her English was fractured at best and difficult to decipher through her heavy Asian accent.

"Can you open up room 24, please?" Kate continued.

The woman eyed each of them with suspicion. "Manager said it was okay?"

"Yes, ma'am. You can go ask him yourself if you'd like. We're with the FBI and are here on an investigation."

With that, the woman seemed assured as to their purpose and reached into her pocket for the keys. She began to walk toward Kate. "Follow me."

Dwight and Nick parted to make way for the woman and Kate and they continued along the exterior corridor toward the end of the complex.

The woman stopped and inserted her key into the lock of room 24. She pushed open the door. "Here you go. It's already clean, so please try to keep it that way."

"We'll do our best, thank you." Kate entered the room, which was identical to the room the maid was cleaning.

A king-sized bed. A dresser was opposite with a television resting on top. Not the flat-screen kind either. This was a good old-fashioned 25-inch Panasonic, circa 1995 by the looks of it. A narrow closet lay next to the vanity niche with a separate room for the commode and shower.

Nick approached the closet. "This room's already been cleaned. I doubt we'll get any prints, but let's take precautions anyway." He reached into his pocket and retrieved a handkerchief, then proceeded to grasp the closet door handle and pulled it open.

Three hangers hung on the metal rod. An ironing board and iron hung on the side wall and apart from that, nothing else remained inside. He bent over, resting his hands on his knees, and peered inside. The carpet was moldy in spots, probably from water damage as the toilet was on the other side. Nothing of note was visible. He reached for his cell phone, turned on the flashlight, and began to shine it on the walls. A few stains, which he dared not guess their origins, peeling paint, and when he shined the light onto the ironing board, he spotted something behind it.

Nick raised again and lifted the board from its hooks, setting it on the outside of the closet. He shined the light upon the wall. "Oh my God."

"What is it?" A curious Dwight began to approach.

"This has to be from Colton." Nick turned to his team. "He scratched a message on the wall."

"Scratched?" Kate began. "Like with fingernails?"

Dwight looked closer. "I'd say so."

The men stepped aside to allow Kate a glance. It was indeed a message and it was scratched by what certainly appeared to be fingernails. Blood appeared sporadically, but wasn't excessive.

The message read, "*He's going to kill me. CT.*"

"CT? Colton Talbot." Kate turned to her colleagues. "This has just become a crime scene and, more importantly, Colton's still alive."

Several hours had passed before the man opened the bathroom door and tossed in some scraps of food, never forgetting to tell him to keep quiet "or else." Colton knew exactly what the "or else" was and so he wouldn't dare disobey. He figured it had to be dark, based on when they arrived. Colton counted, as best he could, the hours from that time until now. The time had to be somewhere between seven p.m. and nine p.m.

His hunger had reached painful levels and so eating slowly was necessary for fear he might not keep down the food. Who knew when or if he would eat next. Colton couldn't shake the vision of the old woman. She reminded him of his grandmother. Of course, at his age, most people with white hair reminded him of his grandparents. Still, she looked kind and he wondered what the relationship was between the man and the kind old woman. Mother? Grandmother even?

How could she not know what was happening only feet below her? The man snuck him in when she was either in another room or perhaps out in the backyard. But Colton's eyes lit up with the slightest glimmer of hope that someone else was here. Because maybe that meant the man wouldn't kill him; not yet, at least. The final destination remained a mystery and he continued to pray that his parents would find him before that time arrived.

When he stopped chewing, Colton heard muffled voices above; very soft and hardly discernable. The man must be upstairs now, talking with her; the old lady. He thought he heard laughter for a moment and he knew it had come from the man. He'd never seen the man smile or laugh or say much of anything, except give him orders. Go here; go there; do this; shut up.

Colton's pulse began to rise at the thought that the man was having fun; laughing and talking while he remained captive in the dank bathroom of an old basement. What if he could escape? What if the man was distracted with all the fun he was having and he could try; just try to leave because staying here was almost worse than death? Colton was beginning to realize that would be his fate anyway and so what was a few days sooner? At least he wouldn't have to obey the man's orders and wasn't that worth something? It was starting to feel like it was to Colton.

He stood atop the toilet and cocked his ear toward the ceiling. He waited but heard nothing. Was it over already? Was the man coming back down? Then there it was again. A deep laughter followed by a few muffled words. The sound of clanking dishes vibrated through the floor to Colton's ear. They were eating dinner, one probably cooked by the nice old lady who didn't know her son or grandson had a prisoner in her basement.

What if he just screamed? Right now. Just screamed as loud as he could. The old lady would do something then; surely she would. She would call the police. Yes, maybe that was the answer. He looked down, thinking about this desperate plan that he was piecing together. Would it work? Or would the man just kill them both? What did that matter to Colton? If the man was a relative of the old lady's, then that was her fault. He had to think about himself because no one was coming for him. No one would save him and so he would have to save himself.

Maybe there was another way. His shoulders dropped when he remembered how little there was around him. So if he tried to break out while the man was occupied with his dinner, would anyone be around to help him? There were a few houses dotted around, but far apart. Maybe even a mile apart, in his young eyes. And what if no one was home?

Colton stepped off the lid of the toilet and sat down on it. It seemed that both of his options would end in his death and that realization fell upon his shoulders, further crushing the boy's spirit; not that much remained after being held captive by the man for how long, he didn't know.

Tears began to overflow and spill down his cheeks. He ran his hand through his thick hair, which was growing matted because it hadn't been washed in so long. In fact, he hadn't bathed since he was taken. The man didn't seem to care.

His sobs, though hushed, had drowned out the man's return down the stairs. It was only when he heard voices from a television that he realized he'd returned. Colton wiped away the tears. He didn't want the man to see his weakness. Any plans of an escape now or at some other opportune moment were all but hopeless. The man had taken from him his courage, and all that remained was a boy; a scared boy whose only desire was that this nightmare would end.

THE LOCAL POLICE arrived at the hotel. Nick was on the phone with Detective Mason while Kate and Dwight assisted them. The growing crowd of hotel guests would need to be contained unless they wanted the media to show up. And right now, that was the last thing anyone wanted. If Lyle Stroud caught wind that the FBI wasn't that far behind, he might do something drastic, if he hadn't already.

Kate approached one of the officers. "We're going to need to get a handle on the bystanders before too long. We don't need this kind of attention right now."

"Understood. I'll extend the tape barrier and have a brief talk with them and the manager." The officer nodded and made his way through the door of the motel room.

Kate went back to her task, but not before being beckoned by Agent Scarborough by way of a knowing glance. She stopped only steps in front of him and waited for his call to end.

"We will, detective, thank you. Bye." Nick placed his cell phone in his pocket and turned his attention to Kate. "Sorry about that. Listen, we're wrapping things up here. Could you go back to the registration office and get copies of any video surveillance they have from when Stroud was here? He says he doesn't know which way they were headed when they left, but we have to be able to glean something from those tapes. If nothing else, I want to be able to show Jake and Rachel the tapes, assuming there's nothing questionable contained in them, and at least give them some hope that Colton is still alive. Right now, they just need something to cling to because I know they're losing faith. We all are."

It pained her to see Nick admit such a thing. She'd never known him to quit on anyone or any investigation. This was different, though, and his gravitas had begun to border on angst. "Of course. I'll go right now."

She stepped outside where the officer had done what was asked and had begun to disperse the crowd. A brief nod of appreciation toward him and Kate continued across the parking lot to the registration office. The chime mounted above the door clinked as she walked inside. "Mr. Truleson?"

Truleson had his back turned, appearing to organize files

behind his desk. At the call of his name, he turned to Kate. "What can I do for you now, Agent Reid? Haven't you all caused enough commotion around here?"

"I apologize, sir, but we are trying to find a missing child. We are sorry for any inconvenience."

It seemed her message was received. "How can I help you then?" Truleson's tone softened considerably.

"I'd like to get copies of surveillance video both from this office as well as the parking lot and any other locations throughout the exterior of the property."

"It'll take me a minute. I'll have to sift through the past few days to find it. We only keep one week at a time, so you're lucky in that event."

Luck didn't seem to capture just what it was Kate was feeling right now, but she acknowledged the man with a kind smile, regardless. The lack of empathy was astonishing. Then again, this was a world in which people rarely spoke to one other, but rather chose to text message or tweet or like on Facebook. It was easy to be emotionally distant, or in Truleson's case, emotionally dead. But she'd come across his type plenty since joining the FBI. People just didn't seem as receptive to the federal authorities as they were to their own local police.

Kate waited at the front counter while Truleson disappeared around the back. She watched the television that was broadcasting *Three's Company*. She could just barely remember the show, being very young at the time. And, most of the humor went over her head.

Several minutes passed, in fact, the show was rolling credits before Truleson's return.

"Okay. This is all I got." He was holding a disk in his hands. "This is your copy."

Kate looked at the disk. She didn't have a disk drive in her laptop and didn't think any of the FBI laptops did. "Do you happen to have any flash drives you could copy this to?"

"Flash drives?" He looked at her as if she were speaking a foreign language.

"Uh, yes, sir. A flash drive. It's a little rectangular thing that gets inserted into a slot on a tablet or a laptop."

Truleson looked down at his disk. "Oh. No. I ain't got that. My systems are a little outdated."

Kate smiled. "That's okay. Would you mind if I just use your computer to take a look? We really don't want to delay this any further."

"Certainly. Come on back." He unlocked the latch on the small door that swung open from the side of the counter. "I'll put this in for you."

The images began to load and Kate studied the date and timestamp of each file, confirming that she was viewing the correct videos. "That's his truck." She pointed to the older model Ford F150. The video was gray, but she knew that was the one.

"Yes, ma'am. That's his vehicle. License plate number VCF-8493. I write 'em down just to be safe."

Kate continued to watch the video. She saw Colton emerge from the back of the extended cab. He was walking slowly but appeared to be lucid. A hoodie obscured his face, but there was no doubt it was the boy. Stroud took his arm and pulled him close, taking control of the boy and walking him toward their room. She covered her mouth and shook her head.

"Are you okay, Miss?"

"I'm fine." She continued to watch and then fast-forwarded, noting Stroud's use of the vending machine on more than one occasion that night. It was, however, the video of their departure that was of most interest to her. "They're leaving."

"Yes. He checked out at ten a.m., just like I told him. He didn't come back in here, though. He left the room key inside and they were gone." Truleson looked at Kate. "If I'd known you all were looking for him; if I'd known the car."

She finally saw an element of humanity appear in his eyes. "It's okay. You couldn't have known." Although she did wonder how it was that nary an eyebrow was raised at the sight of a thirty-something man with a young boy who looked to be of no relation whatsoever. Then again, she was used to being suspicious of people. It seemed all this man wanted was his room's rent.

The truck began to back out of the parking lot. Kate leaned in and watched it turn east. "What's east of here?" She whipped around to ask Truleson.

"Not much, till you hit round the Lake Manassas area, and that ain't much bigger than here."

Kate ended the video and retrieved the disk. "Can I still keep this? There may be something else of interest on here."

"Like I said, that's your copy."

She rose from the chair. "Thank you, Mr. Truleson. I appreciate your help." She began to walk out without waiting for a reply.

Her steps took her quickly back to the room where Nick and Dwight were speaking. "Hey." She moved in toward them. "They were headed east. The manager said there wasn't much until a place called Lake Manassas about forty miles away."

"Could be where they were headed." Dwight reached for his phone. "I'll put a call into State Highway Patrol and have them be on the lookout."

"That was still two days ago," Nick replied.

"If he's heading east, which would still fit in with the call Mason got from the hotline, we'll get everyone on their toes and hope someone spots them."

8

The room had been scrubbed of any evidence they could find. The tapes scoured for information. Stroud was the man they were after, but maybe, if he was getting some kind of help, that might be revealed. It was a stretch, but they seemed to be two steps behind and the team was growing frustrated, especially Nick. His fuse was short and his temper long and that was a union primed to ignite a hellfire of self-destruction. And God help anyone who would try to extinguish it.

A brief moment of reprieve arrived when the team needed food to see them through the day, and a drink wouldn't hurt either. Kate sat at the high-top table of a nearby chain restaurant alongside her colleagues. "It shouldn't be this hard. We know the car, we know the direction they were headed. We should've found him by now."

"We know the car he *was* in," Nick began. "If he caught wind that an Amber Alert went out, chances are good he's already dumped it. That being said, don't discount what the both of you did here today. We're closer now than we were." He raised his glass.

"My concern now is that he's going to start getting antsy," Dwight started. "If he thinks we're close, he might accelerate his method."

"You talked to his co-workers. What about family? Has anyone reached out to his parents? Background indicated they were still alive. And that he has a sister," Kate said.

"Mason took a trip yesterday while we were at the dairy farm and spoke to Stroud's parents. Father's is in a nursing home—Alzheimer's, so he wasn't much help. And when she spoke to his mother, she did what most mothers would do."

"Defended him," Dwight said.

"Exactly. Even though her son had already been in prison for a felony sex offense. In her eyes, he seemed to do no wrong," Nick replied.

"How could any mother defend such actions?" She was slightly biased, considering her once-strained past with her own parents. "What about the sister?"

"Haven't found her yet." Nick grabbed a newly arrived chilled bottle of beer and gulped it down. "Mason said the sister had been married a couple of times, had a few drug possession charges, changed back to her maiden name, and hadn't filed a tax return in four years. Her team went to her last known address, but she no longer lived there. She seems to have dropped off the face of the planet."

"You and Detective Mason seem to be getting along well," Dwight said.

"She's a good detective. I think her team is a little on the defensive since we got officially involved, but they're cooperating," Nick replied.

Kate eyed Dwight, recognizing his intentions. Perhaps this hadn't been the best time, but when was it ever a good time to have a life outside the Bureau? They both knew Nick hadn't been the same since Georgia left. Kate had only met Detective Mason one time, but she couldn't get a read on her. Professional, and courteous, but held back from revealing any sense of her personality. Maybe she had with Nick. It would come as no surprise. Nick was an attractive man; single, great job that paid well. But he was a no-strings kind of man and not a lot of women appreciated that quality, except Georgia, and she broke his heart. Most women Nick's age were divorced with kids and looking to find a man who could commit to a ready-made family. Hell, most men Nick's age were divorced with kids too and they were looking for the same thing. He was a man in a class of his own; an anomaly that required a deep understanding of what drove him. Kate knew. She knew because it was what drove her. The day he asked her to consider joining the FBI, Kate knew it was because they were so much alike.

After a final swig of her beer, Kate encapsulated what they were all feeling at that moment. "Let's hope they're making better progress than we are right now."

Scott Talbot, a gangly teenage boy who often couldn't be bothered with the likes of his younger brother, now sat alone in his bedroom, headphones on and listening to rap music. He didn't hear his mother shout through the door that it was time for dinner. It wasn't until he heard her raised voice behind him that he realized she was there.

"Time for dinner. Now come downstairs, please. I've asked you three times." Rachel turned around and headed back into the hall and down the stairs.

Scott pulled the headphones from around his neck, placing them on his floor. He sat there, leaning against his double bed, knees raised high, and stared off into someplace only he knew.

He wished he could take it all back; all the mean things he'd said to Colton. All the nasty tricks and pranks he'd played. He'd take it all back just to see his brother again and he sometimes wished it had been him. He was older, taller, and felt he knew the ways of the world and would have been able to fend off a would-be abductor.

But that wasn't life. Abductors didn't go after the ones who could take them on. They went after the young, and the weak, preying on their naiveté and their kindness. Scott pounded his fist against the carpeted floor. His face turned red and his eyes welled. He blamed himself for not picking up Colton from practice. He shouldn't have left him to walk home alone.

Scott glanced at his open bedroom door. He was angry with them too—his parents. They shouldn't have made him responsible for his little brother. Colton was their responsibility and instead, they trusted Scott with his care.

Finally, the tears came, as they had every day since his brother's disappearance. His anger was directed at everyone, himself included. He just wanted Colton back and all his mother could do was make dinner and yell at him to come downstairs.

Scott wiped away the tears and pushed off the floor. His fists curled into tight balls of white-knuckled anger. If he didn't calm down, he knew he would punch a hole in his wall. He couldn't let his parents see him this way. It would only add to their distress and he didn't want to be the cause of that. No matter what, they were all he had now, and he was all they had; their first-born son. What Scott couldn't be sure of was if he would ever be enough for them.

As he wandered down the stairs, Scott entered the kitchen, where dinner awaited him. He noticed the FBI agent. Scarborough, he recalled. It seemed everyone was looking for his brother and no one was doing their jobs very well, not even the man who now sat at their dinner table in the same spot as Colton usually sat. He looked at his parents to silently convey this travesty, but their unspoken reply meant he should say nothing. They hadn't told the agent, that much was clear. The seat had been left vacant since Colton disappeared until now.

"Did you wash your hands?" Rachel asked.

"Yes, Mom." He rolled his eyes and sat down at the table. He was fifteen, for God's sake. He knew how to clean up for dinner.

"Mr. Scarborough stopped by and will be staying for dinner." Jake patted Scott on the back and took his place at the head of the table.

"Great." Scott turned to the agent. "Hi." A teenage boy's irreverent tone emerged.

"Hi, Scott," Nick replied without instigating any further conversation.

They began to eat dinner and the sounds of forks scraping along plates filled the room with what would have otherwise been absolute silence. Scott directed a look to his mom, and then his dad. Neither appeared to want to speak about the elephant in the room. In fact, whenever Scott was around, they said as little as possible about the investigation. It was as though they thought he couldn't handle it. Like he didn't know his brother was missing and probably dead.

"So," Scott stabbed his fork into the thick breast of chicken, "having any luck finding my brother?" He shoved a piece of meat into his mouth and glared at Nick. "That's kind of your job, right?"

"Scott." Jake aimed his sights on his son. "Apologize to him."

Nick preempted the occurrence of any such thing. "No, it's okay. He's right. It is my job." He looked to Scott. "I'm afraid I don't have much new information about your brother. We are getting close to finding the man who took him, I can promise you that."

Scott dropped his shoulders. "I'm sorry, Mr. Scarborough. I know you're trying to find Colton and so is everyone else. It's just." He shook his head.

"You're angry, frustrated." Nick locked eyes with the boy. "I understand that more than you know, Scott. Look, you want to talk to me or ask me about something, if your parents are okay with it, I'm happy to tell you what I know." Nick turned to Jake. "Your parents are just trying to protect you and shield you from the worst of this. But I think maybe if you knew just how hard everyone's been looking for Colton, it just might make you feel a little better." He returned his attention to the kid. "And if I can do anything to make you feel better and help you get through this, then I will, without hesitation."

"Thank you, Nick," Rachel replied. "Let's finish dinner and then, Scott, if you'd like to sit down with all of us in the living room, Nick's going to update us on what happened today. You do have a right to know, a right to be involved, and I'm sorry. We're sorry; we haven't been doing a very good job of that." Rachel reached for Jake's hand and unveiled a warm but hesitant smile.

At the end of the meal, they gathered in the living room. Rachel brought in some coffee while Jake held a tray of cookies.

"In case anyone wants a little something sweet," Rachel said.

Nick retrieved his laptop, which contained a copy of the surveillance video from the motel. "I thought you had a right to see this. My team and I were here today after we received confirmation that Stroud's vehicle had been spotted. The hotel manager was able to capture Colton on video. Unfortunately, the manager was unaware of the Amber Alert at the time."

The video loaded and a near-empty parking lot flashed onto the screen. Nick turned his laptop at an angle so that the three could see. "Remember that this was two days ago."

Scott moved in between his parents as they looked on, waiting to see a glimpse of Colton for the first time since he'd gone missing.

The video played on and within moments, the hazy headlights of a truck cut through the darkness outside the motel's office.

"That's the vehicle we're on the lookout for." Nick pointed to the screen. He began to fast forward the video just a little, as it seemed Stroud remained inside the truck for some time before finally emerging.

"Oh God." Rachel cupped her mouth with both hands.

"That's him, isn't it?" Jake said. "That's Lyle Stroud."

Nick concurred. Moments later, Colton stepped out under Stroud's watchful eye.

"Is that him? Is that Colton?" Rachel asked. "Oh, my boy." Her fingertips just touched the screen.

The video played on, showing Stroud walking inside the office and reappearing moments later, only to step back inside the truck and pull away.

"Where's he going?" Scott pushed in for a better look.

"There are other cameras in the lot. Stroud is about to drive to the front of the room," Nick replied.

And he did just that. Stroud stepped out of the truck, scanned the area to ensure no one was around, and finally, he stepped around the rear passenger side and pulled Colton out.

"Goddammit. I'm going to kill that son of a bitch." Jake's lips snarled and his eyes turned dark as he watched Stroud lead his son into the motel room.

"He's alive, Jake. We have to remember that at least he's alive," Rachel said.

Nick ended the video. "There isn't much more to see. They left early the next morning. We know Stroud was headed east and we're doing everything we can to find him."

"But like you said, this was two days ago. Why haven't they found them yet?" Scott's eyes revealed confusion, hurt, and uncertainty. He was grateful to see him alive but took no comfort in the knowledge that no one could offer assurances that that was still the case.

"There's a good possibility that Stroud has become aware of the Amber Alert and that he may have dumped the vehicle for another," Nick replied.

"So you're back at square one." This time, Rachel's irritation emerged.

"No. Not at all." Nick closed the lid on his laptop and stowed it away again. "He's left a trail, albeit not a strong one, but it will have to be enough for now. He can't hide. His face is out there now and so is Colton's. Because of this, I don't think he'll get away with staying at a motel or hotel."

"Where's he going to go?" Jake asked.

"He's going to have to stay off the grid. He may look for a friend, possibly a relative. Although we have been speaking to his relatives, as of yet, they've offered little in the way of any useful information. I know the police are speaking with other known associates and former prison mates. I'll be informed of anything that would be of interest. In addition, Detective Mason should be getting a call from the ME." He looked at Scott, unsure if this information should be conveyed, but decided not to hold back. "We're trying to establish a timeline from the day the girl was kidnapped until..."

"Until he killed her," Scott added.

"Yes. I'm afraid so. It'll give us an idea of his M.O."

"How soon before we know?" Jake asked.

"Could be as soon as the morning. But I promise you, as soon as I know, you'll know." Nick paused for a moment. "I should go. I thought you should hear this from me and, frankly, I'm not sure the others are willing to keep you as up to speed as I am. I think you deserve to know anything and everything relating to the investigation."

"We appreciate that, Nick. Really. As hard as it is," Jake shook his head, "at least we aren't being left in the dark to wonder." He stood up from the side chair.

Nick placed his bag over his shoulder. "I'm sure you're all exhausted. Thank you for dinner, Rachel. I haven't had a home-cooked meal in a very long time." He leaned in to kiss her cheek. "Scott. Any time you have a question, I don't want to overstep my bounds, but if it's all right with your folks, you can call me." He handed Scott a business card. "That's my personal cell phone."

"I'll walk you to the door." Jake made his way to the foyer.

As the two approached the front door, Jake pulled it open. Nick stepped outside where the night had turned as black as it could be. No stars in the sky and a moon remained hidden from the view of this home.

"Nick?"

He turned around. "Yeah?"

"This timeline, this pattern you're looking for. Based on what you know right now, how long does my boy have?"

Nick inhaled a breath of the moist night air that was strong with the scent of churned-earth. "I won't know for sure until the ME confirms it."

"Nick, please."

"Two days, maybe three." He shoved his hands in his pockets. "Goodnight, Jake."

9

A knock sounded on Kate's door. She noted the late hour and grew concerned that perhaps Nick had had a rough time over at the Talbot's place and was coming over for some support. But then, she remembered he stopped doing that sort of thing a while ago. In hindsight, she kind of missed it.

She rose from the sofa and made her way to answer it. Glancing into the peephole, she reared back in surprise and unlocked the door. Her lips pulled into a broad smile as the door opened, revealing the unexpected guest. "Well, what are you doing here?"

"I figured you were probably having a tough week and I thought I'd surprise you." Mike leaned in to kiss her. "You don't mind, do you?"

"Are you kidding? Come in." She stepped aside, closing the door behind him. Kate noticed the bag over his shoulder. "How long will you be gracing me with your presence?"

Mike lowered his bag on the floor. "I don't know, a couple of days. That is if you don't mind. Things are kind of slow back home and I have a lot of vacation days I haven't taken."

The timing wasn't great, but then, it rarely was. And while she'd mentioned to him at the beginning of the week that a visit would be a challenge, she was glad to see him now and glad he ignored her.

"Don't mind at all." Kate made her way into the kitchen. "Can I get you a drink? Are you hungry?"

"I'll take a drink. I ate before I got on the plane." He followed her to the kitchen. "How's things going with the investigation?"

Kate opened a bottle of Canadian Whiskey and poured two fingers' worth in each glass. Some occasions called for wine, but when she was in the middle of the storm, the hard stuff filled the bill. "I feel like the closer we get, the farther away he is." She handed him a glass and the two made their way back toward the sofa. "He's heading east, at least, he was two days ago. The boy was still alive then, but God knows if he is now. There's a BOLO out in three states and an Amber Alert. They've had one lead on the hotline, but no luck. Nick thinks he dumped the truck for something else."

"That would make sense. I'm sure he's seen the Amber Alert and it would've given away his vehicle information." Mike sat down next to Kate. "I'm sorry. I hope they find that boy soon." He took a drink. "Any news of the cause of death of the girl?"

"We should know something tomorrow." Kate placed her hand on his knee. "I don't want to think about this anymore tonight. Tell me how you're doing." A thin, weary smile appeared.

"Pretty quiet, which I can't say is a bad thing."

Mike was different from her in that respect. And while she understood the feeling, her preference was to be in the thick of things. That was when she was at the top of her game. Nick appreciated that about her. She suspected Mike did as well, but perhaps hadn't been as keen on getting to know that part of her. Kate took risks, sometimes unnecessary, and Mike had seen that first-hand, but the structure of their current relationship made it such that he didn't see that side of her on a daily basis.

"Are you sure it's okay that I'm here? I know this case has got you hopping. I hope I'm not intruding."

Kate raised her hand to his cheek. "I'm glad you're here, Mike. I would tell you otherwise." She kissed his lips, which felt cool from the drink and were sweet like the whiskey in it. This man before her now cared deeply about her and she about him. There would come a time when decisions would need to be made, but Kate wanted to live in this moment and not think about the rest of it. Mike's embrace was warm and inviting. His thick arms wrapped around her, cocooning her small frame. Although not as susceptible to feelings of passion as she once was, Kate nevertheless felt a yearning to be with him. Heated desire seemed unattainable to her now, but there was no denying her feelings for Mike were real.

He removed the glass from her hand and placed it on the coffee table. With a telling gaze, he stood, taking her hand and lifting her from the sofa. They stood toe to toe, inches from one another's lips. And with an urgency that often accompanied a new and long-distance relationship, he raised her in his arms so that her toes only skimmed the floor. A gentle sway followed as they stepped out into the corridor. He pressed her against the wall, letting the weight of his body fall upon hers just enough that she felt his passion that remained strong for her.

A smile formed on her lips as Kate pulled gently away from the kiss. "I'm so glad you're here."

"Me too."

THE RUSTY GREEN 1965 Chevy pick-up turned into the parking lot of the Serene Park Motel and crawled to a stop in front of the office in the spot marked "Manager." Kenny Fulton yanked his keys out of the ignition and stepped out of the truck. His treasured black snakeskin boots pressed into the soft blacktop that had been heated by the blazing sun even though it was only ten a.m. He looked up into the bright sky, eyes squinting. "God damn heat!"

A generally unpleasant young man, Kenny often had a difficult time finding the good in anything, even a sunny day because it was too hot for this time of year. He pushed the truck door shut with a resounding boom and walked toward the office entrance.

Peering inside the glass door, he noted his assistant manager doing nothing but reading some damn magazine. Kenny walked inside. "Morning." His firm tone confirmed his displeasure.

"Oh hey, Kenny." Rickey was the night manager. A younger and rounder man who could easily take on the likes of his daytime counterpart yet was still somehow always intimidated by him. Perhaps it was because Kenny's parents owned the motel. Perhaps it was just Rickey's personality. He didn't seem keen on confrontation. "Is it that time already?"

"Sure is. I see you've been busy." Kenny walked to the coffee maker and poured himself a cup, but when he took a sip, he nearly spat it out. "What the hell? How old's this coffee?" He turned to Rickey. "Damn it, Rickey, you're supposed to keep a fresh pot at all times for the guests."

"Geez, I'm sorry, Kenny. You're right. I'll make one now before I head out." Rickey emerged from behind the counter toward Kenny. "We've got eight vacant right now. Everyone who was supposed to check out today already has, so that should make it easier for you." He dumped the remaining coffee into the trash.

Kenny's annoyance with him was reaching new levels as he watched the man fumble and continue to make a larger mess than was necessary. He could feel his blood pressure rise and decided to leave well enough alone and get to work. "What about the cleaning schedule?"

"Marguerite's making the rounds now. I think she's in 265 at the moment." Rickey wiped his hands on his jeans. "Okay, you're all set. I'll be taking off now." He began to walk back behind the counter toward the small office.

"Don't forget to punch out," Kenny said as he logged into the computer.

Rickey reappeared with pursed lips. "That's what I was doing." He fumbled with his keys and made his way toward the exit. "I'll see you later."

Finally, Kenny was alone, which was how he preferred it. His parents made him manager about a year ago when it seemed they realized he was never going to get out of their house. Now he was forced to pay rent, although it wasn't much. At twenty-eight, Kenny didn't have much ambition. He always figured someday his folks would turn the whole place over to him and then he'd make some real changes. He'd make this place what it once was—a destination. Now it was just another run-down motel where cash-strapped travelers pulled in for the night. The pool needed to be re-plastered, and the rooms were in disrepair. But for $49.99, you could lay your head down for the night, so long as the springs in the beds didn't keep you up.

Kenny perused the lobby. "Oh, to dream." He picked up the two-way radio and clipped it onto his belt. It was time to make the rounds.

The unoccupied rooms were the first to be checked. He had to make sure they were properly cleaned, and nothing missing or damaged. It was the responsibility of the manager to schedule repairs and things of that nature. Kenny might not have been ambitious, but he always stayed on top of his duties.

He walked along the ground floor, under the shade of the second-floor walkway. Room 134 was empty so he used his master key to open it up. They hadn't even gone to the credit-card-style locks, which would be first on Kenny's list of improvements. Nothing out of the ordinary inside. Everything seemed to be in its place. The bed was made, although not precisely to his liking, about which he would discuss with Marguerite. But all else was as it was supposed to be and Kenny moved on.

Around the corner, toward the elevator, was one of the ice machines. The clunky sound it was making made Kenny stop. He stood in front of it, hands at his hips, and studied the appliance. Pressing his hands against the front of it, he noted it was cold, which was a good thing. He leaned down toward the dispenser and looked inside as best he could. No blockage. That was good too. Still, the machine made a strange sound.

Kenny moved closer and spread his arms wide to place his hands on either side. He began to feel around, but nothing. Moving to the right of it, he was about to pull it out to examine the backside and that was when he saw it. He leaned back and stared at it. A note; a sticky note, to be precise. Kenny lifted the note. It was from the motel. A notepad that they kept in each room for the guests.

"I'm Colton Talbot. I've been kidnapped by Lyle Stroud. Call 911."

Kenny read the note again as though he'd misread it the first time. "Holy shit." He'd heard the name before on the news, just a day or two ago, he couldn't be sure. "Holy shit. The kid was here." He quickly made his way back to the office, but not before reaching for the radio. "Marguerite? Marguerite, please come to the office ASAP."

Kenny started to race back, his boots striking the concrete and his keys rattling on his belt loop. He looked around as though under surveillance. The kid was there and no one called the cops. How could this have happened? He began to think that Rickey was to blame. That he hadn't noticed a kidnapper checked in with his victim in tow.

The front office was just ahead. The radio chimed in. It was Marguerite. "I'll be right there. Just need to lock up 265."

He didn't respond. Instead, he pushed his way inside the office and jogged to the counter to check on the computer. He knew the kid's name. He'd seen the Amber Alert. But what was the name of the kidnapper? Even if he knew that chances were the man wouldn't have used his real name to check in. "Damn it." There was no way to know when the boy had left the note. Kenny was going to have to call the police.

Marguerite arrived. "What's going on? Is everything okay? Were we robbed?" She stepped up to the counter and waited for her boss' reply.

Kenny looked at her with wide eyes. "You hear of that kid who was kidnapped? That Amber Alert for Colton Talbot?"

"No—no I don't think so. Why?"

"He was here."

"What? When?"

"That's what I'm trying to find out. I was looking at the ice machine on the ground floor by the elevator. I found this." He placed the note on top of the counter.

Marguerite picked it up. "Oh my God. Have you called the police?"

"Not yet. I was trying to find out when he would've been here." He looked back at his computer screen. "But I don't have a name. Do you know what's going to happen if we let a kidnapper stay here? We'll be on the goddam six o'clock news!"

"Kenny, you have to call the police now!"

He pounded his fists on the desk. "I know that, damn it!" Kenny was scared. Scared he'd be blamed for this, scared for the kid whose written words haunted him. And scared of what it might do to the motel's reputation; one that he had hoped to improve. "Okay, okay. I'll call now." He picked up the desk phone and dialed 911.

~

Nick's landline buzzed with a call from the receptionist. "SSA Scarborough, I have a Deputy Lewis on the line for you."

His brow furrowed at the unexpected, unknown caller. "Okay, put it through, please." Nick placed his hand on the receiver. "This is SSA Scarborough."

"This is Deputy Sheriff Lewis with the Stafford County Sheriff's Department. I'm calling regarding the missing person's case involving Colton Talbot."

Nick sat up straight. His heart pounded from fear that they'd found his body. "Yes. We're working on that investigation, deputy. Do you have some information?"

"I do, actually. We received a 911 call from the manager at the Serene Park Motel about five miles outside of town. Apparently, the manager found a note left by the victim, Colton Talbot."

"What did it say?"

"Just gave his name and that he was kidnapped by Lyle Stroud."

Nick's heart skipped and it took a moment for him to absorb the news. "Just a note, that's it?"

"I'm afraid so. We're heading out to the scene now to gather as much information as we can. That's the reason for my call. Since this is your deal, I thought you should know."

"Thank you. Yes, my team and I will be there as soon as possible. Can I get a number where I can reach you?" Nick began to write down the number. "Thank you. We'll see you soon."

He immediately made his way to see Dwight and leaned into his open doorway. "Got a call from Stafford County. Some hotel manager found a note from Colton Talbot."

"I'm ready when you are." Dwight grabbed his keys.

They walked into the bullpen as Kate was returning from the breakroom with a bottle of water in hand. She spotted their approach. "What's going on?"

"We're heading down to Stafford. Someone found a note written by Colton. Sheriff's already heading there."

This might give them another clue as to which direction they were headed, provided a date could be gleaned from the manager. The hope was that it was after the previous location, which it seemed would make sense, considering this place was east of the other motel.

"All right." She reached for her bag and they headed to the parking garage. "When did this happen?"

"Apparently, the manager found the note a few hours ago, but he has no idea when it was written," Nick replied.

"Let's just hope that it was yesterday."

10

The hotel appeared in the distance. A white rectangular sign with a silhouette of mountains behind the words "Serene Park" and a red flashing "Vacancy" sign stood in solitude against the blue sky. Kate's first impression was that it appeared to be a seedy motel in some B-horror movie. But that thought had to be discarded because, in those movies, everyone died.

Several police cars were already in the parking lot and sheriff's officers were milling around, seemingly unsure of the end-goal. They knew that Stroud had been there and so expected to find prints and the like, but what next? That answer, it seemed, would need to be provided by Kate and her team.

"Looks like the party's already started." Nick shoved the gear stick in park and cut the engine. "Let's go talk to the man in charge." He stepped out of the vehicle and peered into the window of the front office.

Inside, Kate noticed a very nervous man with sweat stains

growing beneath each arm. "That must be the manager," she said to Dwight.

Nick was already making his way to the man who appeared to be the officer in charge. "Deputy Lewis?" He offered his hand. "I'm Agent Scarborough. We spoke on the phone."

"Yes. Thank you for coming down." The deputy glanced over Nick's shoulder to Dwight. "You're with Agent Scarborough?"

"Agent Jameson and this is Agent Reid."

Once the pleasantries were exchanged, the deputy began, "We've spoken with the manager over there. He doesn't seem to have any idea when Lyle Stroud was here. The guy next to him is the night manager and he seems just as clueless."

"Any surveillance video?" Nick asked.

"Afraid not. This place is pretty dated." Lewis gestured to Kenny. "I guess the kid over there says they've been slowly working on upgrades, but their computers are almost four years old."

"So they don't know which room Stroud was staying in?" Kate asked.

"That's a big fat no as well."

"I assume the rooms have all been cleaned recently." A thought was forming in Kate's mind that just might get them somewhere. "So I doubt we'll find much there. You mentioned to Agent Scarborough that Colton left a note from a notepad inside one of the rooms. It had the hotel's name on it."

"That's right."

"What are you thinking, Kate?" Nick asked.

"I say we look at the notepads in the rooms and see if we can find one that has an impression on it. You know, look to see if the writing left an impression on the sheets below. At least we'll know which room they were in and that would narrow down who was staying there and when. It isn't much, but it's all I've got right now."

Colton's stomach ached with hunger as he waited for his first of only two meals to be brought into the increasingly pungent bathroom in the basement of some old woman's home. A new day had dawned and he only figured that because of his sleep patterns. His eyes couldn't distinguish between night and day in this room, but his body apparently could. He wondered how the hell she could not know he was down there. He tried to stay active, often running in place just so he could feel his heart beat in his chest. But as he gazed into the small mirror, he saw his face had grown pallid, dark circles formed beneath his eyes, and he was weakening despite his best efforts. Perhaps that was what the man wanted; a weak, frail boy who could no longer put up a fight. Not that Colton did anymore.

The note must not have worked and he'd risked so much to put it there. The night before they arrived here, the man had gotten a room in another run-down motel that Colton thought was on the way here. He didn't know why the man didn't come straight here but didn't ask the question.

But the note had been his one chance. The time had come for the man to do as he wanted, but he needed to use the bathroom first and left Colton alone for only seconds and those seconds were not wasted. He hopped off the bed and grabbed a pad of paper he'd spotted on arrival. A pen lay next to it and he quickly scribbled the words. When he heard the toilet flush, Colton yanked the sticky note from its pad and jumped back onto the bed. He stuck it to the bottom side of the table next to the bed and prayed the man wouldn't find it. He didn't think he would, though, because he'd already had a few of the mini bottles of booze. He always did beforehand.

The next morning, just as they were about to leave, the man was preoccupied with a piece of paper in his hand. Colton didn't know what it was except that it looked like a list; a grocery list. He didn't know and didn't care. As he waited for the man to get up, Colton sat alone on the edge of the bed and reached for the sticky note.

When it was time for them to leave, the man did as he always did, walked to the vending machine, and plunked in a few quarters to retrieve a soda and chips. They began walking toward the parking lot and passed by an ice machine. With the note in the palm of his hand, Colton pressed it against the side and continued to walk beside the man until they reached his truck.

But it seemed it had all been in vain. He'd even given them the man's name and they still weren't here. And his hope had dwindled.

The man never seemed to leave the house, which made any attempts at escape or even of being heard, a futile effort. How much longer was this going to continue?

The door handle turned, pulling Colton out of his trance. He gazed upon the brassy knob as it twisted, listening for the click of the catch when it would open. He rushed to the corner between the tub and the wall, pulling his knees close to his chest. The man liked to knock him around a little and this was the best way to shield himself from the worst of it.

The door opened on creaking hinges, the dampness of the bathroom having rusted them. And there he was.

"Here, eat this." The man set down a small plastic plate on which a sandwich rested, along with a few thin potato chips and an applesauce cup. He looked at Colton, his eyes examining every inch of him.

Colton pulled his knees closer, as though the man's eyes had the ability to physically control him. He trembled, waiting for what the man would do next. It was then that an unexpected burst of conviction escaped. "Why don't you just kill me?" The hate in Colton's eyes pierced the man's vacant expression. He'd grown tired of that expression and something inside him snapped. "You're letting me starve to death anyway. What's the fucking point?" It was the first time Colton had ever said that word in front of an adult. He and his friends often used it around one another to prove how grown-up they were. Only now did he understand its true meaning.

The man's eyes narrowed into mere slits. "Boy, you don't tell me nothing. You don't talk to me unless I say so. I thought you figured that out by now. The fuck you think you are?" He stepped inside the room, closed the door, and squatted in front of Colton. "Your time's coming, boy. Don't you worry about that." He held his stance, staring into Colton's eyes.

Colton stared right back.

The man formed a wry smile and nodded. He pushed up again and stood tall over Colton. "That's what I thought." A final huff of his breath and the man turned away, leaving again.

Colton's head dropped and his pulse began to slow again. It

took all his energy to look the man in the eyes and it was everything he had inside him. He stood up on shaky legs, reached for the plate that balanced on the edge of the tub, and began to eat.

Colton opened his eyes. He had fallen asleep, probably from the adrenaline he'd exhausted from his encounter. The footsteps sounded above him and he knew that meant dinner for the man and the old woman. It must be nighttime again.

He considered his options as he did nearly every second of the day, only since they'd been here, and continued to search for a way out. Planning, scheming for a way to escape from the man. In the end, he couldn't muster the nerves. In the end, he was still a twelve-year-old boy, afraid and missing his family. But desperation was settling in his bones and he expected death would come at the hands of the man sooner rather than later anyway. So what did it matter?

"Here I go again," he whispered. It was the same conversation, over and over in his mind. He glanced upward to the ceiling and listened to the muffled words, some mild laughter and this made him wince. If he could just get her attention. He knew the risks, but then, what if he succeeded?

Colton rose from the towel on which he rested. His knees ached from being bent for too long and his head spun as he stood. Weakness was consuming his body and soon there would be no fight, or even thoughts of fight left in him. He steadied himself until his head cleared. A curtain hung, pushed to one side of the tub and shower unit. Colton eyed the plastic, moldy liner and drew his eyes upward toward the rod. It hung inside two brackets that were bolted into the wall. The rod itself rested in the cradle of each bracket. On examination, it appeared the rod could easily rise from those cradles.

Colton stepped onto the edge of the tub, bracing himself with his arms, which just spanned the length of it. The tips of his fingers touched each side. Once steadied, his right hand raised to the rod and he pushed up on it. The rod lifted. Colton smiled. He tried the other side and that side lifted as well. He then removed his hands and shifted his balance to his legs, which still had some strength because he ran bases a lot and Coach would often make them run laps if the boys were misbehaving.

He pushed up on one end of the rod until it was free and slowly lowered it until the opposite side was forced from its cradle. The rod was heavier than expected, but that was because of the curtain on one end. It was difficult to balance.

Stepping off the edge of the tub, Colton stumbled but didn't fall, nor did he drop the rod. If he made any noises now, his plan would fail. He set it on one end and let the curtain slide off. It felt like plastic, but that didn't matter: it would do the job. The adrenaline surged once again, making him lightheaded, but only for a moment. His mouth dried instantly and his tongue stuck to the roof of it. "Calm down." His body wasn't listening.

Diversion. It was just supposed to be a diversion so that the old woman would hear and insist on coming down to the basement. What could the man do then? Sure, Colton knew he would pay the price, but the damage would be done. And if he couldn't escape, then he would make sure the man would get caught. It was all he could hope for now.

Colton inhaled a deep breath and squeezed his hands

tightly around the rod. Raising one end above his shoulder, he slammed it against the small mirror and a great crash sounded in his ears. His eyes were closed as he smashed the mirror but now opened to see the damage. Shards lay in the sink and on the floor.

He heard a chair screech hard on the floor above and voices that grew louder. He'd done it. The old woman had heard and they were coming down. How was the man going to get out of this one? Colton smiled as his chest heaved and his eyes widened, staring at the door, waiting for it to open. The rod was still in his hand, he had a weapon. But wait, glass would be better. He reached for a shard and cut his hand. No matter. He would slice the man's throat with it when he came near.

The basement stairs exploded with heavy footfalls. This was it. Colton braced himself. His feet, shoulder-length apart. His grip on the broken piece of mirror, though drawing blood, was firm. Shouts. He heard shouts and it sounded like the old woman.

Colton was ready.

Kate studied it closely to be sure, but it appeared she'd found the notepad. "I think we got it." She turned to Nick and Dwight while they surveyed the room with the single queen-sized bed. "Come take a look." She stood back as they both approached and hovered over the white slips of paper with the Serene Motel logo on it.

Nick raised the pad toward the light and examined it.

Imprinted on the thin paper were the words Colton had written. "What do you think?" He handed it to Dwight.

"This is it. Let's get this to the manager and find out when this room was rented last."

Kenny appeared to have calmed down during the couple of hours his lobby had been inhabited by several sheriff's officers and a team from the FBI that was searching his rooms. He feared they might find other, perhaps more incriminating evidence as to the type of clientele that he catered to. Not that he wanted it that way, but they had to keep the doors open, and that sometimes meant renting to less desirables with a criminal past. Still, it wasn't his fault if his guests brought in illegal drugs or worse. He noticed the FBI agents approaching and his pulse began to rise.

The bigger agent pushed through the door, his broad frame practically obscuring the woman behind him, who Kenny thought was much too pretty to work for the FBI. Although he would never express such a thought out loud for fear of being called sexist, which he was. Finally, the last to enter was the more sophisticated-looking man. Built, but not husky and a little older. He had one of those V-shapes that Kenny admired, but he still thought this one was arrogant and definitely the leader of this little trio.

"We found it." Nick approached Deputy Lewis, holding the notepad. "It was in room 124." He turned to Kenny. "Can you find out who's been in that room before and after May 18th?"

Lewis and the agents swarmed around Kenny, who wanted

to piss his pants right now because he'd never been through anything like this and it scared the hell out of him. Still, he tried to man up and began to search the recent guests of room 124.

Kenny punched in the dates and a screen appeared. "Okay, so it looks like we've had three guests in there two days before and yesterday, the 19th."

"He would've most likely stayed only one night." Nick leaned over Kenny's chair for a better look.

Kenny punched in a few more commands. "Looks like they all stayed for only a night. That's usually the type we get around here. But we have some names here. Oscar DeLuca, Marco Rojas, and this last one has two people on it, a Stan and Delilah Smith." He turned to Nick. "Although I don't think that's their real name. We get those types too."

"Uh-huh." The name Marco sparked a memory and Nick referred to Dwight. "What was the name of that guy we talked to at the dairy farm? Wasn't it Marco something?"

"Yeah. Marco Rojas, that's right. That's got to be him. He's using his co-worker's name."

"He did here, anyway." Nick returned his attention to Kenny. "What's the date?"

Kenny leaned in and his eyes squinted. "He checked out yesterday."

Nick slammed his fist down on the high-back fabric chair that Kenny was sitting on, nearly shaking him off. "God damn it! We missed him by a fucking day!"

"Let's step outside, Agent Scarborough." Dwight jumped in to calm his partner and the three walked outside.

"I'm sorry. I didn't know," Kenny said.

"Calm down, Nick," Dwight began. "We're close. He left yesterday."

"Yeah, that's great, but we have no goddamn idea where the hell he's going." Nick placed his hands on his hips, appearing infuriated at the complete debacle that this case had become. "Son of a bitch. We were this goddamn close and he slipped through our fingers again." He turned toward the lobby door. "Maybe if people paid some fucking attention to something other than themselves!" His raised voice would have easily carried through the glass door and he made no apologies for it.

Kate regarded Dwight with great concern. She'd seen Nick angry before, but this was different. He was losing perspective and distance and that was when mistakes happened. "What about the other manager, the kid?" Kate needed to quickly diffuse this. "He would have been the one checking him out. Maybe he saw Colton, or at the very least, he might've seen the car he was driving. We can confirm then if he's in the same vehicle."

With a calmer tone, Nick agreed. "You're right. Let's see what he knows." Nick turned on his heel and walked back inside. "Kenny, would your night manager have been the one to check out Marco Rojas yesterday?"

"Yes, sir." Kenny was sweating again after watching the agent flip his lid.

"We need to see him right now."

Kenny picked up the radio and called Rickey, who was meandering around somewhere outside, trying to avoid the tense scene.

"You think he'll be able to ID Stroud?" Deputy Lewis asked.

"Better than that, I'm hoping he'll tell us what kind of car he was driving. If the son of a bitch got rid of his old truck, we can update the Amber Alert and the BOLO. We're a still day behind, but it's better than nothing."

"Rickey says he'll be here in just a minute, Agent Scarborough."

"Thank you. In the meantime," he said to Dwight, "I'm going to give Detective Mason a call and let her know what's going on. I'm hoping like hell she's making some progress on her end." Nick stepped back outside to make the call.

"You did good, Kate." Dwight rested a hand on her shoulder.

She watched Nick as he stood outside on the phone. "Yeah, well, a day late and a dollar short, right?" Kate returned her attention to Dwight. "I've never seen him like this before. He's too close. He flies off the handle at every obstacle. I'm not sure how long he can stay objective and focused."

"There've been plenty of times you were too close and he let you do what you needed to make things happen. Just give him the benefit of the doubt. He won't do anything to compromise the investigation."

"Is he really close with the Talbots?"

"I'm not sure how close. I can't recall him talking about them, or his buddy, Jake, but then, Nick doesn't talk about much else besides work. So, that doesn't mean anything." Dwight noticed the kid approaching. "Looks like our guy is here."

Rickey approached Nick and the two stood outside for a moment before entering.

"So, you remember him?" Nick asked as he walked back inside.

"Sure. He was kind of bald, a little heavy-set, maybe mid-thirties? Could be younger, but the bald head made him look old." Rickey moved toward the counter that Kenny still sat behind.

"But you didn't see a kid with him?" Nick continued.

"No, sir." Rickey looked up as though in deep thought. "No. Definitely no kid."

"Rickey, you remember what that man was driving?" Kenny asked and immediately regretted interrupting the agent.

Rickey looked up again, only this time placing his fingers over his thick chin. "Let me think. Yesterday morning, must've been early 'cause I just finished making another pot of coffee." He looked at Nick. "It was early, well before the ten a.m. checkout time."

"Rickey, do you remember the car he was driving?" Nick appeared impatient. "This boy's life is in danger and I need you to think hard."

Rickey swallowed and appeared anxious to say the right thing.

"Just answer the question," Kenny said.

"It was, um..." Rickey paused, squeezing his eyes shut. "It was a truck, blue, I think. Yes, it was a blue truck."

"Sounds like the same vehicle," Dwight said. "Didn't you say Mason got a tip on the truck yesterday?"

"Yes." He continued to press Rickey for answers. "Was it older?" Nick asked. "Come on, you have a clear view into the parking lot. You have to remember."

Kate wondered why he was hounding the kid. It was clear Stroud was in the same truck and the kid was scared out of his mind. "It's okay, Rickey. We think we know what it is."

"Just answer the question." Nick ignored Kate's words.

"I'm trying. I swear it. Blue, that's right. A blue Ford truck, I think it was. I remember the Ford nameplate on the grill. It was one of them extended cabs. That's right. I remember now."

"Thank you, Rickey." Nick patted him on the back. "You did good." And just like that, he appeared to be himself again.

Kate wondered what the hell just happened but worked to move past it. "You think he'll be going to another hotel? There isn't much of a distance between these places. I don't understand why he's stopping. It seems an unnecessary risk."

"Maybe not," Nick began. "He's on the move, staying off the roads as much as possible, and he has a destination. Signs are lit up all over the highways and state routes flashing the Amber Alert. Driving is too dangerous. Where he's headed, I can't say, but he's trying like hell to stay low and throw us off. I need to call Mason back and relay the news. This son of a bitch can't hide from us much longer."

11

C**olton waited for** the door to open, but the commotion outside continued. Things crashed to the ground, shouts from both the man and the old woman. There seemed to be a struggle between the two of them and Colton feared the old woman was losing. Who was she to him? His mother? Aunt? Too old to be a sister. But now he feared for her life just as he feared for his own. She was screaming now. Oh God, he was going to kill her and it would be his fault. He pounded on the door with the rod and yelled at the top of his lungs. "Help! Help me!"

A great thud sounded and Colton's shoulders dropped. That was no piece of furniture or decorator vase falling to the ground; that was a person and he knew it could only be her. The noise stopped.

Colton jumped back when the door unlocked and flew open with a furious whoosh of air. He almost dropped the rod and shard of the mirror but managed to cling on to them because they were all that stood between him and the bloodied, deranged man who stood before him.

"Look at what you made me do, you little fucker!" The man stepped aside and waved his arm at the sight of what was just beyond the door.

Colton peered out and revulsion masked his face. The old woman lay on the floor, her arms spread wide, but her legs close together. At first glance, she appeared to be mimicking the Crucifixion. Blood shrouded her face as though it had been poured over her and her silver hair was now stained red with clumps of broken flesh and brain clinging to it. Her eyes stared off into space, hollow and unmoving.

His eyes shifted back to the wild-eyed maniac who seemed ready to pounce. Now Colton knew the true horrors the man was capable of committing and realized he had to fight. He tightened his grip on the household weapons and waited.

"You did this! You killed my grandma!" The man stepped inside, lumbering toward Colton. "You should've kept quiet, kid."

Colton swung the rod with his right hand while plunging the shard toward the man with his left. An elegant move that could have come straight from the likes of a great battle of swords. But this was no sword and Colton was no swordsman. He was just a kid fighting for his life.

The rod bounced off the side of the man's head. Its plastic composition and his too-light swing weren't enough to do damage. The shard was his only hope, but the man pulled back and he missed his target. He tried again and this time connected, but only managed to slice away at the man's t-shirt. Blood from Colton's hand ran down his arm from the grip he had on the shard and while adrenaline surged with power through his lanky frame, it wasn't enough to keep the pain at bay and he dropped the mirror.

The man stepped further inside and closed the bathroom door; a fiendish leer plastered on his blood-spattered face.

"THANKS FOR COMING BY, AGENT SCARBOROUGH." Mason led the way to her office while Nick trailed behind. "I know your team is working hard on this investigation and we very much appreciate it. This was a good find." She held her door open and Nick walked inside.

"We've reached out to the State Police and asked them to assist with reviewing DOT cameras, but he's been staying off the highways so far as we can tell. I just wish we had better news. I've got my people working with the deputy as well and so we're ensuring all the authorities are on the same page." Nick waited for Mason to sit down behind her desk before he sat across from her. "So the ME got back to you?"

"Yes." Mason reached for her cell phone and placed it on the desk. "I got this message shortly after we talked. I'm afraid it isn't good news, but take a listen." She pressed play.

"Detective Mason, this is Dr. Pendergast. I have the results of the autopsy on the victim in question. I'll email you the full report, but in short, we calculated the time of death to have occurred on April 28th, at approximately 9:30 p.m."

Mason ended the message. "I'll shoot you a copy of the report as soon as I receive it, but she was taken on April 23rd, and that means..."

"That means, if Stroud is sticking to his M.O., Colton has a day at best. Considering the circumstances and the fact that Stroud knows we're on to him. He had all the time in the world with his first victim. He may feel more pressure now."

"Exactly." She looked at the time on her phone. "Listen, you want to grab a bite to eat? I haven't eaten all day."

"Sure." While Nick didn't have an appetite for food, he was more than ready for a drink and the idea of a fresh perspective from Detective Mason was appealing. He would have to update the Talbots and was hesitant to disappoint them once again. This meant he could stave that off for a time. He couldn't endure the look in Jake's and Rachel's eyes each time he told them they were getting close and to be patient. What a crock of shit that was. He knew it and they knew it. So yeah, dinner was exactly what he needed right now.

A QUIET CAFÉ nestled between an Irish pub and an antique store that had closed for the night was where they settled on as they drove through downtown Fairfax. Mason offered to drive since Nick made the trip down to see her and he didn't argue. She pulled alongside the curb, stepping out to feed the meter.

"I could've gotten that," Nick said as he approached.

"I got it. It's no problem. If we're longer than two hours, I'll let you feed it. Deal?" Mason walked toward the café.

"Deal."

The place was busy but not so much so that they'd have to wait. There was no time to wait and Nick just wanted a drink and then get the hell out of there and back to the office. Nick spotted the perfect table and when the hostess approached, he pointed toward it. "Can we sit there?"

"Of course, sir. Follow me."

Nick pulled Mason's chair out for her.

"Thank you." She sat down and adjusted her seat.

The detective had a nice smile and the way she looked at him felt good. He'd noticed her stolen glances toward him more than once since their first meeting. It had been a while since a woman looked at him like that. "I hope this is okay. It's a nice view." Why was this beginning to feel like a date? He wondered.

"It's perfect."

Small conversation dominated the first ten minutes before their entrees arrived. Nick did everything he could to not discuss the case, although it clearly weighed heavily in each of their minds.

"Is there anything else I can bring you?" the waiter asked.

"This will do, thank you," Nick replied. At her insistence, Nick had begun to refer to Detective Mason as Andrea and so he felt obliged to offer the same level of familiarity. "Andrea?"

"I'm fine, thank you." She began to raise the glass of wine. "I suppose we'll save the toasts for when we find Colton." A small, tender smile appeared on her lips.

It was the first time Nick noticed how perfectly full they were. Just enough to make him wonder what they tasted like. Then again, he was already on his second whiskey and that might have had something to do with it. Kate was always worrying about how much he drank. But she wasn't here right now. In fact, last he had heard, good ol' Mike was in town and so she had someone to talk to and a warm body to lie next to. Yeah, the whiskey was kicking in all right. "So, Andrea, what do you do for fun?" He regretted the question as soon as it rolled off his tongue. Trite and absurd, all things considered.

"I'm afraid there isn't much time for fun, and I bet you're in the same boat."

"I guess so. Do you have any kids?"

"No. I'm divorced but fortunately never reproduced with the likes of my ex-husband. But we won't go into that." She studied him for a moment. "Somehow I don't think you're a small-talk kind of guy, Nick. Just think of me as a co-worker. I don't need you to sugarcoat a conversation. If you'd like to let off steam about the investigation, I understand and, honestly, would expect it."

Nick acknowledged her candor and wasn't surprised by it. It had been less than a week, but he'd seen her no-nonsense style first hand and it was refreshing. "Okay. I don't feel like we're getting close. I feel like Lyle Stroud is slipping through my fingers and I'm going to have to tell my friend that his son is dead. That I was helpless to stop him. And that's a pretty shitty thing to have to face." There, he'd said it. An admission he'd kept from his own team because he always felt obliged to keep up the morale. That was his job. He and he alone shouldered that responsibility and this time around, it was bone-crushing.

"Yeah, it's a shitty thing," she began. "A position that I often find myself in and it doesn't matter what anyone else says, the reality of telling someone they'd lost a loved one, seeing the pain in their eyes, well, that's the worst part about this job." She took a sip of wine.

A silence fell between them, save for the sounds of background noise from the restaurant patrons and the occasional clinking of a glass.

Nick felt that familiar loneliness creeping in. When thoughts of a woman who knew nothing of his feelings crawled through his brain, all he wanted to do was drown them in the smoky, spicy burn of Johnny Walker Red. And if it drowned the thoughts of the boy too, then all the better. He was tired, but looking into the still-fresh eyes of the woman across from him, maybe she could be his savior, at least for tonight.

"Hey, you ready to get out of here? I'm going to have to head back to the office soon." He glanced at his watch. "But, um, I might have a little time."

Her eyes revealed that she understood his meaning and she raised her hand for the check.

The door of her apartment flung open and they almost tumbled inside. Nick pressed her against the wall, kissing her full lips, and now he knew they tasted like the silky, buttery wine she'd had at dinner.

She pulled back for a moment. "Wait." She locked the deadbolt and took Nick's hand, leading him to the couch. Unbuttoning her blouse, she exposed the perfect heart-shaped cleavage that peeked out from her satin, flesh-toned bra.

Nick kissed the top of her breasts, pushing back all other thoughts but this one. That he was about to have sex with an attractive, intelligent woman who understood exactly what this was—a release; one that they both needed.

When the moment of passion ended, Nick rose from the

couch and reached for his pants that were crumpled on the floor. A few loose coins fell from his pockets and after he pulled them up, he grabbed the fallen change and shoved it back in. His holster rested on the seat of the chair kitty-cornered to the sofa. He hadn't yet said anything as he pulled himself back together. He wasn't sure exactly what to say. Thanks? That would make him sound like a douche. Which, maybe at this moment, he was. "I'd better be getting back to the office."

Andrea secured her blouse again and buttoned her suit pants against her slim waist. "Sure. I'd better check in myself."

Now he felt bad because he thought she was making that up. Maybe not, but he supposed it didn't matter in the end. "I had a nice time."

Andrea Mason was a big girl and knew how to wear her big-girl pants. "Same here. I'll walk you out." She started toward the door and pulled it open while Nick was still several feet away. "I'll be in touch if I hear anything."

"Sounds good." Nick gave her a gentle peck on the cheek and smiled. "I'll see you later."

Kate had returned home for a late dinner with Mike. He was due to catch the red-eye out of town and back to Jacksonville, so they didn't have much time left.

"I'm sorry it's so late." Kate pierced a piece of steak onto her fork.

"You've apologized three times already since you got home. You don't need to do that. I knew things were crazy for you right now. I'm just glad we got to spend some time together."

"It's just disappointing when you leave."

"Listen, Kate, I know we haven't talked about this lately, but have you given any more thought to what your plans are for this place?"

"You mean, the lease?" She already knew where this was going.

"Yes. Did you decide if you're going to stay here another year?"

His eyes were full of hope and she loved that about him, but she hadn't decided. In fact, she hadn't thought much about it at all. Time was running out. She had one month to come to a decision. And in her world, everything could change in a month.

"I'm sorry, Mike. I haven't had a chance to really lay it all out. I mean, I think it's time to buy, considering my probation is almost up. No point in throwing money out the window every month." Her pragmatism was coming through in spades and she tried hard to separate Mike's needs from those of her own because, in the end, she wouldn't let a man decide her fate, no matter how strong her feelings were for him. She'd grown from the woman she once was. There was no time for flights of fancy, believing in the "one." She'd had that and it was gone now.

"So, you'll move? You'll buy a place of your own?" Mike looked as though he had more to say on the matter but held his tongue for her reply.

Kate looked around the house and smiled. "This place has been good for me, but I guess there isn't much point in staying unless Mrs. Mitchell wanted to sell, but I doubt that. It's a good income for her; she owns it outright."

Mike knocked back a sizable swig of beer from the half-empty bottle. "I guess what I'm getting at is I'd like to know how I fit into the equation. I know it's only been what, five or six months? But I think you know how I feel about you. I think you feel the same."

"Yes, I feel the same." It was no longer a question of money for Kate. Her permanent salary would be substantially more than her probationary one and she still had Marshall's stash, although she'd still considered buying a new car with that. Either way, it wouldn't be as much of a financial burden on her anymore. She was free to go in whatever direction she chose. "I don't want you to leave your job for me, Mike. I guess that's what it really boils down to. And, I'm going to be in this field office for the foreseeable future. Are you prepared to leave behind the life you've built? The career you've built? To come here and start over?"

"Kate, I'm a small-town cop. I'm not going to make sheriff because the sheriff isn't going anywhere—ever. I'm thirty-four, and I have no kids." He captured her gaze at these words. "Changing isn't a problem for me. I don't look at it as giving up anything. I look at it as gaining you—gaining a life with you." He raised his fork again. "Besides, I could get a job with Metro Police. I may have already made a call or two."

She tried to conceal her mild surprise. They had talked about this and so of course he would look into such things, but this caught her unawares. Kate really had no idea what she wanted or what she wanted from him. Her conflict came not from a lack of feelings for him, but from a fear of losing someone she loved again. It was capricious at best and irrational at worst. Nevertheless, that was how she felt. She simply couldn't answer him, which spoke volumes.

"You know what, forget what I said." Mike began to walk back his words. "You're involved in a case right now and this isn't the time. I get that. These aren't decisions that can be made on the fly or in the afterglow of lovemaking. These are serious considerations for both of us and I'll leave it at that for now."

She sensed his frustration but didn't want to pursue the conversation any further. "So, you all packed and ready to go? Looks like we'll need to head out in twenty minutes or so."

"Yeah, I'm ready," he replied.

12

The blood ran from his hands beneath the running water and into the sink, creating a crimson-veined pool that slowly drained away. He gazed into the mirror and a pale face glistening with sweat and blood spatters stared back at him. His chest still heaved from both the thrill and the physical exertion, leaving him with a euphoria that would carry him through the grueling tasks ahead.

The death of Lyle's grandmother was to be expected, however, he hadn't wanted it to be so soon. He knew the moment he arrived at her home that it would mean her life. But she was the only relative he knew they wouldn't find. His father's mother had been abandoned by her husband while he remarried another who helped raise his father. Stroud had spent time with her over the summers while he was growing up but hadn't seen her in more than ten years.

He had loved her, or what he recalled love once felt like. But the years of prison had turned him into something less than a man who developed a cold detachment from all things human. There was no denying his chosen path in life would culminate in such a transformation. After all, he was in prison for a reason, but in those early years, he hadn't the stomach to commit the acts that came so easily for him today. In those early years, his true desires had yet to fully surface. It had initially been a game of revenge that had grown into a craving; a desire to fulfill a goal concocted by his twisted fantasies that had been nurtured behind bars.

And Stroud knew how to game the system as well. His parole hinged upon successful counseling and good behavior, both of which were easily mastered and manipulated. And the counseling failed spectacularly in its attempt to squelch the fantasies that played in his mind at the mere sight of children. They didn't know just how drawn to them he was and had no idea who they'd unleashed upon an unsuspecting public. Blame for his distorted views could perhaps fall on the shoulders of the boys who'd once bullied him in school. Perhaps bullying wasn't the right word. Raped was the right word. And he fantasized about controlling the children as he had once been controlled by those boys. But he was otherwise not abused as a child; physically, sexually, or emotionally by any relative. And certainly not by the grandmother he'd just murdered.

As a young adult, Stroud initiated his game of revenge. He'd sought and achieved retribution on those boys and that should have been enough to stem the growth of what had now become his obsession, but it hadn't. He'd gotten away with it and that brought with it a thrill all its own. The second time, though, he wasn't so lucky. A random kid he'd seen in his neighborhood. A young preteen girl who'd managed to pry away from him before he could do any real damage and she told her parents. Stroud went to prison for that attack.

For whatever reason, a gene defect? He didn't know, but he and his sister seemed to deviate onto paths that society would deem repulsive and cast them away to rot inside the cracks into which they'd fallen. That combined with years of exposure to a prison society that further dehumanized all contained within, the transformation into the man reflecting at him now wasn't as much of a leap as one might expect.

Stroud turned off the water and grabbed the hand towel that hung on the wall only inches from him in this tiny bathroom upstairs from where the real mess still needed to be cleaned. The idea had crossed his mind that outsiders, passersby, might have heard the commotion, but the basement in this old house, which was comprised of well-insulating brick and concrete, made that a less likely scenario. Still, he couldn't risk anything and was in a very vulnerable position right now. The girl had been easy to dispose of, but now he had two bodies and the kid was almost as tall as he was; slight but troublesome just the same.

He stepped outside where the murky sky with its scattered stars barely illuminated the quiet, rural community. The neighbors were few and far between, even better, but Stroud continued outside, stepping off the wooden porch and was now exposed. He looked left, then right; no one could be seen. His days here would be numbered, however, because Grandma played Bunko with a few other blue hairs every Saturday night and when they came ringing the doorbell, he'd better be halfway to Timbuctoo.

The truck was in front of his grandma's car beneath the

carport in an attempt to keep it hidden from the road. It was far too risky to continue to drive it any longer. He'd seen the Amber Alert and stayed off the roads as much as possible, but he would have to leave again and that meant ridding himself of the old truck he prized. The question still rose in his mind. How did they know it was him? How could they have identified him only days after he'd taken the boy? Something had to have been left behind; he had to have been careless and now they knew who they were after. It was a costly mistake in any event, but now he questioned whether or not those smart-ass cops found what he kept in his house. Because if they did, it would destroy everything he'd worked for up to this point.

The hour had already grown late and he would not leave tonight. Stroud went back inside to get the keys to Grandma's car. Her 2003 Olds Cutlass was about to be his newest mode of transportation. It was a wonder she still drove, but she had been a tough old woman. He cast his gaze down for a split second while a brief flash of sympathy passed through him. She was his family, after all, but the feeling didn't last long.

Inside the house once again, he stood at the door of the basement and looked down the stairs. What was the point of cleaning up the mess? Hiding the bodies? The cops knew who he was and were looking for the kid. Wouldn't take much to put two and two together, even for those fuckheads. But he knew his luck would run very thin after this little discovery.

He'd seen the cops on TV talking about the kid. The parents pleaded for his return. Now that the kid was dead, Lyle Stroud was about to be the most wanted man in the state, and so he could do one of two things.

Pouring a glass of water from the pitcher that still sat on the dinner table, he considered his options. Stay and most definitely be captured. Or do what all his prison buddies talked about doing; go out in a blaze of glory. Was it his style? Not really, but he didn't like the idea of putting his hands up in surrender either. He reached into his pants pocket and retrieved a slip of paper. A pen was nearby and Stroud began scratching on the paper, crossing off the second name on his list. First the girl, Emily Aldrich, and now the boy, Colton Talbot. He scanned the names to see who was next. He called this his "endangered species" list.

He'd already passed the point of no return and going back to prison would be easier. Then again, he'd suffered at the hands of the inmates who took it upon themselves to dole out justice for child molesters. Now Stroud was a child killer. His time in prison would be short-lived and that didn't mean on Death Row either.

He studied his list again. It had been carefully cultivated after months of online searches. Looking for those who flaunted their privileged lives. Kids who thought they were better than everyone else, just like those boys in the ninth grade had done. Team captains, winners of all the popularity contests, rich parents. This was his ultimate game of revenge. A goal to rid the world of selfie-taking little shits who had no idea what hard life was really like. Stroud hated and coveted them, and wanted to fill them with pain that *he* would dole out. Sexual desire played a minimal role. It was how it made him feel afterward that was better than any orgasm.

"I keep going." He set the glass down after gulping so much water that his stomach began to hurt. Dying was an almost certainty, so why go out like a prison bitch? Stroud would finish what he started.

KATE SAT in Nick's office, waiting for the briefing to begin, not that she expected much if any, fresh news. Another day had passed and still no truck matching their suspect's. She believed, after the last motel, that they were too close not to find him, but it had become clear Stroud was in hiding. He had to have seen the news stories and figured the entire damn state was looking for him. The team's initial fiery hopes of finding Colton alive had dwindled to a mere ember that had nearly extinguished.

The reason for the meeting? She believed Nick was about to suggest they head back to Winchester to search Stroud's place. Mason's team had already done it, but Nick knew Kate had something special. Something that made it possible for her to find clues others had missed. It didn't always work out that way, but most of the time, it did. She'd grown to accept it as divine intervention, of sorts, and never dismissed the possibility that she had an angel on her shoulder pushing her in the right direction. She would never admit this out loud, but Nick had seen it first-hand on more than one occasion. Why he'd been dismissive of her lately remained largely a mystery to her, because this was something he should have authorized the moment they took the lead. Instead, he'd been relying on information from Fairfax County Police. They were doing their job, but he'd failed to utilize his team, meaning her, in the appropriate manner.

"Good morning." Dwight entered and took a seat next to Kate. "You manage to get Mike to the airport all right?"

"It was a late flight, but he made it back home."

Dwight studied her for a moment. "You two still getting along?"

"Of course, yeah." She shifted in her seat. "I just have some decisions to make and I'm not sure I'm ready to make them."

"I see." Dwight looked as though he was about to ask another probing, personal question when Nick walked in.

He dropped a file on his desk. "This is the report from the search Fairfax County conducted on Stroud's residence after his identity was revealed." Nick pulled the report from the file and spread it out on his desk. "I'd like you two to take a look. They still have forensics looking into his computer, but apparently, whatever he kept, he kept it on cloud servers and not his hard drive. All we have is the picture of Emily Aldrich from his locker. But if he kept a picture of her, it means he was probably stalking her beforehand. If that's the case, then he kept a picture of Colton Talbot somewhere and probably followed him too."

"Did he have a connection to her at all? Family friend? Anything like that?" Dwight asked.

"None that they've found. She lived miles from his home, so I don't know how he found her or why. That's what we need to find out. And, there may be something left behind at his home. We can't afford to overlook anything right now. I'm not sure how much time Colton has."

"What would make him revert to his old behavior? It had been a year since he got out." Kate held the picture of Emily in her hand. "Wasn't he required to attend counseling as a condition of parole? Wouldn't his counselor have seen this change?"

"It was group counseling, and according to his parole officer, Stroud was highly cunning. A sociopath with manipulative skills that were above par. Unfortunately, the parole officer learned this too late," Nick replied. "He could easily have hidden his desires as a result. That may be how he survived prison, considering his crimes and how the hierarchy of prison dictates child abusers to be the lowest of the low."

"So he was granted parole based on lies and manipulation," Kate said.

"And that he'd served his sentence and was a model prisoner," Dwight continued.

"Right. Then he'd be required to continue with counseling as a condition of release, and he's a registered sex offender and ex-con at this point. So how and when does he begin to rediscover his desires?"

"I don't think they ever went away, Kate," Nick said. "I think he's been biding his time, waiting for the right moment to make his move, or he simply saw an opportunity and was drawn to this girl."

"That doesn't explain why he went after Colton Talbot, some eighty miles away," Kate said.

"No, it doesn't. However, I suspect he realized he'd crossed the line and knew there was no going back home. I don't know why he chose to stop in the suburbs of Fairfax County." Nick appeared to be losing hold of his emotions but quickly reeled them in. "I'm hoping the three of us can find something in Stroud's house. Something that might give us a clue as to what his plan is and what lies east." Nick rose from his chair. "We're all failing the Talbots right now."

Detective Mason was going to meet them at Stroud's home within the hour. Kate was glad to be along for the ride this time and hoped that Nick was returning to his old self; the man who insisted Kate was meant to be a Federal agent and practically coddled her through the process of making that happen. Although she didn't want to dismiss her own abilities, Nick had, nonetheless, made it possible for her to be here now. With her probationary status on the line, she needed to be in the field again to prove to ASAC Campbell that she deserved to be here.

The case was getting to Nick and Kate feared his impulsivity could jeopardize the investigation. Perhaps he would go too far with his usual bending of the rules. But, if she had any say in the matter, she wouldn't let that happen. Finding Colton was equally as important to her as it was to Nick, whether he knew that or not.

Upon their arrival, an officer stepped outside to greet them. "Detective Mason will be here soon. I just got off the horn with her."

"Great. Thanks." Nick scrolled through his phone without so much as a glance at the officer. "Can we go inside?"

"Oh, sure." He pushed open the door. "Sorry about that. So, you guys work in BAU?" The officer's eyes appeared with some sparkle in them, as though he envied them.

"The Washington Field Office of the BAU, yes," Dwight began. "Under Agent Scarborough's residency."

"That means we're sort of an assistant branch of the BAU. Each field office has a resident agent, but BAU headquarters is in Quantico," Kate added.

"That's pretty cool."

The officer was young, maybe even a rookie. "How long

have you been with Fairfax County?" Kate wanted him to feel like he was a part of this too and she was genuine in her question.

Once inside, he closed the door behind them. "It's my second year on the force. I was in the Reserves for a while, did a stint in Afghanistan, and became a cop after that."

"Thank you for your service."

Nick looked over his shoulder at Kate, as if, in that moment, he realized his callous attitude needed to be checked. He displayed a brief smile, then returned his attention to the interior of the home.

The officer's radio buzzed in. "Grayson here," he answered.

"Be there in five."

The voice on the radio sounded familiar to Kate.

"Ten-four." He eyed Kate. "Detective Mason is almost here. Won't be much longer."

Within the time she'd specified, Detective Mason had arrived. "Sorry, I got delayed." The detective stepped inside the home and brushed her dark blonde hair from her eyes. Breathing heavily as though she'd run all the way here, she turned to Nick and extended her hand. "Thanks for coming down, Agent Scarborough, but as I mentioned on the phone, my team went through this place with a fine-tooth comb, however, you're welcome to have a poke around. Hey, extra sets of eyes can never hurt." She turned on her heel. "Why don't you guys follow me?"

"Thank you for your help, Officer Grayson," Kate said as she pulled up the rear.

The house had clearly been scoured, from what Kate could see. No personal items remained. No pictures or knick-knacks or even a dirty dish in the sink. "So, the report you sent to us, included all the forensics?"

Mason turned to Kate. "What we have, yes. We're still waiting on hair samples that were found in the carpet fibers and a complete report on the findings from his computer. No cell phone was found, but I believe we've already handed over his phone records. Once Agent Scarborough discovered Emily Aldrich's picture at Stroud's workplace, we came back and made another sweep, trying to determine if the girl had been brought here before he decided to drive south and abduct Colton Talbot."

"I doubt that." Nick studied the fireplace mantel, although nothing remained on it. "He'd have had to back-track to do that and he didn't have that kind of time. Where are the pictures of his family? I saw in the report that this mantel had a couple of frames on it."

"There were pictures here, yes, but they weren't his family. Looked like they were friends." Detective Mason moved in for a closer look, brushing against Nick's arm.

He unveiled an awkward grin at her obvious gesture. "You're telling me he had friends?"

"Seems so. Why? Does that seem out of character from your profile?"

Immediately, Kate thought of Georgia. There was no need for a profiler in this particular instance because they knew who they were dealing with and what his criminal background consisted of, but she thought of her just the same.

"My guess is he was just putting on airs for unexpected visits from his parole officer or counselor. Make it look like he had friends and was getting along well with life outside of prison."

"But you obviously don't think that," Mason said.

"No. Not this guy. My opinion is that he shouldn't have ever been released, to begin with." Nick began to head toward the hall. "Kate?" A toss of his head meant she needed to join him.

She followed him down the hall and into what appeared to be Stroud's bedroom.

Nick turned to her. "I want you to spend some time in here. If there's anything to be found, it'll be here."

"What makes you think that?"

"Like I told the detective, Stroud was putting up a front, but he still would've needed a place to call his own, where he didn't need to hide his true self."

Nick had just confirmed his faith in her was alive and well and if he thought she could find something in here, then she would. That familiar little twitch in her mind began to flutter. "Okay. I'll have a look around."

"I'd better get back out there. We can still look through the rest of the house." He placed a hand on Kate's shoulder. "Come find me if you need me."

Kate was left to do what could be the impossible; find something that might not be there to find. But she'd been here before —many times and right from the very beginning. Right from the day she saw the necklace on that woman. It hadn't occurred to her then, but that was when it started.

A bed was positioned on the opposite wall but had no covers on it. They would've taken any bedding for analysis. She moved to the closet; no clothes inside, not even a hanger. Every dresser drawer had been emptied. The place was cleaned out. Perhaps she and Nick had given her too much credit.

Kate slipped her shoes off to walk barefoot on the thick pile carpet. Maybe she'd come across something stuck in its fibers. She wasn't going to find any jewelry here. No red herring that would send them in the wrong direction. After several minutes, she was beginning to grasp at straws. So she stopped, closed her eyes, and cleared her mind. "I have to find Colton. I need your help." It was the first time she'd asked him for help. She'd spoken to Marshall many, many times, but this—well, she was desperate.

She opened her eyes again with a renewed perspective. Kate walked toward a small en suite bathroom and stepped inside. It was just as empty as the rest of the bedroom. Bright yellow tile covered half the wall all the way around and climbed up to the ceiling where the shower stood. A mirror hung above the sink. She stopped for a moment in front of the mirror. Was that? She moved in closer and smiled. Partial fingerprints on either side of the mirror, as though someone had lifted it from its hook, appeared before her.

Not wanting to contaminate anything, she looked around the side of the rectangular mirror and then the other side. Kate immediately walked out of the room and back into the main living area where the others remained.

"Agent Scarborough, can you come back here for a moment, please?" She turned and walked back without waiting for a reply.

He began to follow, nodding to Dwight to do the same. The two entered the room, but Kate wasn't there.

"I'm in the bathroom," she said, hearing their approach.

They joined her inside.

"Something's behind this mirror. Anyone have gloves?"

Nick pulled out a pair and slid them on. He stepped closer to get a better grip on the mirror and carefully lifted it off the wall. Kate and Dwight had spotted what was there but waited until Nick could see as he lowered the mirror.

"Well, God damn." He looked to his partners. "What've we got here?"

13

The burgundy Olds Cutlass was parked beneath a tree, which made the car appear almost black in the shade under the midday sun. The narrow street was usually lined with parked cars, but the weekday meant most of those cars were parked at various places of employment. Stroud no longer had such a place and money was running very tight at the moment. His grandmother kept a stash in her bedroom and one in the kitchen. He'd taken all of it but knew it wouldn't last long. His hand rested atop the rolled-down window, a lit cigarette dangled between two fingers. He stared at the apartment building across the street, wondering if his sister still lived there. Although he began to suspect that if she did, cops might be waiting—or watching.

If his sister did still reside in the building that was unmistakably government housing, she'd likely be high as a kite, so taking money from her would be all too easy, but the question still floated in his head. Was he being watched right now?

Probably not because they'd have swarmed him already. They were looking for a man who had a kid. He no longer had that kid, but once they found the dead boy, Stroud knew things would change.

He stepped out of the car, tossing a look in each direction. Assured no one was watching, at least from the street, he walked across, his gait affected by the blow to his right leg the kid managed to get in before the end. A nasty bruise had formed on his knee and a burst of pain surged with each step. He tossed the cigarette to the ground after a final puff and placed the sunglasses over his eyes. The sun still scorched his balding head and he cursed the heat.

The door to the building required a key to enter, and there was an intercom fixed to the wall with names written beneath of the occupants. He scanned the list. Her name wasn't there. "Fuck." Lyle returned to the car, still monitoring his surroundings. The entire country was about to know who he was and sitting in that car, with an unhinged mind, he perfected his plan that would send shivers down the collective spine of society. He was the devil and there was no point in denying it.

One of Detective Mason's officers arrived with a crowbar. It was all they had on hand, but it would do the job.

"Let's open this up and see what we find." Nick's tone was almost giddy with anticipation, a marked shift from his earlier deflated manner.

Kate knew something of relevance was behind the mirror and now waited to be proven right. A piece of drywall had been haphazardly hung over what appeared to be a cutout for a medicine cabinet that was now covered.

The officer began to hammer away at the wall, careful not to go too deep as to potentially damage whatever was contained inside. The drywall came down quickly and in a sizeable chunk. White dust floated into the air and soon fell upon the porcelain sink below, blanketing it with its powder.

"Hold up!" Nick raised his hand. "That'll do." He approached the opening, pulling away at the jagged pieces on the sides. As he got a closer look, he turned to Kate and shook his head.

She moved in closer. "We'd better tag this. Detective Mason?"

"I'm on it." She walked out of the bathroom with her officer in tow. "Let's get Forensics down here." While pleased by the find, her eyes conveyed regret over her own negligence.

"What the hell are we looking at here, Kate?" Dwight asked although they all knew the answer.

Several images of young kids and online posts or articles were inside the opening. Some stuck to the wooden studs, some fixed to the drywall on the back. The interior was almost completely wallpapered with the clippings.

"We thought this was all random, but it isn't." Kate peered inside again. "These kids. He's been watching them."

"I have a feeling we'll find a picture of Colton Talbot," Dwight replied.

"Son of a bitch has been finding kids online." Nick leaned in farther but didn't touch anything, not until Forensics could photograph and bag it all.

"We could find a blueprint here. Whatever plan he's

concocted," Kate began. "We think he took the girl first and then Colton. We'll have to look at these others here and see if any of them are missing."

"And, we need to find out who's next. We need names. Until we can get a closer look, we have no idea who these kids are." Nick turned to leave. "Stroud's only just begun."

"Should I knock again?" Mrs. Hirsch turned to her friends. Although her eyes drooped with age, there was no denying the concern they held at this moment.

"You know Eileen, she's probably got the T.V. too loud and can't hear us. Go on, try again," Mrs. Gunderson said.

The other two elderly women nodded their agreement.

Another knock, but still nothing. "Well, now I'm getting worried. I know she keeps a spare key around here somewhere." Mrs. Hirsch began to search the porch for signs of the key and the other ladies joined in.

"I found it! Come on, then, let's go see what she's up to." Maggie Hirsch was as close to Eileen Abbott as two women could be without being related. This was their weekly Bunko game and Eileen always insisted on hosting.

"Eileen?" Maggie stepped inside the foyer. She turned to her friends. "Must be in the kitchen." She continued through the hall.

Plates were on the table along with food that had obviously been there for a while. "Oh my. Eileen?" Her voice raised in panic. "Where are you?"

The other women felt the same panic and began to call out for their friend, but there was no answer.

Louise Gunderson was the first to reach the basement stairs. "Eileen? You down there?" Her nerves seemed on edge as her voice fractured. She turned back to find the other women, but they were looking elsewhere. It would be up to her to walk down these steps.

She reached for the handrail and began her descent with careful consideration of each step. Her knees ached from arthritis, but the pain seemed to disappear behind her racing pulse. "Eileen? Honey, you down here?" She continued and was approaching the final few steps. An odor reached her nose and she flinched with disgust.

Upon reaching the bottom of the stairs, the horrific scene revealed itself. A voracious scream clawed from her throat. Moments later, the footsteps of her approaching friends sounded loudly above.

"What is it? Louise, what's going on?" Maggie rushed down the stairs and clutched her chest at the sight of Eileen splayed out on the floor surrounded by blood that had soaked into the carpet and appeared more like tar. "No, no, no!" She ran to Eileen.

"Don't touch her, Maggie!" Louise cried out.

"Call 911!" Maggie turned toward the steps but caught sight of the bathroom. "Oh Lord, oh no." She moved closer.

"What is it?" Louise stood frozen on the last step.

Maggie shook with horror as tears streamed down her deeply-lined face. "God help us, there's a boy down here."

~

Detective Mason offered the use of the department's conference room to review the items retrieved from Stroud's home. It was clear she was shouldering the blame for the screw-up, although, in Kate's eyes, they hadn't. No one would have thought to look behind that mirror and while she would never have revealed just what made her look, she didn't blame those officers.

"We didn't think we were dealing with an internet predator. Turns out, we were wrong." Nick rested his elbows on the table and leaned in for a closer look. "How the hell did he find these kids? What was he looking for?

"And what are these? Posts or blogs or something?" Dwight held up one of the sheets of paper.

Kate leaned in to take a look too. "Hey, there's a name here." She pointed to the post. "This looks like maybe something from a school article or Facebook page. Just a first name, Sophie." She examined the contents on the table again. "Damn, which one of these girls is Sophie?"

Nick rubbed his forehead. "Christ, I don't know." He rummaged through the images until he saw it. Colton was in his baseball uniform, holding a trophy. The caption read, "MVP at Springfield Little League playoff tournament." His eyes drew up slowly. "This was how he found him. A picture of Colton and his location right below it."

Kate noticed an immediate shift in Nick's demeanor. This was the moment she knew would come. It was as though he was splintering right before her eyes. Anger darkened his brow while despair weighed down his shoulders. She placed her hand on top of his. "We'll find Colton. We'll find out who all these children are and make sure they're safe."

Nick brushed off her concern and turned his attention to the detective, who'd just returned.

"We found Colton's picture," Kate began. "Below it stated where he was from."

"Find any other names or locations of these kids?" Mason asked.

"We have another first name, but nothing more. Not yet."

Mason brushed her hair from her eyes again. It must have been a nervous tick. "Jesus. How the hell did I miss this?"

Nick looked at her with some sympathy. "Anyone could've missed this, Andrea. I just hope these other kids are still alive."

"And that we find out who they are," she replied. Silence swept over the room. "Listen, why don't I have some food brought in? You guys must be starving." She left without waiting for a response as though she was trying to disguise her own overwhelming feelings.

"You got some kind of sixth sense, Kate," Dwight grinned.

"I don't know about a sixth sense. I think it's more like a guardian angel."

"Well, whatever it is, I'm glad you're on our side."

While they continued to piece together Stroud's plan, Detective Mason returned with an unmistakable look.

"What is it? What's going on?" Nick asked with an urgency that shot through him like a bullet.

"Colton Talbot is dead."

THEY ARRIVED at the home of Eileen Abbott, grandmother to Lyle Stroud, whose relation had been quickly revealed with the use of the FBI database. An oversight Detective Mason again shouldered. Kate stood on the porch of the home and stared inside, her eyes glazing over the officers collecting evidence and snapping pictures. The real horrors lie below and she needed to muster the strength to see that.

It was the worst possible outcome, but one the team had expected. Too much time had passed and she knew the critical hours in any abduction were the first forty-eight. It had been six days since Colton was abducted and they didn't yet know how long he'd been dead.

"I need to go downstairs," Nick began as he approached Kate. "I have to see him."

"No, you don't. Just let them do what they need to do to get him out of there as quickly as possible." She held his shoulder to prevent him from entering the home. "I'm sorry, Nick."

"We found out too late. If we'd known what he was doing—hunting down these kids—we might've stopped him."

"I don't think that would've been possible. He might know who they are, but we still don't, except the ones who are already gone."

Nick pulled away from her. "I have to go in there."

Kate closed her eyes in defeat and with a moment to regain her composure, she followed him inside. Just as she reached the top of the stairs, Dwight called out her name and she glanced over her shoulder to see him appear from the dining area.

"Hang on. Where's Nick?"

She pointed down the steps.

"Jesus."

"I tried to stop him."

"Stopping him when he's got his mind set is like trying to

stop a speeding train." He folded his arms and cast his gaze at what lay below. "I'll go down. You stay here and see if these guys need anything."

Dwight slowly made his way to the bottom of the steps. Mason was already down there along with the coroner. Kate didn't need to go; there were enough people already crowded around the gruesome scene and her presence would only add to the congestion. And frankly, she didn't want to see Nick's face. This was breaking him and she already saw a glimpse of that at the station when they got the news. He needed to be pulled from the case; that would be the right thing to do, but she doubted Dwight would make any such recommendation. And there wasn't a chance she would; not after all he'd done for her when she was desperate to find those who sought to bring her harm. A betrayal like that would be unforgivable.

Nick was starting back up the steps but kept his head down. His pace was slow, drained of life. He raised his eyes to Kate. "They're bringing him up now."

THE HOSPITAL DOORS parted and Nick was the first to enter. Kate was only steps behind him but saw Colton's parents several feet ahead waiting in the lobby. Grief had already begun to consume them and the moment they all feared had arrived.

There was nothing Kate or Dwight could do but stand aside and let Nick be the one to take the brunt of the parents' sorrow. He'd already insisted on the drive over and they weren't going to change his mind. Kate's mentor stood not confident and sure-footed, but damaged, knowing what needed to be done.

Nick approached Jake and Rachel. "I'm so sorry." His expression remained steadfast, but his eyes revealed his pain.

Rachel stepped closer and raised her hand, slapping his face with the strength that comes from overwhelming agony.

A mark immediately appeared on his cheek, but Nick didn't flinch; instead, he absorbed the blow as though he'd deserved it.

"Rachel!" Jake pulled her back.

"You promised you'd find him. You promised you'd bring him home safe." Rachel's sorrow filled the entire room. Her anguish penetrated the very souls of all who stood near.

Kate turned away with welling eyes. She didn't want to take anything from this woman who needed this moment of temporary release; one of many that would come in the weeks and even years ahead. She would not rob her of that with her distraction.

"Rachel, this isn't Nick's fault. He did everything he could." Jake embraced his wife and looked at Nick. "I know you did everything you could."

Nick inhaled a deep, controlling breath. His own emotions seemed ready to spill, but like Kate, he wouldn't let that happen. "I know I let you down and I hope one day you'll be able to forgive me."

"Can we see our boy?" Jake asked.

"Yes. Follow me." Nick headed toward the corridor, passing by Kate and Dwight. He locked eyes with Kate and a brief, knowing exchange of emotion drifted between them.

Detective Mason soon approached. "I'll give them a minute before I go back."

"We all held out hope for Colton." Dwight turned his sights as Nick and Colton's parents disappeared beyond the doors.

"The most important thing now is to identify the other children in the photos and online posts. We still have a chance to save them."

"I'm going to step outside for a moment." Kate walked through the near-empty lobby and stepped outside, the sticky air immediately clinging to her skin. With no one in sight, she set free her emotions and fell back against the smooth stone wall only feet from the entrance. Her heart broke for those parents and for Nick. It didn't matter that she was the one who found the evidence that could still save the other children if they acted fast enough because it was too late to save the one who mattered most to Nick.

Kate retrieved her phone to call Mike but decided that perhaps now was not the right time. He would offer comfort to her and she wanted that, more than anything, but she was needed inside. Nick was going to need her. And so, she cleared her throat, dabbed her eyes with her fingers, and walked back in to face what would come next.

On her return, Nick was talking to Dwight and Detective Mason. Kate approached. "Are they still back there?"

"Yes. They need to say goodbye." Nick held Kate's gaze.

She knew what he felt, but could do nothing about it. "Of course."

"We should probably head back. It's late," Dwight said. "We can get an early start on ID'ing the other kids, but I know we all need a few hours' rest. Then we can track Stroud down before he finds his next victim."

"That's a good idea," Mason replied. "Agent Scarborough, can I speak to you for a moment?"

The two walked outside, leaving Kate and Dwight to

wonder what she needed to discuss that couldn't be discussed in their presence.

"Listen," Andrea began as the doors closed and they were alone, "I know what you're going through right now, and if it wouldn't be too awkward, you're welcome to come stay with me tonight. I'm only ten minutes away and I can get you back down to the station early." She glanced through the glass at the other agents. "I don't know how that would fly with your people, but I imagine you probably don't care about that right now."

Nick turned briefly to see Kate and Dwight huddled together in conversation. They didn't seem concerned by the two of them alone outside. Or if they were, they weren't showing it. He pressed his lips together in a thin smile, although his eyes still revealed the devastation of this latest blow. "I appreciate the offer, Andrea, but I just don't think I can be around anyone right now. I need a few hours to clear my head. I doubt I'll sleep, but I have to refocus so we can find Stroud before he takes another child." He closed his eyes. "I let them down in the worst possible way and I need some time to come to terms with that. Please don't be offended."

"No. I'm not offended." She raised onto her toes and kissed his still-reddened cheek. "Try to get some rest and I'll see you in a few hours."

14

"We **could get** a hotel," Dwight began as he opened the door to Nick's SUV. "Or you guys can crash at my place. I'm closer than driving back to Woodbridge."

"Maybe a hotel isn't a bad idea," Kate replied. "I just want to put my head down."

"That's fine. The closer we are, the better." Nick keyed the ignition and pulled away from the hospital.

Kate searched on her phone for the nearest hotel. "How about the Holiday Inn? It's two miles from here."

"Perfect," Nick replied.

They arrived in minutes and entered the lobby. The time had already passed one a.m. and they would need to be back at the station no later than five. Not much time, but enough to clear their minds so they didn't make any mistakes. They couldn't afford not to find Stroud when they had no idea who or where those children were. It had just become a race for time and their weary faces revealed anything but.

"I'm just gonna grab a drink to quiet my mind." Nick started to walk into the lobby bar, which was only open until two a.m. "You guys can go on up to bed. No need to wait for me."

"I'll join you," Dwight replied.

"Me too. I wouldn't mind a drink to help me sleep." The idea had been appealing. Taking the edge off in this moment was very much needed. And she knew Nick needed it, even if she disliked it when he turned to alcohol for an answer. Right now, though, she wouldn't nag him about it.

"Jack and Coke, please," he said to the bartender before turning to the others. "What do you guys want?"

"That's fine for me," Dwight replied.

"Same here."

"Are they transferring the body tonight?" Dwight asked.

"No." Nick grabbed the glass the bartender placed in front of him. "Not until the autopsy is complete."

"Right. I'm sure that didn't go over well."

"It didn't and I don't blame them." Nick tossed a swig back.

Kate studied Nick's face and couldn't recall ever seeing him quite like this. "So, we'll catch some sleep, then head out early, back to the station to meet with Mason?"

"Yeah. First thing we need to do is ramp up our search efforts for Stroud. He's now killed three people and I have no idea if he's even still in this state. It might be easier to find him than to find the kids in those pictures. Without names and locations..." He trailed off, tossing back the rest of his drink.

"We won't have much time to rest, but a few hours will

help." Dwight glanced at his watch. "I'm going to head up now. I can't keep my eyes open." He pushed off the barstool.

"I'm right behind you." Kate looked at Nick. "You should go lie down. There's no telling when we'll get another chance."

"I don't think I could sleep if I tried." He raised a finger to order another drink.

Kate slid her arm around his to lock onto him. "Come on, Nick. You have to try." She looked at the bartender with eyes that intimated another drink wasn't necessary.

"She's right, Nick. Let's get some rest." Dwight reached out for him.

"Hey, I got this, okay." Nick raised his hands in protest. "I don't need you two dragging me out of here." He grudgingly rose from his seat. "Happy now?"

The elevator ride was painfully silent and Kate could feel Nick pulling away even further than he had in recent months. Dwight seemed to have felt it too.

The doors opened onto their floor. "Goodnight." Kate walked past the two of them toward her room near the end of the corridor.

"Goodnight, Kate." Dwight inserted his key and opened the door to his room, but not before turning back to Nick.

"You'll be okay?"

Nick's room was a few doors down. He simply nodded and walked away.

Kate locked her door and slid her shoes off, padding her way toward the bathroom. As she stared into the mirror, the image reflecting back was not of a woman filled with determination, as she had always been when working on a case such as this. The woman before her appeared grave, despondent, and worst of all, lacking faith.

Yes, she'd been the one with the big find today, but she was too late. The boy was dead and her dearest friend, the one who'd been there when she was at the lowest point in her life, appeared to lose all hope. It was his breaking point and she feared he would not be put back together.

Her eyes welled as she tried to remember that other lives needed saving. Other children were being hunted and they were the ones who would have to stop Stroud. But she wasn't sure Nick could do it. Not after today.

She pressed a cool cloth on her face and returned to the bed. The unexpected overnight stay meant she would have to shed her clothes and hang them up for tomorrow. Kate crawled into bed and wondered if sleep would come. Her cell rested on the nightstand and she considered calling Mike, but he would surely be sleeping. It was almost two in the morning. And, he would only worry about her, so maybe it was best to wait until daylight. A thin smile only briefly appeared at the thought of him, then Kate closed her eyes.

A knock on the door took several moments to register in Kate's hazy, sleepy mind. She glanced at the clock. It was four a.m. Was it time to leave already? She'd only just fallen asleep, it seemed.

Kate sat up, feeling slightly dizzy at the disruption, and made it onto her feet when the knock occurred again. Realizing she was only in her underclothes, Kate grabbed a towel and wrapped it around her lower half as she was still in the camisole she wore beneath the blouse that hung in the closet.

She peeked through the security lens and immediately opened the door. "Are we leaving?"

"You need to come with me. It's Nick."

Dwight's expression sent off alarm bells in Kate's head. "Hang on. Let me slip on my pants."

He turned away while she dressed, but she was back in an instant.

"Is he okay?" She followed him into the hall.

"That depends on your definition of 'okay'." Dwight pulled out the room key. "He's drunk off his ass."

They entered Nick's room. The bar refrigerator was open and everything inside it had been strewn through the room and emptied.

"Oh my God." Kate moved quickly toward Nick, who was on his back, his legs hanging off the bed. She turned to Dwight. "Did you wake him?"

"I did, but he must've passed out again when I came to get you. I got a strange text from him and came right down after that."

"What the hell are we going to do? We have to be at the station soon."

"I know. Listen, I need you to stay with him. I'll go downstairs and get some food and coffee. I noticed a Starbucks kiosk near the lobby. Just wake him up and try to keep him alert." Dwight turned on his heel. "I'll be back as soon as I can."

Kate walked into the bathroom and grabbed a washcloth, soaking it under the sink with cold water. She returned to Nick, who was still out cold and pressed it against his forehead. "Nick, wake up. You need to wake up."

He moaned and began to speak but was incoherent.

Kate moved the cloth to his neck and this seemed to jolt him and his eyes opened.

"What the hell are you doing?" He flinched.

"What did you do, Nick?" She pressed the cloth against his skin again and this time, he pushed it away and began to rise.

"Stop it, God damn it!" He was upright again and examined the aftermath of his binge through bloodshot eyes. "Jesus." Tears began to spill as he pushed his hands through his tousled hair. "I can't do this, Kate. I'm so fucking tired of this shit."

"What are you talking about? You've been through this before. It's not easy for any of us. Just give it time. This pain will pass."

"Not this time." He turned his attention to her. "I couldn't save my friend's son. You saw how they looked at me; like I failed them in the most horrific way any human being could fail another."

"I know this is hard," Kate began.

"You of all people should know just how fucking hard this is. So I got drunk. Big fucking deal."

Kate was witness to his emotional rollercoaster that had turned from anger to sorrow to anger again. "You're still drunk. That's the big fucking deal. We can't stop now and you know that. But what you're doing—what you've done here? It's only making things worse."

Nick hunched over, his hands pressed against the top of his head. "Christ. It was the one thing I should've been able to do. It's my goddam job."

"Yeah, well, it's mine too. Okay? You're not the only one who failed the Talbots." Nick wasn't one to fall prey to self-pity and Kate hoped that by pointing this out, he might pull himself out of the black hole in which he'd begun to spiral down.

He raised his head—a pitiful expression through glassy eyes stared back at Kate. "Georgia was right to leave me. She saw who I really was, what I really felt."

"What? Georgia was the one who screwed up. Look, Dwight will be back soon with some food and coffee and we'll get you sobered up, okay?"

"She knew I was in love with you even before I did."

The door opened swiftly with Dwight's return. "You're up. Good. Drink this." He shoved the coffee into Nick's hand and turned to Kate. "I got one for you too, if you're interested."

"Yeah, thanks." She reached for the cup, but her head spun with confusion. Had she heard him right? His words were mumbled through the haze of alcohol.

"Are you okay?" Dwight asked. "You look like a deer in headlights. What happened?"

"Nothing." She pushed off the bed and moved toward the chair that was shoved beneath a desk. "Thanks for the coffee. How long you think before he sobers up?" She cast a brief look at Nick, but he didn't look back.

"Soon, I hope. We should really be back down there no later than six. We've got a lot of ground to cover today." Dwight turned to him. "Drink up, buddy." He stepped toward Kate. "This was about the kid, wasn't it?"

"This one's knocked him off his feet." Kate looked at him again, but he still wouldn't make eye contact. She didn't know what to do, what to say. *He's drunk*, she thought. *It's just the booze talking*.

She couldn't think about this now, not when they were on

the hunt for Lyle Stroud. They had to stay on his trail or risk losing him again. And that couldn't happen. She wouldn't let it, even if that meant carrying the weight of Nick's burden on her shoulders. Whatever just transpired had to be pushed aside because her friend was in pain and he was drunk and she had to help fix him.

THE SUN WAS JUST PEEKING out over the eastern sky when they arrived back at the station to see Detective Mason.

"How you doing?" Dwight was behind the wheel while Nick continued to dry out.

"Better. I'll be all right."

"Well, you still look like shit."

"Thanks." Nick looked through the side-view mirror at Kate.

She caught his gaze, but he quickly returned his attention to the front. "I see Mason out front now." Kate noticed the woman as she stood outside the station doors with a coffee in hand.

She began to walk out to meet them.

Dwight opened the door and stepped outside. "Morning. You ready?"

"As I'll ever be." Mason turned and the two walked side by side. "You guys manage any sleep at all?"

"Some," Dwight replied without acknowledging what had happened. No one would know that they'd spent the past two hours trying to sober up their boss.

Inside, the early hour seemed of no consequence to the many officers working hard to help find the man who just killed a boy and was looking to kill more. Kate almost felt guilty for leaving at all. "We're going to need to take a two-pronged approach. Keep searching for Stroud and find out who those kids are and make sure they're safe," she said to Mason.

The team made their way into the bullpen where the images and maps and anything else that pertained to Stroud's whereabouts lay upon a table. It wasn't exactly the way things were usually laid out back at the WFO where they had space and privacy to create a board and a timeline. Here, the officers were crammed into a bullpen with a few low privacy walls between the desks and were open for suspects, victims, and the like to waltz right through. Not exactly the best place to line out what one was working on. Not to mention, most of these guys worked multiple cases at once. But they did the best they could with what they had.

"As you can see, we've already tried to begin making sense of the information you all found in his home," Mason said.

Kate leaned in for a closer look. "What about getting some checkpoints in place? Can we reach out to State Police and get them up on the major highways, particularly leading out of state?" She looked at Dwight. "I can also get Vasquez to give us a hand with coordination."

Nick walked toward the table and began to study it closely. "I count five children in total and he's already taken two of them." He pushed aside the photos of Emily Aldrich and Colton Talbot. "Let's piece together this information and see if we can find out if these posts and articles connect with any of these three remaining kids. Names, locations; that's what we need right now." He turned around to Kate. "State Police should implement checkpoints in addition to the BOLO already out. The only thing we have on our side right now is that we can safely assume he's taken his grandmother's car." Nick began to walk toward Mason. "We'll need your department's full support as well as the State Police and our office." He turned to the officers in the room. "We'll divvy up into teams. One to search for Stroud and another to find those kids. We have to find them before he does."

Detective Mason approached her team and began to dole out tasks.

Nick approached Dwight and Kate. "Kate, talk to Vasquez, get her on board with the plan, and have her help with coordination efforts between the jurisdictions. Also, let's see if we can have them issue a statement to the press. I think it's important that Stroud knows we're on his tail. The Amber Alert's been canceled, so the public needs to know that he's still out there. The more eyes watching, the better."

"Understood." Kate made her way into the lobby and back outside to make the call to Agent Vasquez at the WFO. She remained hesitant at what had transpired this morning and it was a feeling she'd have to overcome. There was no room for childish games and while she still reeled at his words, Kate tried to remember they came from a man who was three sheets to the wind at the time. A man she cared for deeply and tried not to let it come between them. The job at hand mattered far more. She began to dial when from the corner of her eye, Nick approached.

"We're going to have to work fast to identify these kids. Get back inside when you can and the three of us will try to piece this shit together. We might have enough to glean locations and from there, we'll need NGI to help us out."

"Got it. I'll be in after I get with Vasquez." Kate watched him head back inside. He seemed unwilling to discuss or even acknowledge what he'd said earlier. She supposed that right now, it didn't matter. It would be filed away for another time. Or maybe it would be better just to forget it happened at all.

Kate soon rejoined the team. "Vasquez is on board and is working on it now. We should have State Troopers setting up checkpoints by mid-day." She sat down next to Dwight at the table.

"Good. Sounds like she's got things under control." Nick watched as the two studied the evidence. "I want to apologize for my behavior. You two got me straight again and I appreciate that. I let my emotions get the best of me." This time, he eyed only Kate.

"We're a team. That's what we do," she replied.

"I'm supposed to be mentoring you and I sure as hell didn't lead by example this morning."

"It's okay, Nick. You're allowed to feel things. This was a tough blow, I get that and so does Dwight. No one is holding it against you."

"Right." Nick reached for a picture of a young girl, blonde, probably early teens. "Have you two noticed that these pictures are of all the kids who are either being rewarded, ribbons and trophies and things, or doing something that has made them stand out in some way? Look." He showed the two the picture in his hands. "This girl is standing next to that elderly woman and holding a certificate."

"Like she'd been rewarded for doing something; charitable work, maybe?" Dwight added.

"What does it say on that certificate?" Kate asked.

Nick held it closer to his face. "I can't tell. The print's too small." He eyed them both again. "Scan it in. Now! We can zoom in on the certificate and it might reveal a name."

Dwight snatched it from Nick's hands. "On it."

Moments later, Dwight returned with his laptop. "I sent this to my email." He retrieved the image and opened it up. "Let's see what we've got." He began to pan across the photo of the young girl standing in front of a building with another woman. The certificate in her hand was highlighted and he cut that part of the image to zoom it in further. The words were still blurry but discernible. "Holy Shit." Dwight leaned back.

"Sun Park Retirement Community." Kate read. "Presented to Sophie Curtis." She leaned in to read the much smaller print. "Outstanding community volunteer of the year." A smile formed on her lips. "Sophie Curtis. We have a name."

"And a place. Same as the name in that post over here," Dwight said. "Let's get an address on this now."

"And pray to God he hasn't already taken her," Nick added.

15

Detective Mason moved swiftly through the halls and back toward the bullpen. She spotted the Federal agents huddled around the conference table. "They picked her and her parents up this morning. The girl is safe."

"If he's as smart as we believe he is, it won't take long for him to realize we found the pictures in his home." Kate turned her attention to the detective. "Has Stroud been spotted in the area?"

"Not that we know of, but I know Agent Scarborough requested CCTV footage around the girl's home."

"I don't have it yet. We should get down there now. He hasn't been there or Sophie would be gone. Or, one of the other kids will be his next target. I'd like to bet on the one we know and keep looking for the ones we don't."

"Is there anything else you need from me?" Mason asked Nick.

"Just keep working to find Stroud. We're running these other images through our databases to see if any of them have been reported missing. No luck on the names of the other two. Thank God we have at least this one. But I'm hoping the search will turn up something." Nick reached for her shoulder. "Thank you. I'll let you know what we find and you do the same."

"Will do," Mason replied.

"It'll take us a good forty minutes to get to Gainesville." Dwight glanced at the time on his phone. "I hope to God he hasn't been there yet."

"If he has, then he already knows we're on to him and if that happens, we'll have lost him for good," Nick said.

THEY ARRIVED at the Prince William County Police station near Gainesville where the girl and her family remained waiting for answers. Nick stepped out of the car, rubbing his temple.

"You want an aspirin?" Kate was already digging into her purse to retrieve them.

He smiled and held out his hand. "Thanks." Nick swallowed them down dry.

An officer, who appeared to be waiting for them, approached. "Afternoon. I'm Officer Arroyo. Chief would like to have a quick word if you'll follow me." Arroyo continued inside until they reached their destination. He opened the chief's door. "Chief? FBI's here to discuss the Lyle Stroud investigation."

"Come in, please. I'm Chief John Deely." He made his way around his desk to greet the agents.

"Agent Nick Scarborough." He turned to his team. "This is Agent Jameson and Agent Reid."

"Thank you for coming down." Chief Deely gestured to the chairs. "Have a seat. We're extremely relieved to have found Sophie Curtis before she became Stroud's next victim."

"The family is here, is that correct?" Dwight asked.

"Yes, sir. But before we go speak with them, I'd like to know if you've received any information as to the suspect's whereabouts. To my knowledge, no one has seen him."

"Yesterday, we found the bodies of two of his victims. One, a young boy, and the other, an elderly woman, his grandmother."

"Jesus," Deely replied.

"That location was west of here and with this recent discovery, we aren't sure where he'll be heading next; or who he'll go after," Nick replied.

"And you've checked the surveillance videos?" Kate asked.

"We're a small town, Agent Reid, and so there isn't much in the way of cameras, except for the banks, ATMs, and town hall. You all think he's coming here, is that right?"

"The important thing is that you've got Sophie Curtis and her family," Kate began. "Did you tell them why they were here?"

"Not every detail, but enough that her parents got the gist." The chief stood up. "I suppose you'd like to have a word. I'll take you back."

They followed him into the hall and toward the back of the station. Kate didn't know just how much the family knew and addressed her concern with Nick. "What are you going to tell them?"

"The truth."

"Yes, but will you tell them about the other two victims?"

"You mean Colton Talbot and Emily Aldrich?"

"Yes." Kate watched his eyes turn cold. Not out of apathy, but out of anger.

"Not in front of their daughter, but they deserve to know the truth."

Chief Deely opened a door at the far end of the building. Inside was what appeared to be a media room, perhaps used for press conferences. Sophie Curtis was sitting in the back row, alone. She looked like any other thirteen-year-old girl. It was clear to Kate that she knew nothing of her predicament, and it was probably better that way.

"Mr. and Mrs. Curtis, I'd like to introduce you to Agent Scarborough and his team. Agents Reid and Jameson."

The wife stood first. A dynamic presence was obvious from even a great distance. Kate approached her. "Mrs. Curtis, I'm Agent Reid. May we speak with you and your husband for a moment?"

"Of course." She turned to her daughter. "Sophie, honey, why don't you go and get yourself a soda and a snack? I'm sure one of the officers out there will be able to direct you to the breakroom."

Sophie rose from her chair, sandy blonde hair resting in a loose braid over her shoulder. She blew the wisps from her eyes and walked toward the door. "Can I get a Snickers?"

"Yes, you may."

A tender smile crossed her lips as she looked at her parents. She appeared afraid to leave their side.

"It's okay, Sophie. We only need a minute," Kate said.

After the girl left the room, her father stood up to meet the others. "Which one of you is going to tell us what the hell is going on?"

THE SIGNAL the TV was receiving was lousy and Lyle pressed the "off" button on the remote. He'd hoped to get updates on where the police and FBI were looking for him, but the only talk of the bodies he'd left in his wake was what the public seemed interested in. Still, he didn't think they knew his plan and he would use this to his advantage.

It was less than an hour's drive from where he was now to where he would find her. A pretty girl; Lyle noticed her two months ago when an online article was posted about her. He studied her picture. She was perfect. Not like the boy, though. No, Colton caught his attention because he seemed so very happy to be holding that trophy he'd won. *"MVP at Springfield Little League."*

If only people realized just how easy they made it for him to find their children. Social media posts, all the bullshit after-school activities where they told everyone their exact location. So damn easy, especially here where there were small towns dotted all over the state. Colton Talbot's team, for example. "Sponsored by your local Ace Hardware store," the caption at the bottom read.

Well, there were only two Ace Hardware stores in the suburbs of Springfield, and, from there, it was a piece of cake.

Now he was ready to continue to the next one on his list. He would wipe that pretty little smile right off her face.

Lyle reached for the car keys that sat on a folding table near the door in the apartment that had once belonged to his sister but now belonged to meth-heads who let him waltz right in at the mention of her name. Apparently, she had a reputation. He'd monitored the area for some time from his car and decided it was safe to go back and see if whoever lived there knew where she'd gone. He was going to need her in the very near future. They recognized him from the moment one of them opened the door and thought it was cool he was on the run. The cops had already spoken to them and they told them she no longer lived there. Now, if there had been anyone else in this apartment, he'd have had to turn and walk away, but by the looks of the building, he knew the type who lived here and decided the risk was worth it. And it looked like today was his lucky day because they also told him where his sister was, last they knew anyway.

He stepped over one of the men who had passed out. The other was slumped on the couch, his slanted eyes watching Stroud.

"Thanks, man." Stroud left the apartment and made his way back to the car. The time was approaching late afternoon. He wanted to arrive before dark to get a good look around and start making some headway in determining where the girl would be. There would be plenty of time for that.

Once inside the car, he lit up another cigarette and pulled away from the curb. The shade that had obscured his vehicle no longer offered any security and he grew concerned that a passerby might have called in the location. Then again, Stroud often counted upon people's obsession with themselves and stood a better than fair chance that not one single person gave his highly sought-after Oldsmobile a second glance.

Lyle rolled down his window and let the warm breeze brush against his skin. The thrill of the hunt felt exhilarating. But he knew caution would be paramount. Two dead bodies, well three, if you counted his grandmother, and they knew his name. Seems they'd been able to put two and two together after all.

"I CAN'T BELIEVE THIS." Mr. Curtis couldn't stand on his own feet any longer and lowered himself back down onto the chair. "What are we supposed to do now?"

Mrs. Curtis still stood firm. Kate was reminded of her own mother, although this woman was much younger. After Marshall's death, Deborah had hardened for the sake of Kate. She was no longer docile, acquiescing to her father's wishes, as she had for so long. No longer pushing under the rug what had been a dark time in their family's lives. Deborah had changed, and Kate was grateful for her strength at a time when she had none. And Mrs. Curtis was no different.

"I assume you'll be keeping us someplace safe until you catch this monster?" Mrs. Curtis stared into Nick's eyes, identifying him as the decision-maker.

"Of course. We'll arrange to keep Sophie and you two safe." Nick directed his attention to Dwight. "Let's get them to a safe house. We'll keep them there until this is over."

"The nearest one is fifty miles away," Dwight replied.

Mr. Curtis looked at his wife. "We can't just hide out." She seemed unmoved and so he began to implore the agents, "We have jobs, for Christ's sake. We'll lose everything."

"We'll lose Sophie if we don't do this." Mrs. Curtis understood exactly what was at stake. "You think he won't come after her again if they don't find him? You want to risk that because I sure as hell don't."

"We'll have one of Chief Deely's officers escort you home to pack a few things and then take you straight to the house. No phone calls, text messages, emails. Nothing. Am I making myself clear?" Nick didn't wait for a reply. "This is the way it has to be—for now." He soon turned to address his team. "Can I see you two alone for a moment?"

The three stepped outside into the corridor, leaving Sophie's parents to absorb the information.

Nick widened his stance, shoulder-width apart, and folded his arms against his chest. "If Stroud hasn't been here yet, we stand a good chance of capturing him if we play our cards right."

"What are you thinking?" Kate asked.

"We set up shop at the Curtis' place. See if he shows up. We get WFO field ops and place surveillance teams in locations where Sophie would normally be seen. Her school, the elderly home where she visits, places like that."

"What about Deely and his people?" Kate asked.

"We can use them. I just need to figure out how. What I don't want to happen is a show of force or an increase in police presence that would raise a red flag with Stroud. He catches a whiff of what we're doing and it's all over. He'll be out of here and he'll change his plans. We can't let that happen."

"We're making some hefty assumptions here," Dwight

began. "Are we putting all our eggs in one basket? We don't know where he's going next or who he's going to track down."

"Until we get the names of the other two, I don't know where else we go from here," Nick said. "We still have state troopers and Mason and half the damn state looking for him. If we have a chance to get a jump on where he might be headed, I don't see as we have another choice."

"What if we go a step further?" Kate's eyes sparked at an idea. "That girl is as tall as me. What if I act as a decoy? Go to the places we know he'll be looking. Not close enough that he'll be able to see it's not her, but from a distance."

Her partners traded glances. Kate raised the corners of her mouth because she could see they were seriously considering the idea.

"I could dye my hair blonde and wear it just like hers." She was glad she'd let her hair continue to grow long, as it once was. "I've always wanted to know what it's like to be a blonde. You know this could work. Look, if Stroud comes here and he can't find any evidence of Sophie, he won't waste his time. He'll move on to the next kid and we don't know who that's going to be. Not yet."

"Again, we can't be sure he's going to go after her ahead of the others. But we do have a chance to shut him down, one we might not get again," Nick agreed. "What do you think, Jameson? You think Kate could pass for a thirteen-year-old blonde girl?"

Dwight examined Kate's face with a half-cocked smile. "It could work. So long as he doesn't get any closer than about a hundred feet from her."

"He gets that close and I'll take him down."

"Damn right." Nick patted her on the back. "Until we know more, we have to at least do something. Mason's team, along with Agent Vasquez, are working hard to identify the others. This is the best we've got for now."

Sophie approached them in the hall. "Can I come back inside now?"

The girl moved nearer to Kate and she began to draw upon the comparison as they stood shoulder to shoulder. "I'm right, aren't I?"

They studied the two of them, who were, in fact, nearly the same height. From a distance, it could work. She'd have to play down her figure and wear loose-fitting clothes. Change her hair color for sure, but as they continued to evaluate the possibility, it seemed they might have a decent chance and it was better than waiting.

"Yes, you can go back inside now, Sophie. Thank you for your patience." Kate ushered the girl inside where her parents were immersed in conversation with the chief.

"Chief Deely, can you send someone to gather their things for them?" Kate began. "I don't think we should risk a patrol car escorting the Curtis' home." She turned to Mrs. Curtis. "They can grab enough to last you a few days."

16

The bathroom mirror reflected a startling image; a blonde Kate, and as she studied this new look, she realized this color would never have suited her and was glad to be a brunette. Her skin had too much olive in it and her eyes, much too dark for such a fair shade. Nevertheless, the change succeeded in the one thing she desired—to appear younger. Not thirteen; not by any stretch of the imagination, but perhaps closer to twenty, rather than her early thirties, which had crept up on her with little notice.

Her hair, towel-dried, she brushed through it and put a blow dryer on it for a few minutes. The time had come for her to make her big reveal. Kate opened the bathroom door where Dwight and Nick waited nearby. While the Curtis family stayed hidden in a safe house, the three federal agents were playing house in their residence.

Kate arrived to their wide eyes and gasps. "Do I look that bad?"

"No. Just—different." Nick approached her and placed his hand on her hair, lifting a section of it to get a better look. "Just never pictured you as a blonde before."

"I don't like it, but then this isn't a permanent change, right?" Dwight asked.

"No, definitely not." Kate walked past them, toward a wall mirror that hung in the dining area. "Just long enough to catch Lyle Stroud." She turned to them again. "So, how do we plan to do that?"

"I got the Curtis' usual schedule from the wife." Dwight sat down at the dining table where Kate waited. "Sophie has dance on Tuesday nights, soccer on Mondays and Wednesdays, and choir after school on Thursdays."

"Geez, when does the kid sleep?" Nick pulled out the chair next to him.

"That's the way they do things now. My kids do the same kind of thing. Unfortunately, I'm not around for most of it. So anyway, that means she'll have soccer practice tonight from 4:30 to 6:00."

"Who usually picks her up?" Kate asked.

"She hitches a ride with a teammate and they're both picked up by Mrs. Curtis."

"But how would Stroud know this?" Kate continued.

"I don't think he would unless he's been watching her for a while. He's got these kids' pictures and is picking them off, but how he finds them, or why, we just don't know yet." Dwight turned to Nick. "Any ideas on where he might go to watch out for her?"

"Sophie was collecting a good Samaritan award at the retirement home. With everything else she does, when does she go there?"

"Sunday, after church," Dwight replied.

"He won't wait that long." Nick appeared to consider their best option. "Sophie's in the seventh grade. Either of you know how many middle schools there are in this town?"

Kate retrieved her tablet and began running a search. "Hang on." She typed in a few more commands before the answer appeared. "Three. There are three here and based on where the retirement home is, it would be fairly easy to discern that she wouldn't travel too far from her community to volunteer. And the retirement home is five miles from here." She looked at Nick. "It wouldn't take a genius to figure out the nearest middle school would be where Sophie would attend."

"But with security at schools these days, he wouldn't be able to get very close without being noticed, especially now."

"He'll have no choice but to follow her from a distance," Nick replied.

"Then that's where I'll come in." Kate glanced at the time. "Do we know when school lets out?"

"3:15, according to Mrs. Curtis," Dwight replied.

"That gives us two hours to get things in place. If we're going to act, it has to be today and it has to be now. Because if we're wrong, he'll be on his way to the next victim."

Nick reached for his cell phone. "I'll have the chief's people approach the school administrators about this. I'll relay the plan and they'll have to convey it to the school in such a manner that they don't feel the need to go on lockdown."

"That's going to be tough. A killer on the loose who's after one of their students," Dwight said. "That's a tough sell *not* to lock the place down. If the community gets wind of it, parents will be up in arms. It'll be a media shitstorm and we'll lose Stroud."

"We have to hope the chief will be able to keep a lid on it. We don't have a choice here." Nick rose from the chair and stepped away to make the call.

Kate watched him leave before returning her attention to Dwight. "What do you think? He was in pretty bad shape this morning." She wouldn't reveal his surprising declaration. "You think he's up for this?"

"I wouldn't put him in the line of fire if I didn't. He needs this. This is what's going to keep him on the straight and narrow. Finding and capturing Stroud is all that matters to him. What happened last night? That was a brief moment of recklessness, one I don't believe he'll repeat." He cast a glance at Nick, who was still on the phone. "Don't worry, Kate. He would never let you down and neither would I."

"Okay, we're set to go." Nick returned to his seat. "Chief says he'll go to the school himself and arrange it. We agreed that you would be allowed inside the school grounds, but only to the extent that you are making your way toward the exit. In other words, you're not to enter any classrooms, the gym, or any other place where you would be near the students. He wants you out in the open and I agree."

"I guess I'd better find some clothes to wear. Hopefully, I can squeeze into something of Sophie's, or we'll have to make a trip to a clothing store. I think I might stand out if I'm wearing my work clothes and high-heels." Kate made her way toward Sophie's room.

Inside, the young teenager's room revealed that she was an

awful lot like most other teenagers. Bright and colorful, her tastes bordered on eclectic with vintage pieces, and by vintage, she owned a record player and modern pieces like Bluetooth speakers and an ergonomic Swedish desk. Or perhaps this was her mother's taste. The rest of the home seemed to be furnished in a similar manner.

But there was no denying the room belonged to a thirteen-year-old girl who had a love of all things boy-band. Kate didn't know who the kids on the posters were. The latest rag-tag bunch of rapscallions Britain had to offer, no doubt. She had to smile because she recalled a time when her own room looked very much the same, except with NSync and not whoever these guys were.

Kate approached Sophie's closet, pulling open the white louvered doors to reveal something akin to Armageddon inside. Clothes hung haphazardly or tossed onto the floor. Shoes were strewn about in mismatched pairs. "Looks about right." She began to sift through them, looking for something she might be able to get into. Perhaps an oversized T-shirt and yoga pants.

Sure enough, she found plenty of those things. Kate slipped them on along with Sophie's tennis shoes, which were half a size too big, and looked into the dresser mirror. With her fingers, she began to braid her now blonde hair over her shoulder, just as Sophie would have, and at completion, Kate studied her reflection. A sense of sorrow passed through her. Sophie's life was in danger, and while the girl was safe at an undisclosed location with her family, she was still the target of a monster who would seek to do her harm. One of many Kate had come across in recent years. She pulled the hair back at her temple to reveal the fading scar left behind by just such a monster. But she had defeated him and the others. It was her job. She knew why Nick had begun to unravel. It wasn't hard to figure out. Kate only hoped that the same would not happen to her one day, but how could it not? Now she had to not only capture this monster but keep Nick from tumbling further down the rabbit hole.

Kate looked at a picture of Sophie and her friends, smiling and happy. That was why she was doing this job. A final tug on the braid and Kate left the bedroom to rejoin her colleagues. They had little over an hour and the strategy needed to be in place.

The time had come to rid himself of his grandmother's Olds Cutlass. After the discovery of the bodies in her home, his truck parked and her missing car, they were obviously aware of what he was driving. Stroud was already en route to find the blonde girl; one of two on his list, and would arrive in just under an hour. He needed to find an easy target. Some old woman's car; a Buick maybe. Something that would throw the feds and the cops off his scent.

Stroud spotted a Walmart and pulled into the enormous parking lot. The place was packed and he needed to stay out of sight as best he could. The fringes were his best bet. The closer to the store he got, the better the chances were of surveillance cameras. He pulled alongside an older model Ford Focus. It was all he could find this far out and was probably an employee's vehicle, which might be a better option. Whoever owned it wasn't likely to come walking out anytime soon. Still, he had to be vigilant. There were five spaces between this car and the next, closer to the store, and so he pulled up on the opposite side.

He stepped out and casually approached, lifting the front passenger handle in the unlikely event it was unlocked. It wasn't. Stroud lowered his hand to feel the underside of the wheel well. Nothing there either. Another casual glance for passersby and he continued toward the back of the car, feeling beneath the rear well; still nothing. "God damn it."

Stroud was running out of options and risked being spotted if he took much more time. Most people probably couldn't pick him out in a parking lot as the man they'd seen on TV, but it was a chance he couldn't take. Around the car he moved, again in search of a spare key hitched on the underside of a fender, but still there was nothing. He was going to have to do this the hard way. He walked back to his car and retrieved a Slim Jim. It would get him inside, but then he'd have to kill the alarm—fast. He'd acquired a great many skills while behind bars and bypassing factory antitheft transponders was one of them. Time was all anyone had inside and a lot of them chose to spend it teaching their tricks of the trade and right now, he was glad he listened.

Within two minutes, he was inside and the alarm was off. His brow dripping with sweat, Stroud kept his eyes peeled for anyone looking to charge at him, but the few people who were around were far away and only cast a brief, unconcerned look in his direction when the alarm initially sounded. Because it was off quickly, they went back to their daily lives, unfazed by the event. The engine sputtered as he pressed down on the gas and reversed out of the spot. The fuel filter sounded clogged and he prayed the damn thing wouldn't stall out on him.

Stroud was finally back out onto the road, feeling more confident than ever. He wasn't sure he'd recall all the steps to boosting the car, but he'd managed with flying colors and felt rejuvenated—ready to take on the world; or maybe just the girl. He needed to keep his head right now if he stood any chance of succeeding. She would keep him occupied for a while, but he hadn't worked out all the details yet, except where he would go. He had money now, but it wouldn't last and he'd have to find another way. It was getting harder to pull off his goal. They were looking for him and he was just one step ahead, giving them a chance to catch up. Once he got her, he'd have to devise a plan better than the last. "One thing at a time," he said.

Stroud continued on the drive and began to approach his final destination. He pulled onto the driveway behind another car and while he couldn't be sure this was the precise location, he had to trust the two drug addicts, and that in and of itself was risky. If this wasn't the place, then he'd be screwed.

The afternoon sun was still high above and he still had time to do what needed to be done, but this was a necessary stop in preparation. He stepped out of the car and, with suspicious eyes, scanned the vicinity. No one was watching, at least, not from the outside.

The front porch was littered with newspapers, cigarette butts, and a few bottles of cheap beer. "This has got to be the place." Stroud flicked his own cigarette onto the ground and tried to peer through the front window, but it was obscured by curtains, not to mention bars on the front. He moved toward the door, pulled open the heavy wrought iron screen, and knocked.

If she was here, she'd be home, no doubt. He leaned his ear against the door for sounds of footsteps, but he heard none. He waited, but still nothing. "Son of a bitch." This time, he knocked harder. "Shannon, open up! It's me, Lyle."

Moments later, he thought he picked up some movement inside. "Shannon?"

"I'm coming," A rasping voice sounded on the other side and, finally, the door opened.

Lyle flinched with shock at the sight of his older sister. He hadn't seen her since before he got out of prison and she looked like death warmed over. He knew then that her addiction was deep. "Shannon, it's me, Lyle. Can I come in?"

She regarded him with apprehension. "What are you doing here? How did you find me?"

"What? No, 'hey bro, it's good to see you. Where the hell you been?'"

"You been locked up and now you're out. So what the fuck do you want?" she replied.

He realized she had no idea the cops were after him or what he'd done and that would make this much easier. "I wanted to see you. Can I come in or you just gonna make me stand out here like a punk?"

She pulled the door open and stepped aside but said nothing and Stroud walked in. He nearly gagged at the smell. A mixture of cat piss, sex, and pot. Leftover food, bongs, and a few beer bottles were scattered throughout the living room.

"How long you been here?" he asked.

"Not long." She closed the door and tugged on the bra strap

that had fallen down her shoulder beneath a dingy grey tank top. "When did you get out?"

That was a tricky question. "Not long ago." He figured the less she knew, the better and easier this would be.

"You want something to drink?" She shuffled toward the kitchen.

Stroud knew he didn't have time to get reacquainted with his sister, nor did he really have the desire to, so he was going to need to expedite this reunion. "Sure, just some water, thanks." He spotted a used needle on the side table and looked for a bag of heroin, but didn't see any nearby. What he did find was a bottle of OxyContin.

While his sister's back was turned in search of a clean glass, he opened the bottle and took out two of the pills. Stroud used the bottle to crush the pills into powder and swept the dust into his hands. As far gone as she was, he didn't think two would do her much harm, except keep her out for a while, which was what he needed.

"Here." Shannon returned with a glass of water and sat down on a folding chair next to the stained floral sofa where her brother sat.

"How long has it been since you last used?"

She furrowed her brow as though insulted by the question.

"I don't really give a fuck. I'm just asking 'cause I wouldn't mind getting a little lit myself, but I don't want to do it on my own."

"Oh. I could use another hit." She walked toward what was probably her bedroom.

Stroud grabbed a nearby spoon that looked as though it had been used for last night's dinner and poured some water into it.

He mixed the powder with the water and then dipped the syringe into the mixture, using the plunger to pull as much of it up as he could. He knew this would be dangerous and originally just wanted to drop it into her water, but he was running out of time and she wasn't drinking any water.

Shannon soon returned with a dime bag of tar and fresh supplies and sat back down. "This is all I got left if you want some."

"Shit yeah. I'll take some of that." Stroud held the needle in his hand, tucked inside his palm, and approached her. It was risky, but she was only half-alert as it was and her reflexes would be slow, probably non-existent, so he decided to take his chances.

She tied two condoms together and began to wrap them around her arm for a tourniquet.

"Here, let me help you with that." Stroud slapped the crease of her elbow where several injection marks were visible to plump up the vein. "Like old times, eh?" He locked eyes with her for a moment of distraction and with his other hand, pushed the needle in, emptying its contents into her arm.

She reared back, her eyes immediately dilating and her back arching. "What the fuck?" She peered at him in shock.

"You'll be fine. Your tolerance must be high as fuck."

Kate stood inside the empty halls of the school dressed to blend in and hair that matched the style of Sophie Curtis. Her classmates, according to the principal, didn't know what was going on, nor why she was taken out of school today. Kate's presence wasn't likely to trigger any questions because up close, she looked nothing like the young girl whom she was portraying. But from a distance, from Lyle Stroud's distance, she could pass.

The final bell echoed in the halls, doors flung open, and kids spilled out into the corridor. Kate disappeared into the herd and followed them through the doors and out into the open. "I'm outside," she whispered in her earpiece.

Two teams were posted in front of the school; WFO agents who had to hustle to get there in time and Nick and Dwight, who waited in his SUV two blocks down where Sophie would normally walk.

"Nothing yet over here," Nick answered through his headset. The other two teams responded in kind. "Damn it. Where is he?"

"He'll be here; he has to be." Dwight looked through the passenger window to the side view. No one was behind them. "He could've gotten rid of the Olds, in fact, I'd wager on it."

"Still, we should see someone lurking around. He'd stand out like a sore thumb."

Kate continued down the wide concrete path that opened up just beyond the gates of the school. She hoisted the backpack further up on her shoulder. No one questioned her, so she must have been on the right track. Either that or they just didn't care, which was also likely in a school full of thirteen and fourteen-year-olds who scarcely looked up from their cell phones.

"I'm leaving the grounds, heading west." Kate made the turn and was now walking in the direction of her partners. "Still nothing?"

"No. He's not here, Kate. Just keep walking in the direction of the house. He might be hanging back until you get further away from the school," Nick replied.

"Ten-four." Kate continued along toward the Curtis home, passing Nick and Dwight without acknowledgment. "Where are you, you son of a bitch?" Kate was nearing the Curtis home. "What should I do?"

"Go inside. It's over. He didn't show."

Kate looked behind her, one last glance to confirm Stroud hadn't been following, but no one was there. They'd baited the line, but he wasn't there to take a bite. She unlocked the front door and entered, relocking it behind her. "I'm in."

"Kate, we're going to make another pass, see if we can spot him. Just stay put." Nick turned the wheel and pulled away from the curb. "Let's hit the next block over and then come back up here," he said to Dwight.

"What about the teams at the school?"

"Give me one more pass, then we'll call it," Nick said again in his earpiece.

Lyle Stroud hung back from the school far enough not to raise any red flags. He retrieved the binoculars and aimed them at the school's exit. Double-checking the time, he'd made it with not much to spare. Taking care of his sister took longer than he anticipated, but no need to get riled up about it.

The school buzzed with the ending bell; a horrible, loud buzz that he could hear from this distance. "Jesus. No wonder they want to get the hell out of there." He zoomed in his binocular lens for a better view. The kids tumbled out, randomly and happily. He kept a lookout for the girl, the one who'd held that ribbon so boastfully in the picture. A smile crept up on his lips. There she was; plain, innocent. She waved goodbye to her friends as she began her trek home to a place where she would drop her things, kick off her shoes, and plop down in front of the TV or phone or computer and vegetate for hours until her parents came home from work. But not today. Today, Lyle Stroud was in town and he was looking for her.

He started up the car when she was far enough ahead not to hear the engine and began to follow her. His palms clung to the wheel, sweaty from the excitement and the heat. The air conditioner blasted on his face, but it did little to soothe the burn in his stomach. It was the burn that drove him further, risking more than he ever had before.

Only a block behind her, he made a quick right when she looked back. "Damn it." Stroud quickly turned the car around and returned to the T-crossing. Before pulling out, he made sure she wasn't looking back again. He would have to take care not to get too close. He saw that she was wearing headphones, probably listening to the shit music they played today. This would work to his advantage. The street in front of him cleared and he pulled back out onto it. She was farther ahead now, but he could still see her well enough.

He was going to have to make his approach before she reached home. That would complicate things far too much and he'd already planned this out with meticulous care. The time had to be now and so Stroud pressed the gas just enough to hasten his arrival. Three hundred, two hundred, now one hundred feet behind her. She didn't turn around this time. One last look to ensure no one was nearby and Stroud pulled to the curb, thrust the gearshift into park, and launched out of the car. He rushed up behind her. She turned around and panic masked her face. But Stroud knew she was too late.

The girl's world darkened instantly and Stroud lifted her from her feet and rushed back to the car, which was, at most, twenty feet away. He ripped open the passenger door and tossed her inside like a rag doll.

Lyle Stroud started the car and with tires inadvertently squealing, he pulled away, his treasure secured inside.

"I THOUGHT he'd be there, damn it. It was our one chance to get a step ahead of him instead of the other way around." Kate felt deflated as she slumped on the sofa.

"So did I, Kate." Nick joined her. "It was a shot in the dark, but we had to try."

"Should we hang around the soccer field and hope he shows up there?" Kate asked.

"I just don't know how he'd know that's where she'd be."

"He could've been watching her for a while. Maybe he knows her schedule."

"Fuck! Fuck!" Nick pounded the sofa cushion before taking a breath. "We keep the family in the safe house and we keep working on finding the others. That's all we can do now. I'll touch base with Mason and see if she's made progress. You do the same with Vasquez and let's hope to hell we find out who those kids are." His cell phone buzzed in his shirt pocket. "Scarborough." He paused. "What? Are you fucking serious?" He pushed to his feet. "No, God damn it! No!" He lowered his phone.

"What is it? What's going on?"

"That was Mason. A 911 call came in about a missing girl. The picture matched one of the other kids and she was notified within minutes about the match. God damn it, Kate, he went after someone else."

17

Detective Mason met them in the precinct lobby and wasted no time. "I've got patrols set up in the vicinity of where the girl was abducted and we know he's got himself another vehicle." Authority resounded in her voice as she began to lead the way back to her office. "The call came in from the area of Manassas Park, right on the edge of our jurisdictional boundary." She regarded Kate with a baffling gaze. "Nice hair."

Kate almost forgot about her brief and unnecessary change of appearance. "We thought he was going after Sophie Curtis. This was my idea."

"Don't beat yourselves up. He may have spotted the trap while you were setting it. The timing was close and you did what you could with the time you had." Mason now stood behind her desk. "At least Sophie's safe. Now we need to find her." She slid the photo of the girl who had just become

Stroud's latest victim. "This is Chloe Schaffer. Dispatch got the call from 911. Her grandmother told the operator she hadn't returned home from school and was worried in light of the news coverage of Stroud. Chloe had been staying with her due to her parents' impending divorce, which had turned ugly. The grandmother lives near the parents' home and so Chloe was living with her until things with her folks settled down."

"There's our answer," Kate said.

Nick glanced at her with some concern. "What answer?"

"TV. Why don't we get these pictures in front of the news cameras? Get their faces out there so someone can identify them."

"It would work," Dwight said. "The problem, though, is Stroud himself. Right now, we have the advantage. We know he has a plan. Those kids' pictures get out in front of the public, he won't go after them. He'll change his plans—randomly go after others and we won't know who they'll be."

"That doesn't help us out right now with finding Chloe. He's got her and he's trying to stay a step ahead of us. We can't let that happen. He won't take his time with her. We've got a day or two at best to find her and to ID the other two kids. If we can't, then one of them will be next and Chloe will be dead," Nick added.

Upon his return to his sister's home, Stroud had hoped she'd still be passed out and he proceeded to drag Chloe inside. If she wasn't, she'd be in for one hell of a shock. And the girl was strong. It took more strength than he'd expected to get her under control, but she was afraid and that fear would keep her in line. He pulled her back toward the bedroom where he'd moved his sister so she could sleep it off, but on entry, a rancid, vomitus odor wafted toward him.

"Shit!" Stroud yanked the girl toward the bed and he leaned over his sister, checking her pulse, but he already knew. Her mouth was foamy and it suddenly became clear that she'd asphyxiated herself probably because he'd shoved too much into her veins. He was no stranger to the hard stuff and he knew how dangerous it was to shoot oxy like that, but he thought she could take it.

Chloe screamed at the sight of the woman on the bed.

"Shut up! Shut the fuck up!" Stroud tightened his grip on her arm and pulled her back into the hall. This was unexpected, but there was nothing he could do for Shannon now.

He pushed open the door of another bedroom where he'd already made accommodations for his prey while his sister was otherwise occupied. The bed had been secured to the floor and he tossed her to the ground at the edge of it where a pair of handcuffs lay. Stroud shackled her to the leg of the frame. "Stay here and don't even think about making a sound or I'll fucking kill you."

An officer rushed through the doors, past inquiring eyes, and made his way through the corridor holding something in his hand. "I need to find Detective Mason." His was not a request, but a demand to another officer roaming the hall whom he happened upon.

"She's with the Feds in the command center." The officer continued past him, glancing back with his coffee in hand.

"Thanks." The young cop entered the command center, which was really a conference room decked out with computer equipment and monitors since the Feds brought in everything they could to catch the man who had evaded them thus far.

He spotted his boss, Detective Mason, standing next to the man he knew to be Special Agent Scarborough. "Detective, I have the video." He handed her the flash drive. "This is from the past eighteen hours, from various locations."

They were well behind the eight ball and Nick hoped that someone caught Stroud on video so that they might know where he was headed and what he was driving. "Let's load it up."

"You mind?" the officer asked a woman who appeared to be FBI, as he didn't recognize her to be one of his own.

"Here." Agent Vasquez, who had recently arrived at Nick's request, reached for the drive and inserted it into the laptop. Within moments, the files appeared.

"They said the files are labeled by date and time." The officer pointed to the first one. "So this would have been from 12:01 am on the 21st."

"Got it." She looked to Scarborough. "I'm going to need help going through these. This will take too long for one person."

"Agreed." Scarborough scanned the room. "Agent Reid, Agent Jameson." He waved them over. "We need some help sorting through this surveillance video."

"Where did this come from?" Dwight asked.

"We have a lot of public security cameras, particularly around the City Center, but we also have access to VDOT cameras and those are included here too. Since you guys have gone all apocalyptic on this, everyone wants to be sure and cooperate," the officer replied.

"Let's split up the files and each take a section," Nick said. "Until someone calls the hotline for the Amber Alert, this is all we've got to find Chloe."

Chloe Schaffer rubbed her sore cuffed wrist with her free hand because she'd already done a pretty good number on it. Her struggles had caused it to swell from yanking it around and the scratches were deep enough to draw blood.

Her only thoughts were of getting out of here before that man came back. The moment replayed in her mind, taunting her. She shouldn't have had her headphones on. How many times had her mother told her it wasn't safe while she was walking because she wouldn't be able to hear cars or sirens? All this time, she thought her mother was just being over-protective, as usual. Since she and her dad split up last month, her life had been a living hell and all she had was her music, and listening to it helped soothe the pain they were causing her.

Now she was here and her parents probably figured she was missing. Chloe knew she had to get out of here or she would die. That man wasn't going to let her go—not ever. She saw it in his eyes.

Looking around, there seemed to be nothing she could use.

Nothing that would break the cuff. Nothing that she could throw to break the window and escape. On second glance, the window had bars on it anyway. Even if she'd broken it, the bars would've stopped her for sure. She knew what men like him did to kids. She was almost twelve and was far more perceptive than she ever let on to her parents. Thanks to the internet, she could get her hands on all sorts of information. Not that it would help her now. Chloe closed her eyes to think. How could she escape? And if she did, where could she go? He'd kept her in the foot well of the passenger seat when he shoved her in the car. She had no idea what direction he drove or how many miles. Time had no meaning because fear took over everything—her mind, her body. She didn't know how long they'd traveled. Still, if she could just break free. Someone would help her, right?

She pulled her arm in an attempt to drag the bed. What a stupid idea. Of course that wouldn't work. God, why did she have to be so stupid sometimes? Chloe squeezed her eyes tightly, angry at her carelessness, angry at her parents for not being home. Grandma must be so upset right now. Chloe felt bad for her because she loved her so much. She was her only grandchild and they were very close. She'd helped Chloe through much of this past month, insisting none of her parents' divorce was her fault.

"But what about this, Grandma?" She shook her head. Chloe looked again at the metal bedframe to which she was unwillingly attached. The leg was bolted to the ground. She scoffed. "Of course it is." So thinking she could drag the thing along was stupid because it was bolted to the wood floor.

"I guess you're stuck here, Chloe Schaffer." She stared at the ceiling, her eyes glazing over the little white balls stuck to the top, like the ceiling at Grandma's. What'd she call it? Popcorn or something? She guessed it sort of looked like popcorn, but really it looked more like beads to her.

It was then that an idea struck. What if he let her out to go pee? Would she have a chance to escape then? Maybe, but it wasn't likely he'd let her out of his sight for long. Even to go to the bathroom. And if he did, she'd have to rely on there being a window-one that didn't have bars on it. Still, what choice did she have?

Chloe called out. "Hey?" she paused. "Hey? I need to pee." The thought had occurred to her that she could scream at the top of her lungs, but she was afraid of him and he would kill her if she did—he already said so.

"What? What the fuck do you want now?" Stroud's impatience was palpable as the door flew open.

"Can I go to the bathroom, please?" She shrank back in fear but raised her shoulders again. "I have to go pee. Please."

Stroud moved toward her, retrieving a key from his pocket. He unlocked the cuff from the bed and helped her up, dragged her, more like.

She winced at the pain from the tight squeeze he placed on her forearm but refused to utter any sounds.

"You won't get out of there." Stroud leaned into the bathroom and pointed to the window. "Bars."

Chloe didn't say anything and quickly realized her plan was about to fall apart. She went inside and he closed the door.

"You have sixty seconds." Stroud's voice echoed inside the bathroom.

She didn't have to pee—at all. She just stood there, waiting for something to happen, an idea, anything that would get her out of here. He wouldn't keep the door shut for long if she didn't start to go to the bathroom, so she pulled her pants down to her knees. Resting her arms on her thighs, Chloe felt something in her right pocket that rested against her ankle. She reached down to feel. A coin. It was a coin wedged into the deepest corner of her pocket. A dime? Maybe. Something small, definitely not a quarter. Chloe knew right at that moment how she was going to escape this lunatic.

She pulled her pants back up and flushed the toilet, not that anything came out, and then washed her hands. "I'm done." She reached for the handle but he pushed it open, catching the toe of her tennis shoe.

He pushed harder until she moved it, but the damage had been done. He'd jammed her big toe, but no matter, Chloe knew what needed to be done.

Stroud returned her to the tiny bedroom with its single bed and cuffed her to the frame again. "You'd better keep quiet. I swear I'll kill you if you make a single God damn sound." He closed the door behind him.

Chloe reached with her left hand and shoved it into her right pocket. There it was. A dime, just like she thought. And it was the perfect size to unscrew the bolts that kept the bed secured to the floor. The only problem was that she didn't know how much time she had before he would return. An hour? A half-hour? Who knew? He would show up when he was good and ready based on what she'd seen from him so far. So either she waited until the inevitable was over and he left her for the night, or try like hell to get out before that happened. She preferred the latter and it was a risk she was going to have to take.

Her fingers were nimble and strong, mostly from the time she spent blogging on her computer. This was something she'd remind her mother of when she escaped, not if, because she wasn't about to give up now. The dime fit perfectly in the straight-slotted bolt, but it was difficult to turn. Her fingers pressed hard and became white until the screw gave way just a little. She'd gotten it started.

Chloe continued to loosen the bolt, not knowing how much time she had before he made another visit. It would be hard to hide her progress if he came in before she was done. There wouldn't be time to tighten it, but she had to stay positive and pray that wouldn't happen.

Her fingers ached with each turn now, but it couldn't last much longer. At least an inch was already sticking out and how long could this thing be? She kept at it, turning faster and faster, glancing at the door between each turn. The bolt was wobbling now, she had to be close. "Come on, come on."

The bolt fell out. It was done and while she wanted to admire her handiwork, there was no time. She pulled her knees under her, twisting her wrist in a painful and awkward position, but it was the only way to get leverage on the bed and lift the leg.

With her right hand, she gripped the metal leg and lifted it. It hadn't raised much and she looked to see what the problem was. She noticed that all the legs were bolted tightly and it would take more force to raise this corner enough to slip her cuff from beneath it.

Chloe tried again, pulling harder this time. Her right hand flattened to the ground so she could slide it out. Higher, she pulled and finally, her hand slipped from beneath it. She was free. Chloe scrambled to her feet, searching the room for a way out. It was going to have to be the window, but how could she get past the bars?

She tiptoed to the window and unlocked it. The noise it made as she pushed it up caused alarm. Had he heard it? Footsteps would sound in the hall if he had and so far, there was nothing. The bars were warm to the touch, having been heated by the sun all day. With a white-knuckled grip, she shook the bars. Some movement, but not enough. She tried again, terrified of the sound she was making. This time, one of the corners wobbled. It appeared rusted and maybe it would be enough to dislodge the bars from the frame. She wished the window was low enough to kick the bars loose, but it was chest-high. Still, if she did get them loose enough, crawling out wouldn't be a problem. Hope began to rise in her and it gave her strength.

Again, she pushed. Again, the bars moved even more. This was going to work. She could see it now. There was maybe one good push left before it would fall off. Then, he would hear that for sure, but it would afford enough time for her to jump out and run like hell.

She pushed as hard as she could and the bars broke free, dropping to the ground outside, with a deep thud. Chloe looked over her shoulder at the sound of footsteps clamoring down the hall.

No time to think, just climb through the window. And she did. Chloe tumbled to the ground outside, twisting her ankle, but she had no choice now except to run. She could hear him opening the door and sprinted with lightning speed to the road. She pumped her legs, a cramp catching her ribs, her ankle throbbing with pain; she ran. He jumped out the window behind her, but she had at least a hundred-foot head start. There was a house ahead with lights on. Chloe knew he would catch up if she didn't get to someone first.

She made a hard turn to the house and pounded on the door, screaming for help. She could see him getting closer. Finally, the door opened.

18

The street was lined with patrol cars whose lights flashed so brightly, that the sky illuminated like Pink Floyd's laser light shows. Chloe sat on the edge of the ambulance that was parked in front of the home she'd run to only an hour before. Although it was warm outside, they insisted on draping a blanket over her shoulders, perhaps to stave off shock. One of the paramedics flashed a penlight in her eyes, made her follow his fingers, and asked her what day it was. Of course, she didn't really know except that it was May something. The events of the past twenty-four hours blurred in her mind and time was indistinguishable.

The kind woman who opened the door found a frightened Chloe, drenched in sweat, looking over her shoulder, saying things like "He's right behind me. Help me." But when the woman stepped onto her porch to see this boogeyman, he was already gone. She whisked the girl inside, closing the door and bolting it shut. Immediately, she called 911 and now the entire neighborhood was outside, watching the events unfold.

"Ms. Shepherd," the officer began, "the FBI is here and would like to speak with you."

Elizabeth Shepherd was a recently divorced mother of two whose children were already grown and out of the house. This home was where she raised them and was married to their father for twenty years. He decided he'd rather live a carefree life with his assistant manager who happened to be much younger than Elizabeth and so this house was now hers alone. The evenings often found her curled up on her sofa, reading the latest Harry Bosch book and drinking a glass of white wine. Which was exactly what she had been doing when Chloe Schaffer pounded on her front door at eleven p.m. on a Thursday night.

She didn't see the man in question and believed she had little to offer the likes of the FBI, but who was she to say no? "Of course." She held a cup of tea in her hands and sat on the edge of the sofa, her tired mind fearing she might not recollect every exact detail but would do her duty.

The officer nodded and retreated out of sight, only to return moments later with a handsome man in a button-down dress shirt and a woman, very pretty, though Elizabeth didn't care for the blonde hair. It didn't seem to suit the woman's skin tone.

"Ms. Shephard? I'm Agent Nick Scarborough and this is Agent Kate Reid. You mind if we ask you a few questions about what happened tonight?"

"No, please sit down." She waited until they took their seats. "I'm not sure how much help I can be. I'm afraid I didn't see much."

"Ms. Shepard," Nick began.

"Please, call me Elizabeth."

"Elizabeth, when you stepped outside to see who was after Chloe, you mentioned you weren't able to see anyone."

"That's right. It was dark and I didn't have my glasses on, so it was difficult to see under those circumstances, but no, I didn't see anyone running after her."

"Chloe said she was only four houses down and I have one of my agents there now. I'm afraid they found a body inside. Were you familiar with that particular neighbor?" Kate asked.

"It's a rental and people come and go every few months, it seems. I've lived here a long time and there are only a couple of us originals left in the community. Most sold during the boom and a lot went vacant when the bust came. That house finally got some tenants about a year or so ago, but like I said, they come and go and I don't pay much attention." Elizabeth studied Kate for a moment. "Do you have any children, Agent Reid?"

"No, ma'am, I don't."

"Well, I have two. They're grown now, but if Chloe were my child, I'd find that man who took her and put a bullet in his head."

"Yes, ma'am. Chloe was very lucky you were home. She's also a tough kid who managed to escape." Kate admired the young girl and had already drawn the obvious comparisons to her own past.

"Her parents will be meeting us at the hospital where Chloe's headed to get checked out now," Nick added.

"Did he hurt her?"

"We don't think so, Elizabeth."

"That is good news, but he's still out there and I hope you catch him."

"Thank you for your time. They'll be clearing out of here soon and you'll be able to get some sleep. I'm sure you must be exhausted."

"After tonight, I don't think I'll be sleeping much knowing someone like that was living four houses down, Agent Scarborough."

"He was only using it temporarily and he won't come back here. Rest assured of that." Nick stood up. "Thank you again for your time and for helping Chloe. You saved her life."

"I think she saved her own life, Agent Scarborough."

A final acknowledgment and the agents walked back outside and into the organized chaos that was a crime scene. A media van had arrived and a reporter stood on the other side of the street where the officers held her and her cameraman at bay.

"What the hell do we do now?" Kate surveyed the scene with her hands at her waist.

"We get Chloe back to her parents, most importantly, then we keep working to track him down," Nick replied. "I don't want to let this trail go cold. Let's go see how Jameson's doing."

They approached the front of the sister's home where Dwight stood outside talking to another officer.

"These guys have been scouring the neighborhood, but no luck." Dwight tossed a glance over his shoulder, toward the house. "Looks like she OD'd."

"Do we know who she is?"

"Forensics ran her prints. She's his sister."

"So he knew where she was and we didn't?" Nick appeared disgusted. "This shit ends now. I'm tired of screwing around with this, dealing with three other damn departments. We can't get shit done and from this point on, we're the only decision-makers." Nick rubbed his forehead. "We search the entire God damn area tonight."

Options were something that Lyle Stroud found in short supply as he made his way the hell out of the suburbs as quickly as he could, avoiding the freeways, but unable to cross the state border. They would have checkpoints or roadblocks for certain. He knew he couldn't slip past them this time. After that bitch opened the door, he had no choice but to run back to the old Ford Focus he'd stolen and get it started so he could get the fuck out of there before the cops came. He wondered if she told them what he was driving. Probably not. She was inside so quickly; she wouldn't have had time to notice. Might be able to give them the color, but that was all.

He didn't count on her escaping. He checked everything in that room. Drilled those holes to bolt down the bed while his sister was in the other room enjoying the high he'd given her, but regrettably, had ended in her death. Two things he hadn't planned on happening today. He didn't think to check her pockets for something as simple as a damn coin. Stroud shook his head. "A fucking coin." Then those bars giving way so easily. He should've known. The place was so run-down; it was no surprise. It was a mistake, going for her so soon after getting rid of the boy. His anger rose, causing his foot to press harder on the pedal.

There were still two on his list, Sophie Curtis and Matthew

Grimes. Each lived miles from one another and Stroud didn't dare head back in the direction of Sophie Curtis. They'd probably already launched an all-out manhunt. His meticulous planning was going up in flames.

The feds and the cops would ramp up their manpower and he'd become the most wanted man in the state; maybe in the country. And his options would diminish even further.

Stroud pulled off the side of the road and into a deserted parking lot of a dollar store. It was almost two a.m. and he needed sleep.

NICK ENTERED the command center where his team waited along with his field ops team from WFO, State Troopers, and the local police department. He approached Kate and Dwight, who were huddled with the other FBI agents. "They released Chloe Schaffer. I just got off the phone with the hospital."

"Thank God for that." Kate turned to Mason. "Did she have any new information?"

"No. I was the one who spoke with her after the doctors checked her out and apart from confirming his identity, she couldn't provide any further details."

"We know he's driving something else, but we don't know what it is." WFO field agent, Calvin Bass approached.

"How do we find him?" Dwight began to pace the front of the room, studying the maps of Stroud's known locations. "He knows he's running out of time and that he stands little chance of getting out of the state."

"You think he'll turn desperate?" Agent Bass asked.

"He's already desperate. We just need to know how desperate he'll become. He'd had this all planned out and while we had the advantage in that he didn't know we'd discovered his targets, we've since lost that because he has to assume we know."

"We still don't know who the last one is." Kate held up the photo. "He might go after him."

"Then we need to get choppers in the air and patrols on the ground and hunt this son of a bitch down." Agent Bass' enthusiasm reeked of a greenhorn.

Dwight shifted his eyes toward Nick, who remained in the back, arms folded, appearing to consider the possibilities. "Agent Scarborough, what do you think?"

"We need to establish better perimeter control." Nick moved toward the monitors. "He was last seen here and fled immediately on Chloe's escape. I know we've got patrols still scouring the area, but frankly, it's been three hours, and daylight's coming. If they couldn't find him, then he's long gone. And we don't know what the hell he's driving. I think our only option to put a stop to him is to get a perimeter control over the entire area." Nick moved to the wall monitors that showed the maps of his previous locations. "I don't know if he'll risk going after the boy now. If he was smart, he'd figure a way out of the state."

"He might try to lay low for a while," Agent Bass replied.

"We can't risk that assumption. But we can hope that his arrogance will cause him to make a mistake. We need to continue to search for the boy's identity and I think getting the county's air unit as well as State Troopers' air unit support is critical."

"Our helicopters are equipped with Forward Looking Infrared to spot heat signatures," the state trooper said.

"Sometimes all those will find are animals, but it's worth having." Nick turned his attention to Mason. "Who do we need to speak with to get your air support on board?"

"Chief will have to authorize. That won't be a problem."

Kate secured her bulletproof vest and other tactical gear when Dwight approached. "I haven't had to strap this on in a while."

"You and me both. But we'll be overhead most of the time. The officers on the ground will be the ones searching the homes and backyards."

"I noticed a few news vans out front," Kate said.

"Yeah, well, so long as they keep their mouths shut so Stroud isn't alerted, we'll be all right."

"Like that'll happen. This will be on CNN for the next ten hours."

"I hope to hell this doesn't last ten hours," Dwight replied. "I'll see you back in the comm. room."

Kate stepped out of the office that had been set up for them and as she made her way through the halls, the scene was much different from before. It seemed everyone on the force had been called in to take part in the search as well as more field teams from her office. She began to feel confident they would find Stroud. And if he survived the day, she'd be surprised.

On her return to the comm. room, the leaders of each team

cordoned off their designated search areas. Nick waved her over.

"We'll be heading up with State Troopers for aerial support. Bass' team will coordinate with foot patrols led by Mason and her sergeant to secure each area as you see on the maps."

"I think that might be a waste of time. The idea that he's staying in the general vicinity goes against all we know about him right now," Kate said.

"Maybe, but we can't afford to overlook anything. He could be hiding out somewhere around here and I don't want to be the one to miss that."

"What can I do?" Agent Vasquez approached.

"Coordinate from here. Keep an eye on the board and let us know if anyone locates Stroud."

"You three ready to go?" the trooper asked Nick.

"Let's do it."

The chopper was already running as it sat in the parking lot of the station. The BAU team made their way inside, followed by the pilot and two other troopers.

"Strap yourselves in, people. We're on our way." The pilot lifted the chopper off the ground and into the bright sky as the sun climbed above the horizon. The day brought with it clear visibility and calm winds and the ride was smooth.

Kate spotted the news vans and reporters vying for position outside the station. This was no longer a local story; this was going to be on the national nightly news and she prayed they'd have Stroud in custody before the broadcast.

"Where're we headed first?" Kate asked Nick.

"Foot patrols are almost in place at quadrants one and two.

We'll go there first in advance of their efforts to see what the Infrared can pick up."

"Will the chief be issuing statements to the press?"

"Yes. He'll need to inform the public that Stroud is here and that we're conducting the search. We don't have a choice. It's a matter of public safety. And, it might work in our favor. The more people who are looking out for him, the better our chances."

"What if he finds the boy before we find him?"

"That won't happen."

STROUD SAT in the corner of the near-empty diner wearing a baseball cap to aid in his disguise.

"Here's your coffee, sir." The waitress smiled, unaware, it seemed, of who she was looking at. "Your food will be right out."

"Thanks." He checked the time on his phone. Dawn had just emerged and he still didn't have a plan on how the hell to get out of here. He'd made it pretty far south, about forty miles from where she escaped. Getting out farther than that would require a highway and he couldn't risk it. His only choice was to try to stay hidden until they believed he'd made it out ahead of them. He sure as hell painted himself in a corner and this was the only way he could see through the problem.

He sipped on the too-hot coffee and flinched before setting it back down. Out of the corner of his eye, he caught sight of a small television mounted on the wall above the breakfast counter. A headline scrolled across the bottom of the screen and although Stroud had youth on his side, his vision suffered mildly, and he struggled to read it. But what he did see was a man standing outside what appeared to be a police station, ready to speak to the crowd of reporters.

Stroud scanned the diner to see if he could spot anyone else watching the TV. A few patrons sat at the counter and cast a glance above, but they didn't appear interested and continued eating, staring at their phones. Of course, whatever this conference was about, it was only a matter of time before it started showing up in people's news feeds. No one needed to watch television to catch the news anymore and most people didn't.

He strained to listen, but the volume was down. It wasn't until a mugshot of him appeared that confirmed his suspicions.

The cameras focused on the police captain or chief, Stroud didn't know which and didn't care when he heard a snippet of a question.

"How could this have happened when the man was in prison for a sex crime? Why was he allowed parole?"

"I'm afraid that's a question for the State Parole board. I'm here to find Lyle Stroud and when we do, he won't get out again. Thank you and we'll keep you posted."

As he looked at the people in the diner, no one turned to him. No one seemed to notice that he was there at all. His stomach rumbled and he needed food, but waiting for the waitress and risking that she might recognize him now wasn't going to work. Stroud had to leave.

He slid out of the booth and headed toward the door when the waitress called out.

"Sir? Sir, your meal is here." She moved in closer. "Sir, you need to pay for this."

Stroud pushed through the doors and rushed to his car. He

pressed the exposed wires together and the engine whined. With the gear shift slammed in reverse, he sped out of the parking lot.

"What the hell?" The waitress shook her head.

Stroud pulled out onto the road and headed west. "Fuck!" He slammed his fist onto the wheel. His brow beaded with sweat beneath the baseball cap and he flicked it off his head. The idea that he was going to have to chance getting out of the state seemed better than having the state on the hunt for him. But either way could be a losing proposition.

He veered off onto a residential side street a few miles from the diner. He had to stop for a minute and think. A train or a bus? He could be at the bus station within minutes. That would get him past the highway patrols. It was possible, assuming he could buy a ticket and board without anyone recognizing him. With this press conference, though, what were his odds?

If they were all searching for him, he needed to get as far away as possible. Hiding out here until it passed no longer seemed a viable solution. By the sounds of it, they were going to search every nook and cranny to find him. "God damn girl." This was all because he let that girl go free. She'd been his undoing and his rage grew.

MID-DAY CAME and went and still no signs of Stroud.

"We need to refuel." The helicopter lurched forward as it headed back to base.

"Either he's hiding or he's already gone." Nick turned to

Dwight. "We need to get on the ground and find this son of a bitch."

"I agree. I feel useless up here." Dwight turned to the Trooper commander. "We're going to revise our tactics and try to make better headway on the ground. We'll still need you in the sky, but we're doubling our efforts here and we could be more effective on the ground."

"Ten-four. We'll be down in five minutes."

The chopper began its descent toward the Fairfax Springfield District Station, the winds knocking it around a little but eventually landing. The agents exited and made their way inside.

Kate's cell phone buzzed and she glanced at the caller ID. "Excuse me, I need to take this." She hung back while Dwight and Nick continued toward the Chief's office.

"Hey. You doing all right?"

It was Mike's voice on the other end and for the first time in two days, Kate smiled. "Yeah, I'm fine. You must've heard."

"BOLOs are out everywhere and I also caught the press conference. I won't keep you. I just wanted to know that you were okay."

"I'm glad to hear your voice, actually. It's been rough going so far. We aren't any closer now than we were this morning and tensions are high around here."

"I'll bet. Listen, I know you're going to do what you need to do, and I won't suggest otherwise. I just want you to stay safe and I'll be here if you need me. I love you, Kate. Goodbye."

"Goodbye hon, and thanks for the call." Kate continued to join the others.

"Everything all right?" Nick asked as she approached.

"Yes. Sorry about that."

He eyed her with mild suspicion which brought on an awkward feeling that reminded her of what he'd said in his drunken state, but rather than make a thing of it, she brushed it aside. "What's the plan?"

It was at that moment when a man walked toward them, taking everyone by surprise.

"Jake." Nick looked at the others and began to walk toward him. "What are you doing here?" He wrapped his arm around Jake's shoulder and ushered him out into the lobby.

"They told me you were down here. Nick, I'm here to make sure Lyle Stroud doesn't get away."

"Man, I know you're hurting, but you can't be here. Look around you. We've got a damn army behind us. We got this."

"I can't sit at home and watch my wife crying every second of the day. My son stays in his room, playing video games and who knows what else. Our lives have been destroyed by this man and I'll be damned if he gets away with it."

"He won't get away, Jake, I promise you that."

"Just like you promised you'd bring my boy home to me?"

Nick couldn't look away. Jake's gaze burned right through him as the words so easily flowed from his tongue. The blame was his and his alone. And Nick would shoulder it—always. "I did promise you that and I have no excuse to give that could ever make up for my betrayal. All I can do now is what you see here. There will be no rest for any of us until he's caught. Lyle Stroud has nowhere to run this time."

Kate and Dwight appeared around the corner and began to approach the two men still deep in conversation.

"What's he doing here?" Kate asked.

"If it had been my kid," Dwight began, "I'd be here too. Come on, we'd better put a lid on this quickly."

"Agent Scarborough, we need to get moving." Dwight turned to Jake. "Mr. Talbot, this isn't the place for you to be right now, no matter how much you might want to."

"Tell that to my wife, Agent Jameson. I'm here just as much for her as I am for myself."

"Then you'll need to stay put here if you insist, and please don't misinterpret my meaning. I'm a father too and I don't think I'd be any different if I were in your shoes."

Kate appreciated Dwight's words. He was the only one out of the three of them who could truly empathize with Jake Talbot. Dwight didn't talk about his kids often, but Kate knew they meant the world to him. It was something she would never experience. "Agent Scarborough, we're ready to go."

"Okay," Nick replied, then turned his attention to Jake. "Please, just stay here, Jake. I'll find him, I swear to you."

19

At the Daybreak Diner, Sarah Hoffman wiped the counter clean of breadcrumbs and soda stains left behind by the lunchtime regulars. The talk show program on the television mounted to the wall behind the counter had been interrupted, and the sound of a "Breaking News" report caught her ear. She took notice of the broadcast and turned up the volume.

"If you see this person, please call 911 and do not approach him. He is armed and dangerous." A mug shot of a man she immediately recognized appeared on the screen.

"Oh my God." Sarah reached for the phone beneath the register.

~

Detective Mason hurried to find Agent Scarborough after

an officer from Loudoun County conveyed the information he'd received from a 911 call.

Kate listened as Mason relayed the news to Scarborough and soon interrupted. "She spotted him this morning. It's already midday. What can we do now?"

"I want confirmation from this waitress or any of the other staff who thought they saw Stroud eating there. And, someone might have noticed the car he was driving." Mason waited for Nick to comment. "You okay with this?" He still hadn't replied. "Nick? You good with this?"

It was as if a switch turned on and Nick returned his attention. "Yeah. We should get down there and talk to the wait staff."

Kate eyed Mason, who, for the first time that she'd witnessed, referred to Nick so casually. She thought she'd picked up on a vibe the other day when they were at Stroud's place but dismissed it. "Agent Scarborough, maybe you should hang back and stick with Jake Talbot for a while? We've got more than enough people to get a handle on this."

Fervor ignited in him as he regarded her comment. "There isn't a snowball's chance in hell that I won't be the one to find Stroud." He breezed past her toward the exit.

The diner was already swarming with media, thanks to an owner who thought it would make for good publicity. Never mind that he and his staff served a wanted killer and didn't take a lick of notice.

"Get the hell back," Nick shouted at the reporters as he made his way inside. "Where's the owner?"

A small man, middle-aged and slender, hiked up his trousers. "I am." He moved toward Nick, hand extended. "I'm Ronald Hoffman, and you are?" He noted Nick's suit. "You must be FBI. No one around here wears suits this time of year."

"Special Agent Scarborough. You mind telling those people outside to get the hell off the property? We have an investigation to run and I sure as hell don't need them disrupting things."

The man appeared to suddenly regret his idea of free promotion and began to walk outside.

A young woman noted the exchange and approached. "I'm Sarah Hoffman. Please forgive my dad. I don't think he realizes exactly what's at stake here."

Nick greeted the woman. "Thank you. You're the Sarah Hoffman who made the call?"

"Yes. I'm the one, I believe, who served the man you're looking for." She led them toward the table where Stroud sat. "He was sitting here and was wearing a baseball cap. St. Louis Cardinals, if I recall. I just didn't realize." The young waitress began to tear up.

"Ms. Hoffman, it's okay." Kate reached out for her shoulder. "Most people don't think they'll ever come across someone like Stroud."

Nick was dismissive and continued to prod the waitress with questions. "Did you see what kind of car he was driving?"

"As a matter of fact, I did, because I was getting ready to serve him; and had his plate in my hand, when he took off. Just left. Didn't even pay for his coffee. I shouted at him that he was responsible for paying for the food, and I made it to the door, but he was already inside his car, fixin' to leave."

"What was he driving, Sarah?" Nick pressed on.

"He was in a white hatchback. American, but I don't know that much about cars and I couldn't say what kind it was, but it didn't look like Japanese or something. It was old, like maybe early 2000s or sometime around then. Small, two doors, kinda damaged."

"What kind of damage?" Nick asked.

"He started pulling out of the parking lot and I saw the passenger door. It was banged in. Had a big dent right there in the panel."

"This is helpful, thank you." Nick began to scan the diner. "Anyone else around here see him?"

"I don't think so. We weren't that busy this morning and they all would've left. I was the only one waiting tables and Rudy back there works in the kitchen, so it was just me."

"Thank you," Kate said. "We appreciate it."

"I'm sorry I let him go."

"He's a very dangerous man. Be glad he left." Kate began to walk away and Nick followed.

"What now?" she asked him.

"Let's get this information out. Update the BOLO and we'll keep looking."

His temperament was borderline callous and Kate didn't know how to rein in his growing fury. He'd made a second promise to Jake Talbot that he might not be able to keep. It would unravel him completely if he let him down again and she didn't think there would be any coming back from that. Nick was a man teetering on the edge and she felt helpless to do anything about it.

STROUD LISTENED to the radio in the Ford Focus as he found temporary refuge parked around the back of a grocery store. He'd repeated his revised strategy over and over in his mind and it was nearly time to put it into action. According to the radio news reports, the entire state was looking for him. The FBI, State Troopers, and the local cops were all hunting him down like a dog.

He stepped out of the car and began to walk around toward the front of the busy store, pulling his cap low on his forehead and doing his best to keep his head down. He stood near a masonry column that would help to obscure his presence.

Stroud waited. He had to find the perfect target. Preferably a middle-aged woman on her own and with a cart full of groceries. She'd be slower to unload and he'd have more time.

Minutes seemed to move much more slowly than he'd anticipated. At this rate, the cops would find him standing right here. He peered across the walkway toward the exit doors and spotted her.

She pushed her haul over the lined sidewalk and onto the asphalt, appearing to struggle to gain momentum. Stroud hung back, confirming no one was watching either her or him. He waited for her to start down one of the rows and when she was far enough from the entrance, he followed.

A final glance at the front of the store and no one had taken notice of him. A couple with a young child was too busy keeping the kid from darting out into the parking lot and a man with a cell phone stuck to his ear pushed a cart with two cases of Bud with his free hand. This was his chance and Stroud continued in the woman's direction.

A glance at the light posts confirmed that no security cameras were stationed. A good thing for him, not that it mattered much because by the time anyone could see what happened, he'd be over the state line.

The woman was placing her grocery bags into the back of her midsized crossover. She was about halfway through when he made it to within fifty feet of her. It would only take a glance over her shoulder to spot him, but if Stroud could count on one thing in people it was that they were oblivious to anything else around them. He shoved his hand into his front pants pocket, pretending to retrieve car keys and walking toward the vehicle next to hers. Fifteen feet away, ten; now was the time.

Stroud dashed behind the woman and thrust his hand over her mouth. "If you scream, I'll kill you. Now get in the car."

The woman froze until Stroud kicked her foot and she nearly tumbled to the ground. He forced her to the driver's side and pulled open the door. "Give me the keys."

She shook her head.

"Give me the goddam keys, or you're dead."

She closed her eyes and handed him the keys.

He pushed her inside and quickly slid into the back seat, all the while, keeping his gun pointed at the back of her head. "Drive."

"Where?" Her voice trembled and her hands shook as she tried to place the key into the ignition.

"Get on the freeway."

The engine started and the woman reversed out and left the safety of the Kroger's parking lot. "Please don't hurt me."

"Then do what I say and don't try to get yourself pulled over."

"Where are we going?"

"Out of this town is all I know right now. Just keep driving."

They reached the freeway and continued north on I-95. Stroud kept his eyes peeled for signs of checkpoints. So far, they hadn't reached any, but he knew it was only a matter of time.

His gun was pushed deep inside the back of the driver's seat, although Stroud tried to keep a low enough profile not to raise eyebrows from passersby in other cars. Now that they'd gained some speed, that would be less of a problem.

The woman hadn't uttered a word and continued with her hands glued to the wheel. An occasional glance through the rearview revealed her captor's malevolent gaze because if she believed he wouldn't make good on his promise, then there was no reason for her to continue.

The road signs above flashed with warnings of Stroud's white beat-up car that he'd recently abandoned. That meant they had no idea yet of what he'd done. He might end up with an hour or two head start and that would be enough.

The sun was behind them as it shone through the rear of his passenger window. It was approaching late afternoon. They were nearing the state border and that would be the real test of Stroud's plan. He needed to stay hidden in the back seat and that meant searching for cover of some sort. There was a good chance the woman's car wouldn't be stopped at all. They were looking for Stroud's car, and so he might not need camouflage. But right now, he couldn't take that chance.

"What do you have in the back besides the groceries?"

"What do you mean?" She glanced into the rear view again, but quickly returned her eyes to the road.

"I mean, do you have any clothes, or a blanket or something?"

She seemed to be searching for an answer that was coming too slowly.

"Come on! What do you have?" Stroud raised the gun to the space between the seat and the headrest, just touching her neck with the barrel.

"Um, I-I think I have a towel, maybe two for when the dog gets in the car."

The gun retreated and her shoulders dropped.

Stroud kept the gun aimed at the seat and twisted his upper body toward the back to have a look. He felt around with his right hand, his short stature working against him. He swatted at the grocery bags until he felt the top of a towel. He took hold of it and dragged it out. The beach towel would do enough if he hunched down into the foot well, making certain the gun remained pressed against the seat, just in case. He couldn't risk her alerting the cops, so if she knew he wouldn't hesitate to pull the trigger, even if it meant his own life, she would cooperate.

"By the amount of food you bought, I'm assuming you have a family—children."

"Yes."

"If you want to get back home to see them, then you just need to do exactly as I say. You understand?"

"Yes."

"We're about fifteen miles from the border. If you're stopped, stay calm. Don't even think about saying a word to them about me, or give them a funny look. I'll be keeping my gun against your seat and believe me, miss, it'll be the last funny look you'll ever give. And I'm sure your kids would miss you very much."

DETECTIVE MASON ENTERED the comm. room with an urgency that alarmed Kate, who noticed her arrival before the others. The detective approached, holding her cell phone.

"Agent Scarborough?"

Nick diverted his attention. "Yes?"

"Chief told me he just received a call from the McLean district. They got a call from a Kroger store manager regarding a car they found around the back of the building. They think it might be Stroud's."

"McLean. That's what, thirty, forty miles east of us. Shit. He's trying to get the hell out of the state. Do they have any security video?"

"They're emailing it now." She moved to one of the computers. "If you don't mind, can I log in here?"

Agent Vasquez nodded and stepped away from the screen. "Be my guest."

She retrieved her email from the main server and there it was. The attachment was from the store manager. "This is it. I'll open it up."

A few clicks and the files lined up, ready to be viewed. She opened the first one. The video was slightly grainy as the sun hindered its clarity. "The inside footage is much clearer, but the manager said they didn't see him in there. Just here." She pointed to the outer part of the frame where a man stood, wearing a ball cap and appearing to disguise his face from the cameras. "That's got to be him."

The video continued as Stroud stood there for some time.

"How the hell did no one see this guy?" Dwight asked.

Finally, Stroud began to move.

"He's following that woman," Kate said.

The team watched closely, waiting for Stroud to make his move. It was then that the woman disappeared from the frame and soon after, so did Stroud.

"That's it? Where the hell did they go?" Nick asked.

"There aren't any cameras at the far end of the parking lot. The manager said it's because most people don't park out that far unless it's really busy and the corporate office didn't want to spring for the extra half-dozen units."

"Jesus Christ! Who was that woman? We need to know now!" Nick's anger spilled over, landing squarely on the detective. "Find out who she is. She probably used a card to pay. Have them match their receipts to the time when she walked out of the store. Get a God damn name!"

20

The overcrowded police station made it difficult to find a place for Nick to cool his head. He seemed to realize he'd reached a boiling point and finally made his way through the back entrance. It seemed the only refuge left.

Kate pushed through the doors of the comm. room in search of him. She stopped one of the officers. "Have you seen Agent Scarborough?"

"A few minutes ago. I think he went out through the back."

"Thanks." She started along the corridor. As she pushed through the rear exit, there he was, propped up against the brick masonry wall, one foot pressed against it, scrolling through his phone.

"Hey." She moved closer, leaning on the wall next to him. "You all right?"

"No. I'm not." He turned to her. "He's going to make it out of the state and we'll have to start all over again. And if he kills that woman?" Nick shook his head. "How the fuck am I supposed to go back to Jake and tell him—again—that his son's killer got away from us when we have so many people looking for him? How do I justify that to a man who's lost his son, Kate?"

To see the torment in his eyes pained her. He'd been there to comfort her so many times and now that the situation was reversed, she didn't know how to comfort him. Part of her feared he would misinterpret her actions, which upset her further because that was exactly what she'd wanted to avoid. Now there was this thing between them and it was preventing her from being there for him as a friend. She needed to talk about what he'd said but now wasn't the time. "I'm sorry it turned out this way. I truly am, and I wish I knew what to say to you. You're my best friend, Nick, and I don't know how to help you get through this."

He reached out for her, wrapping his arms around her neck, and pulled her close.

She felt his weight rest upon her and she hugged him back. "There's nothing you can do or say that will help Jake get through this. I wish to God there was."

He pulled back and held her gaze. "I failed him, but not only him; Emily's family and now this woman's family." He broke the stare. "So many times, I've been here in this very spot and each time, I've been able to come back from it. Tell myself that I did what I could for the victims. I just don't think I can keep feeding myself those lies."

The door burst open and Dwight appeared. "We got an ID on the woman."

They quickly returned inside.

"Olivia Rice, 42, stay-at-home mother of three." Dwight pointed to the monitor. "This was where her car was last seen. It's a 2010 Honda CRV, license VBJ-5311. The store's purchase records confirm she was the one who Stroud followed. The only lone female to check out at that exact time."

"Where is this? And how long ago was this image taken?"

"We reached out to her husband, who's on his way to the McLean station," Detective Mason began. "Her phone has a GPS tracking app and he's bringing in his now. He said she just crossed over into Maryland. He figured she'd just decided to do more shopping and didn't think to check her location until he got the call from us."

"God damn it!" An unexpected burst of anger sprang forth from the otherwise levelheaded Agent Jameson. "How did she get past the checkpoints?"

"Because no one was looking for her or her car—until now," the detective replied.

"We know where she is, and that's a good thing. Stroud may not realize this yet." Kate turned to the detective. "When is her husband due to arrive?"

"Any minute. Once he does, the chief there will give us a call and we'll have to do this over the phone. There's no time to wait for him to come here. We'll lose half an hour, easy."

Within a few minutes, the call came in and Mason put it on speaker.

"Detective Mason, this is Chief Gardner. I have Mr. Rice here." His voice faded for a moment while he spoke to the man. "Sir, this is the detective I mentioned. The FBI is also involved in the search for your wife."

Detective Mason began, "Thank you, Mr. Rice. We don't have any time to waste. Do you have the tracking information?"

The line crackled with background noise while the man retrieved his phone and opened the app that showed his wife's locations over the past several hours. "This is it here."

"What are you looking at there, chief?" Agent Scarborough asked.

"He's on the I-15 over the border into Maryland. Looks like he's headed toward the outskirts of Baltimore."

Nick looked at the detective. "Do we still have access to the chopper?"

"Yes." She immediately picked up the phone and made the call.

"We know where she is and that they're still on the move," Dwight replied to the speaker. "So long as they're driving, we know she's safe."

"I'm sorry, Agent, but you don't know that at all. He could've already gotten rid of her and kept her purse for money and her cell phone along with that." Mr. Rice's voice trailed off, sounding as though he was verging on tears.

The sun was working its way down the horizon behind them. Stroud peered over the driver's seat and noticed they would have to stop for fuel in the not-too-distant future. They could go maybe another fifty or sixty miles, he figured, before they ran out. That would put them well into Westminster, which was where he'd wanted to go.

The woman was getting tired too. She probably ran out of

adrenaline and was running on empty now. Her shoulders drooped, and her wrists relaxed on the wheel. Even her face appeared less tense. The muscles and veins in her neck no longer bulged either. She must have felt his stare and glanced through the rearview again, quickly returning her eyes to the road.

"Just keep driving. I'll let you know when we get to where we're going."

"I'm down to less than a quarter tank."

"I know that. I'm not fucking stupid."

She recoiled.

Stroud made it across the border and that was his priority. He had to give the cops some credit, though and figured they discovered his car and knew the woman was gone. They'd be looking for them both by now. He couldn't keep her for much longer. Alive or dead, that was the decision he still had to make.

His eye wandered toward the rear passenger window. It was that time of evening when the eyes struggled to adjust to the dimming light and everything was harder to see. He peered through, seeing nothing more than burning city lights as they started to turn on. There would have to be a place where he could leave her. He could kill her, but the idea wasn't as appealing as she wasn't to his usual liking. It would be out of necessity and while his mind flashed with images of her head dripping blood from having blown her brains out, it wasn't his usual flush of excitement. He could do it just for spite. To get back at those asshole FBI agents and cops hunting him down like an animal. And he'd already proven he could beat them at their own game, hadn't he? A small chuckle escaped him as his eyes lingered on the blurring lights passing by.

"Take the next exit." Stroud returned his attention to the matter at hand.

She didn't ask any questions this time, instead, did exactly as he instructed. The next exit was just ahead and she veered off the highway. They were heading into Reistertown, in the suburbs of Baltimore. That was where he could finish what needed to be done.

"Head right." Stroud had studied the maps long ago, and planned his route for each and every one of his victims right from the start, with few exceptions, one being his sister's move. And even though his plans had been irreversibly altered, this one need not change. A park lay a few miles ahead where he could easily disappear into the night, at least to lose whoever would try to track him down. But then, if she were to remain alive, she would tell them where he was.

Perhaps he'd now provided an answer to his own question. A loose end like that could mean his capture.

"They turned off the highway." Dwight noted the moving blip on the screen. "He's headed into the northern Baltimore area."

The husband had allowed the FBI to log into his GPS app account so that they could keep an eye on her location and track them down.

"We need to get Baltimore PD there right now. They're our best chance at stopping him," Detective Mason replied.

"Kate, make the call. Is the chopper here yet?" Nick asked.

"Yes," Mason replied.

Within minutes, the agents were airborne once again, but there was a sense of urgency even greater than before. They knew the challenges that lay ahead and that Stroud was smart enough to find a way out.

"We should be there in forty minutes," the pilot said.

"That's too long." Nick turned to Kate. "Any word from Baltimore?"

"They're on their way. I've got the captain on standby to keep us updated. They'll find him."

"That's what we thought yesterday." Nick returned his attention to the front of the chopper, peering through the windshield as though he'd be able to spot Stroud from that distance.

Kate directed a troubling eye to Dwight. There were so many variables in this scenario that it was impossible to predict them all and right now, they'd only counted on the one—that Stroud had kept the woman alive.

"PULL OVER HERE." Stroud waited until she pulled alongside a small community park that had been vacated thanks to darkening skies. He stepped out of the rear passenger seat, shifting his gun to the front and yanking the driver's side door open. "Get out."

The woman's eyes grew wide as she slowly stepped out into the warm night air. The streetlamp ahead burned a dim amber glow, hardly casting enough light by which to see. It was one of those low-glow designs that was meant to cut down on light pollution. But what it did was allow them to blend into the scenery. "What are you going to do?" Her fear was transparent, even with her semi-firm stance.

With the gun still aimed at her head, Stroud tossed his gaze in the direction of the park. "Start walking."

She took small steps, but he nudged her in the back.

"Faster than that." Stroud eyed the surroundings, checking for witnesses.

Moments later, they'd entered the tree-filled park and moved behind the playground where a few benches were tucked away beneath the shade trees. He could hear the woman's breathing intensify. She was starting to panic and he couldn't afford for her to let out a scream.

He reached for her shoulder and spun her around. "I'm sure you're ready to go home to your husband and your children, so remember that it's in your best interest to do exactly as I say and don't make any noise."

She nodded.

Stroud rested the barrel of his gun against her chest and began to slide it down until he reached the collar of her shirt—a V-neck top that revealed modest cleavage. "As I said before, you're not my type, so if you're thinking what I'm sure you're thinking, you can stop." He stepped back and looked her in the eyes. "I'll be keeping your car and you'll be staying here."

Her face was masked in relief.

"But if you scream for help before I have a chance to leave, then I swear to you, I'll find you and your family and kill all of you. Do I make myself clear?"

"Yes."

"And if you think I'm not smart enough to find you,

remember that I've been on the run for a week and the cops haven't found me yet. Believe me, I'm smarter than you think."

"I don't think that—I swear. I just want to go home."

"Good." He glanced at his watch. "Your purse is still in the car?"

She nodded again.

"Then I'll keep your cell phone just to be safe." He began to walk away but stopped short. "Oh, and there's one more thing." Stroud swung his arm wide, striking the woman's head with the butt of his gun. Her knees buckled and she collapsed to the ground. "That should buy me some time."

Stroud again scanned the area in search of any onlookers but noticed none. He jogged back to the car and slid into the driver's seat. Her purse rested on the passenger seat and he shoved his hand inside, searching until he retrieved the woman's cell phone. Several missed calls and text messages. It was then that it occurred to him they could be tracking him through the phone's GPS. Perhaps he wasn't that smart after all.

"Shit!" He was pissed he hadn't realized this before, but his only goal had been to get out of the state and he'd lost sight of anything else. But now, if they were tracking him, cops could be there at any moment. He opened the door and dropped the phone to the ground and stomped on it until it was smashed into several pieces. He didn't know how much longer he had to get the hell out of there, but there was no time to think about it anymore.

He keyed the ignition and pressed hard on the gas pedal, waiting for this large vehicle with its small engine to kick into gear. "Come on!" Finally, he spun out from the side of the curb and was on his way.

Kate's cell phone buzzed in her pocket and it took a minute for her to realize it wasn't the vibration from the helicopter. "It's the captain." She answered. "Agent Reid here. Is your team close to the last known location?" Her words caught Dwight's attention and he turned to her with trepidation.

"Okay. Call me when they are and let me know what you find. We'll be there inside of fifteen minutes."

Dwight reached for Nick's shoulder to get his attention and then nodded to Kate. "What happened?"

With both of them staring at her, Kate swallowed hard before she could speak. "Captain said the signal died."

"As in no longer moving or gone?" Nick asked.

"Gone. Like the phone's been shut off or destroyed."

"Damn it. Are they close?"

"A few minutes away."

"If that woman's dead, I swear to God I'll fucking kill Stroud myself." Nick balled his hands into tight fists. "I'll fucking kill him."

21

The chopper began to descend toward the site below where Baltimore police surrounded the area and an ambulance waited.

"Looks like we're the last to the party." Dwight unbuckled his seat belt and prepared to exit while the helicopter was just touching ground. "I hope to hell they found her alive."

The pilot cut the engine and the team exited, keeping their heads low as the blades slowed overhead.

Nick peered over his shoulder and waved to them "Over here." He returned to full height when he cleared the chopper and jogged toward the back of the ambulance, whose doors were open. "Where is she?"

An EMT stood just outside the doors and noted the FBI letters on Nick's vest. "Inside. She's hurt, but she'll be okay."

"She's alive." He turned back to Dwight and Kate. "She's still alive." Nick raised the corners of his mouth in what appeared to be a moment of relief.

"Where's the captain?" Kate asked the man who offered the welcomed news.

"Over there, by the trees." He pointed in the direction of the wooded area.

Kate made her way toward him, leaving Nick and Dwight to get the rundown on Mrs. Rice's condition. "Captain McKinnon, what happened?"

McKinnon stood next to one of his officers and turned his attention to Kate. "Agent Reid? Looks like Mrs. Rice is a very lucky woman. She's conscious and was able to tell us what went down. Stroud took a swing at her with the end of his gun and knocked her out cold—long enough for him to take off in her car after he smashed her cell phone. We've got all units out looking for her car. I've got all my men searching the area."

"How long was she unconscious? How much ahead of us is he?"

"We arrived on scene when she'd already regained consciousness. She was sitting on the bench and was still pretty out of it. A dog-walker spotted her and asked if she was okay. She figures she was out for at least ten minutes, maybe fifteen."

"Long enough for him to clear out."

"I'm afraid so. And my guess is, he probably dumped the car and is either on foot or looking at public transportation."

"You think he'd risk showing his face?"

"It's getting late and the later it is, the less busy the buses and trains will be. Commuters are already home by now and so unless he's recognized while buying the ticket, he would stand a fairly good chance of getting out that way."

Kate eyed the area, pondering their options. They were so close to him now and to let him slip again would most certainly mean putting the boy at risk; the one they still had yet to identify. But he wouldn't dare cross back over the border into Virginia.

Her expression revealed instant recognition. "Oh my God. We've been looking in the wrong place. Stroud wanted to come here all along. The boy must live here."

"What's that?" The captain's attention had been diverted.

"Nothing, sorry, but would you mind meeting with my team for a moment?" Kate started to walk back toward Nick and Dwight.

"Not at all."

They approached the two agents.

"How is she?" Kate asked.

"She'll be fine. They're going to take her to the hospital now. The husband's been made aware."

"We've been looking in the wrong place for that boy," Kate started. "Vasquez has been searching the databases, reaching out to the schools, checking for a passport or other forms of ID, looking for a match to the boy, but we were wrong. Stroud wanted to come here; he just needed safe transport." She studied her colleagues, who seemed to grasp her concept. "That's why we haven't been able to find him. He doesn't live in Virginia; he lives here."

Lyle Stroud had the A/C blasting and wasn't sure if it was the heat outside or his nerves making him sweat. He needed to get out of this car because that was what was going to get him caught.

Stroud picked up his list and held it against the steering wheel as he drove, glancing at it briefly. A single name remained and he had no idea if the Feds had tracked the kid down or not. He had to assume they tore the shit out of his house by now. He shouldn't have left the pictures there, but then he hadn't planned on them discovering his identity. Stroud believed he had covered all his bases. It should've been an easy plan to execute. Different places, none of the kids knew one another or had any connection to him. They would've been untraceable.

He'd made a grave mistake early on, somewhere along the line, but didn't know what it had been. They weren't far behind and if they had figured out who those kids were, they'd be at the boy's house when Stroud showed up. If they hadn't, he could finish what he started, except for Sophie Curtis. She was one lucky kid. One thing was certain, though, this would be his last hurrah.

The question now was whether Stroud should take the risk. He'd studied the boy, learned his habits, and even engaged him on social media once. The kid was bright, though, and never showed back up in that chat room.

He was so close now that he could almost taste it, and his desire grew for this final thrill, even if it wasn't supposed to be the end of his plan. Continuing on, as he had wanted, choosing others in different places, working odd jobs and staying on the move and just picking off those kids one by one; that had been his true heart's desire. The list he had now? It was only phase one. His "endangered species list" would've grown until he was satisfied he'd controlled them and consumed them until they were nothing but shells and then discarded them with the trash as he had been. He would take the risk again because he knew it would be the last. He had no more tricks up his sleeve and no other place to go. "I ain't no one's prison bitch."

Stroud flicked his cigarette out the window and continued onto the outskirts of a darkened parking lot in a strip mall. He killed the lights and rolled forward to a stop. There was no time to steal another car. He could, however, take the plates off of one and put them onto the Honda. It would, at the very least, buy him some time. He stepped out of the car and made his way, as stealthy as possible, toward a nearby vehicle. This one was a newer model Chevy Tahoe. It would do.

He returned to the Honda in search of a screwdriver or something that would be a good substitute. The woman's car was clean, no trash. He checked the glove compartment, but all that was inside was the car's manual and insurance information.

With the center console panel raised, he peered inside. A coin. He spotted a penny and he had to laugh at the irony. He was in this predicament for just such a thing. The girl had escaped by using a coin to loosen the bolts and he'd seen that very coin lying next to the leg of the bed frame. It was an ingenious idea that he would now find himself considering.

With the coin in hand, Stroud began to remove the plate cover. It read, "My other car is a boat." *Typical,* he thought. A noise sounded in the distance, and he stood but didn't see anything around. He continued to the task of removing the car's plate.

Once the change was made, Stroud started up the car and drove north, in the direction of the boy, Matthew Grimes. He looked at his list to see the schedule of the kid's locations he'd jotted down. Tonight, the kid would already be home by the time Stroud made it there. That would present a few minor problems, not the least of which was the fact that his parents would be home.

He continued in the direction of Matthew Grimes' house. He would draw near, then leave the car and make his way on foot as close as he could get. If the cops were waiting, he'd see them before they'd see him if he was on foot.

Surface streets offered better routes than the highway, which would surely be patrolled, so Stroud opted for the longer route. He meandered toward the suburb where the boy lived and stopped at a red light. A car pulled alongside him. Stroud cast a sideways glance, but the driver in the other car was oblivious as usual. He figured if only a quarter of the people in this country paid attention to their surroundings, crime would drop substantially. "Thank you, smartphones."

The light turned green and the other car pulled out ahead, which was fine by him. The next right was where he would abandon the Honda and take to foot. Stroud made the turn and realized there wasn't a good place to leave it. Sure, he could leave it roadside, but it would be easily spotted, if anyone, like cops, were looking. A change of plates would divert them, but only temporarily.

He peered through the windshield in search of a better location and noted an alleyway. "Perfect." It was behind a row of stores and was probably there for the dumpsters. Stroud drove into the narrow alley until it widened enough that would allow him to turn around. He parked at the edge, against a wall. The lights of the stores were off and they appeared to be closed.

Stroud exited the car but didn't lock it. If he needed to bolt, every second would count and he highly doubted anyone would try to take it. He wasn't planning on being very long.

With his baseball cap pulled low again, Stroud made his way to the end of the alley and veered left toward the boy's street, which was about two blocks away.

The night hadn't brought with it cooler temperatures and Stroud began to sweat through his shirt. Another turn to the right and he'd be on the street. This was the moment Stroud needed to remain confident. It would only take a brief look-see if there were any cops around. And so he continued, after taking a deep breath to settle his nerves. Several more steps and Stroud didn't see anyone around. No neighbors or cars on the road. It was as if the street shut down at nine o'clock at night. The house was in view now. He stopped. Lights were on, but no cars in the drive. The kid just might be alone.

"This is the kid he's going after." Captain McKinnon zoomed in on the monitor in the conference room of his station. "What we know now is that whoever he is, he must live somewhere inside the area where we found Olivia Rice."

"We need to access NGI." Dwight turned to McKinnon. "Is your department utilizing the program?"

"Yes. When it became fully operational last year, we signed up. How will it benefit us in this scenario?"

Nick began to approach. "We had limited our search criteria to Virginia since the other victims were in the proximity of roughly 150 miles. We did not need to assume he would venture out. And that was our mistake. Now, with the use of NGI, social media, airport travel, any place where this kid would've been caught on CCTV. The program will be able to run facial recognition."

"The intent of NGI wasn't to integrate it with those systems, with the exception of airport security. The use of it in this manner is risky, which was why we hadn't before," Kate replied.

"Agreed, except that the Privacy Impact Assessment hasn't been completed for this program yet," Nick replied. "There is currently no oversight program in place, which leaves the door wide open."

Kate knew Nick often crossed the line when it came to obtaining information. However, she was hesitant in this instance because privacy concerns were a huge issue that the Bureau battled on a daily basis. "Agent Scarborough, if we use the program for purposes it wasn't intended for, we'll be vulnerable to litigation, both personally, as well as the Bureau, if privacy advocate groups get wind of it." She also understood that Nick's letter of censure already put him in danger of any further involvement in this scenario.

"This boy's life is at stake and I sure as hell don't want to be the one to look his parents in the eyes and tell them that we had a chance to save him, but we were too worried about being sued by the Electronic Frontline Organization and groups like that." His temper was rising. "But, Agent Reid, if you'd like to make that call, I'll defer to you."

Fuming, Kate held his gaze, which was growing darker by the minute. She was trying to protect him and he either didn't see that or didn't care. Perhaps she shouldn't care either. They could save the boy, but there was no guarantee they'd find anything. "Just do it then. We're out of time."

Dwight logged in and began typing on one of the computers in the back of the room. "I've already got this digital image in the system since we've been looking for him and it appears this picture is from a social media post. We might have luck here."

They all waited for something to pop up. Something that would give them a name and a location.

"Captain, where are we on the search for Stroud? Can you follow up with your team?" Perhaps Nick had begun to see that maybe breaking this rule could be avoided.

The captain retrieved his radio. "Four-four-two, come in. This is Captain McKinnon."

"Four-four-two here. Go ahead."

"Do we have a location on the 2010 Honda CRV?"

"We're patrolling a ten-mile radius in the vicinity of our previous victim's location. Nothing yet, but we will be broadening the search."

"Ten-four. Thank you Four-four-two." McKinnon turned to Nick. "They're still searching."

Dwight continued to access NGI and enter the parameters. Minutes passed with a painful lethargy. "Hang on, I got something here."

Kate leaned over his shoulder. "What am I looking at?"

"This is a Facebook post—public—on April 5th. Looks like it came from a relative's account. Maybe his mother?"

"Who is he?" Nick moved in to examine.

"The account is under the name of Claire Grimes. The post reads, 'Matthew striking it up at the bowling alley." Dwight turned to Nick. "That's the kid. Matthew Grimes."

"That has to be his mother. Run both names and get a location ASAP!"

With a feverish pace, Dwight keyed in the names and waited for the massive brain behind the NGI database to spit out a location. "Claire Grimes lives at 3259 NW 1st Street, Owings Mills," Dwight said.

"That's not far, twenty minutes, tops." McKinnon picked up his radio again and made the call.

"Do we have a phone number? Anything we can do to warn the mother?" Kate asked.

Dwight continued to type on the keyboard. "Here. This is her cell phone." He turned the monitor toward her.

Kate immediately dialed it, her heart pounding with anticipation. She prayed they weren't too late. The line rang. One, two, three times. "God damn it. Voicemail." She ended the call. "Captain, how close are your units?"

"They'll be there in three minutes."

"Good. Tell them not to approach the home, but try to get a visual inside."

"What? Why?"

"Because Stroud will kill the kid. We need a coordinated approach."

"Agreed," Nick replied. "We burst in there with guns blazing, he won't hesitate to take out the boy. We have no choice but to assume he's already there."

"And what if he's not there?" McKinnon asked.

"Then we'll get the family someplace safe and be ready for him."

22

A **shock wave** jetted down his spine as he stood watch outside the boy's home. It was that customary tingling and bolt of energy that came when the time was near. But he had to be sure the boy was there—and alone. He'd taken cover behind a tall, wide shrub between the home and a neighboring house. He double-checked his gun was at the ready.

Another survey of the immediate area confirmed no bystanders and no cops, but how long he had, Stroud couldn't be sure and so a decision must be made. He stepped out from behind the shrub and began making his way toward the home. A light in the front window burned with a soft white hue that spilled through the slats of the closed shutters.

He was next to the garage now, hiding behind the stone column. If only he could see through the garage window for a car, but the windows were too high. Even if he could manage a peek inside, the garage was dark and it would be difficult to see a car anyway. When he believed it was safe to continue, Stroud moved toward the front of the home and stood near the porch steps. A deck spanned the entire length of the front of the home and he could approach from the far right side, remaining obscured from the view of the front window and anyone who might be approaching from the street. He leaned toward the window, listening. Only a low, muffled sound emerged and sounded like a television.

He had but one chance and the time had come to take it. If the parents were home, he'd simply make up an excuse and leave. If they weren't, then he'd take his shot. Stroud stepped toward the front door and knocked with three firm thumps of his knuckles.

The faint sound of footsteps approaching made Stroud's pulse rise. He swallowed hard and hardened his stance, ready to push his way inside. But the door didn't open. The steps ceased to make any further sounds. Something was going awry. It occurred to him that if the boy was alone, he might not be willing to open the door to a stranger. The door had a peephole and he might have already gotten a look and opted to pretend no one was home. If that was the case, it would all but confirm that the parents weren't home. A much easier, and much more desirable scenario.

Stroud waited a moment longer, then turned and stepped down from the porch. He walked around the side where he would not be spotted and waited for the kid to make a choice. He hoped a call to the police wasn't in the program. The kid was thirteen; smart enough to know what to do in a situation such as this. Then again, this was a safe neighborhood and the chances the kid would know Stroud was on the loose was slim. The last anyone reported was that he was still in Virginia.

The question now was, how to get inside. Now that he felt comfortable with the certainty that the parents weren't home, he would need to find a way in. Time was still critical and the cops could show up if the boy made the call. However, Stroud had no intentions of taking this kid anywhere. It was an unavoidable deviation from his initial plans. He would do what needed to be done without delay because he knew his chances of getting away clean this time were slim and none. It didn't matter now. Stroud had nothing to lose by getting caught.

Stroud began to walk toward the back of the home where a red cedar gate hung between wooden posts of a picket fence that could be scaled but with some difficulty. A certain level of physical fitness was required when endeavoring to capture preteens and young teenagers. He tried the latch, but a long bar hung across it. It wasn't going to be that easy. The fence was short, maybe only five feet in height and Stroud was five feet nine.

Stroud gripped the top of the fence posts, their pointed tips difficult to hold on to. But he pulled himself up with the strength of his arms while his sneakers slid against the smooth surface. He needed traction but had none. His arms bore all the weight as he pulled on them to lift himself higher. *Just a little more*, he thought.

His waist reached the top and from there, he lurched over the edge, counterbalancing the rest of his weight before finally flipping over to the other side. The thud of his fall sounded loudly in his ears and he quickly got to his feet and pressed himself against the sidewall of the house. A moment passed while he waited for someone to come outside, but no one did.

Stroud dusted off his jeans and stepped with caution toward the rear entrance of the home. While he hadn't heard the presence of a dog, there was no way to be sure one wasn't in that backyard, but as he proceeded, no dog came running. He could have easily broken the dog's neck in any case.

A sliding glass door extended the length of the covered patio in the rear yard. There would be no need to break the glass. Stroud knew how to lift the slider from its track to gain entry. Another handy-dandy trick he learned in prison.

The door was obscured by window coverings and now it would be all too easy to get his hands on the prize. Stroud approached and began to lift the far end of the glass door until the wheel raised a few inches. The lock would then disengage and pulling the door away would be no trouble. He did just that and slid the door back about a foot, enough for him to slip through.

As he emerged beyond the curtain, a surprise awaited him.

"Stop!" The boy held a large butcher knife in his hands. With wide eyes and a pale face full of fear, his voice cracked. "I already called the police. Get out of my house!"

"Well, aren't you a smart one." Stroud moved a step closer and removed his baseball cap. A sign that he wasn't going anywhere.

"I told you! Leave!" His hands gripped the knife with such force that it turned his knuckles white and returned a red hue to his cheeks.

"So, you called the cops, huh? I guess we ain't got much time then."

KATE REFASTENED her vest and was again ready to apprehend Lyle Stroud. McKinnon's team was only two minutes from the residence when the call came in from dispatch. The boy had called 911. Stroud was already there.

"Let's head out, Reid." Dwight walked past her in the corridor, already prepared to go.

She followed him, tugging on her vest to ensure it was secured. Her gun was holstered and she was ready to take Stroud down. And when they reached the lobby, Nick seemed ready to do the same. She feared what he might do, given his state of mind. Once he got something in his head, no one could convince him otherwise; not her and not Dwight. But she couldn't think about that right now. Her priority was to save Matthew Grimes and she hoped it wasn't too late because if it was, there was no telling what would happen.

"We're leaving." Nick checked his weapon and secured it again before walking through the door.

He hopped into the driver's seat of one of McKinnon's patrol cars and Kate had a rare opportunity to sit next to him. She looked back at Dwight in the rear seat with inquiring eyes.

He nodded.

It seemed he might have wanted her there to keep Nick in check. She doubted she had that sort of sway over him.

Nick started the car and roared out of the parking lot, heading toward Stroud's location. "Who's the officer in charge on scene?"

Kate retrieved her cell phone and made the call. "Jackson. I'll touch base now." She got him on the line. "We're on our way.

Is your team set?" A silence ensued while she waited for a reply. "Good. Hold your position until we arrive. The boy's alone with Stroud. We need to take every precaution." She ended the call. "They're setting up a perimeter around the home. They're on foot so as not to alert Stroud to their arrival and have eyes inside the living room, but haven't placed the boy yet."

"Okay."

She watched as he kept his eyes glued to the road, never glancing at her or Dwight. This was a very bad sign. "Nick, I know what you're feeling right now and I know what you want to do."

He shot an abrupt glance at her. "I'm not going to do anything stupid. And I'm sure as hell not going to let you do anything stupid either. Not with six months left on your probation."

She turned to Dwight for confirmation he was telling the truth, but it seemed neither was quite sure.

"With Baltimore PD in place, how do you want to approach this?" Dwight asked.

"Stroud's going to know we're there. I'm sure the kid told him he called 911 and so he's going to be on the lookout. What I don't know is what he plans on doing with him. Keep him as a hostage or shoot him to make a point."

"That'd be a suicide mission," Dwight replied.

"He may have no intentions of going back to prison," Kate began. "I think we make our presence known and get him to start negotiating."

"We'd have to have something to offer him and there's no chance the DA will offer him any sort of deal. Not after the bodies he's left in his wake. I refuse to accept Colton Talbot's killer will get life in prison instead of the death penalty on account of the DA allowing him to strike a deal to save someone else's kid."

There it was. Kate knew what he wanted to do. While she wanted nothing more than to see Stroud dead, unless it was self-defense, Nick would lose everything if he was the one to pull the trigger.

He'd been so concerned about her probation that he didn't seem to consider his own shaky status since receiving the Letter of Censure. Campbell wouldn't abide by another episode of questionable field behavior from his top resident agent.

"This is the street." Nick killed the lights on the vehicle and made the turn. He coasted along, slowing as they approached. Two houses down, Nick pulled to a stop and cut the engine. He radioed Jackson. "We're on scene."

Kate spotted Officer Jackson emerge from the neighboring home and make his approach. He made his way toward Nick's side and leaned in through the open window. "What now, Boss? I've got three men in position. Front and sides. No one in the rear. We gonna do this or what?"

"Has Stroud made an appearance? Peeked through the window? Anything?"

"No, and from what we can tell, there seems to be very little movement inside."

"Are we sure he's still there?" Kate asked.

"It's possible he got out ahead of us, but we're on standby until we get the word."

Nick began to open the door. "You go around back. We'll stand at the front and announce ourselves. I'm not going to be busting down any doors and forcing Stroud into panic mode."

They came out of the vehicle and Nick drew his weapon. "Let's do this."

Jackson pressed on his earpiece. "Standby." He ran ahead and toward the back of the house.

The others had weapons drawn and quickly made their way toward the Grimes' front door. Dwight and Kate flanked Nick as they stepped onto the porch, at the ready.

Nick leaned in, trying to listen for voices inside. He turned to Dwight and shook his head. "FBI. Open up."

They had their guns pointed at the door, ready to fire, but no one opened it.

"FBI. Lyle Stroud, we know you're in there. We've got half a dozen officers out here waiting for you. It's over. Don't make things worse for yourself."

Kate's nerves stood on end as footsteps approached. She couldn't be sure, but it sounded like more than one person. That would mean they weren't too late.

The handle turned and the door began to creak open just an inch.

"Looks like you finally found me. Took you long enough. Now take care because I have a gun to this boy's head and I know you don't want him to get hurt." He continued to open the door until he revealed himself and Matthew Grimes. "I did have to disarm him, so apologies for his appearance."

The boy's stomach had been slashed and blood seeped through his torn t-shirt.

"Don't worry, though, it's not a deep cut. He's one tough little dude. Came at me with a knife."

"Please, help me." Matthew's voice was small and childlike.

"Drop your weapon, Stroud. There's no getting away this time." Nick raised his gun to the man's forehead.

Stroud began to step back, dragging the boy along with him. "Well, at least I got to have a bit of fun with him." He kissed Matthew's cheek.

Nick pushed inside and released the safety on his gun, heading straight for Stroud.

"I don't think you want to get any closer than that, agent. I got bullets in here. You want me to prove it?"

"Scarborough, hold back." Dwight moved in next to him. "Put your weapon down and let the boy go. You know what'll happen if you don't."

"You gonna shoot me? You think I give a shit about that? Let's see, what are my options here?" Stroud looked at the boy again. "Rid the world of this little shit, or let him live and go back to prison until they execute me, which will be at least ten years."

"Put your gun down!" Kate aimed her weapon at his heart.

"Oh, you gonna chime in now, missy?" He studied her for a moment. "Aren't you a pretty one?" He turned to Nick. "Must be hard for you to concentrate at work with a partner like her. Damn." He leered at Kate again. "Bet you're a real wildcat in the sack."

"Let the boy go or I'll shoot you myself." Kate released the safety of her own weapon.

"Stand down, agent." Nick appeared at the end of his rope. "This is your last chance, Stroud. Drop your weapon and let the boy go. I won't ask again."

Officer Jackson came up from behind Stroud through the rear entrance and caught the eyes of the agents in front and knew what he had to do. Before Stroud could react, he'd grabbed hold of his arm and yanked it back, pulling it away from the boy.

"Matthew, move!" Kate lowered her weapon, ready to pull the boy away. She reached for him and managed to step back from the chaos that had erupted.

Jackson struggled to take Stroud's weapon. Nick rushed in to help and while Stroud's head was turned in defense of the officer's advance, he smashed his weapon against the man's skull. Stroud collapsed to the ground and fell unconscious.

Jackson regained his balance. "Thanks, man." He pressed again on his earpiece. "Stand down. We got him."

Matthew clung onto Kate's shoulders, trembling and drenched in tears.

"You're okay, hon." She squeezed him back. "It's over now. You're safe. We need to get you to a hospital, okay?" She gently pushed him back to look into his eyes, tried to calm him, and briefly examined the wound on his stomach. "Where are your parents, Matthew? We need to find them."

"They're at some work thing my dad had. I didn't have time to call them, just 911."

"You did the right thing. Come on now, we'll get you taken care of. You did good." She kissed his forehead.

Jackson kicked Stroud in the gut. "Get up, asshole."

He moaned as he came to again and looked up at the men who hovered over him. A bloody smile spread on his lips.

Nick turned away from him. "Let's throw him in the car and get him the hell out of here."

23

The captain waited for them to haul Stroud in when they returned to the station and he took the man into custody. He would be transported back to Fairfax County first thing in the morning.

Kate was exhausted and none of them had slept in almost forty-eight hours. It had been decided that a few hours of rest were needed before the sun came up.

They'd traveled together to the nearest hotel, and this time, Dwight was staying in the same room as Nick. It was a decision he initially rejected, but reluctantly agreed to, figuring they had a right to insist.

As they reached their floor and the elevator doors parted, Nick stopped in the hall. "I'd like to have a quick word with Kate if that's all right. I'll meet you in the room in a few."

Dwight subtly regarded Kate and she nodded her approval. "Okay." He headed down the corridor alone.

"You mind if we talk?"

"Not at all." Kate led the way in the opposite direction and just a few doors down from the elevator was her room. She retrieved her keycard and opened the door. "Come in." Her stomach jumped into her throat and she tried hard to swallow it down as he walked past her and dropped to the edge of the bed. This was going to be a conversation two days in the making and the time had come to have it out.

"You haven't said anything about—earlier—and I just wanted to thank you for that." He looked up at her with eyebrows slightly raised in a request for leniency for his behavior. "What I said..."

Kate sat down next to him. "You were drunk. You blamed yourself for Colton's death. Nick, I know you weren't yourself." She wanted to let him off the hook. Whether or not he meant what he said didn't matter because she wouldn't—couldn't let that happen. He was her closest friend and the two had been through hell together, but she couldn't let herself fall into another relationship with a man who had been a mentor. She was hardened now, not discounting what her relationship with Marshall had stemmed from, and she wasn't that person any longer. Walls had been built from the rubble of the tragedies she'd already suffered and it was doubtful she could ever love anyone the way she loved Marshall. Even her current relationship was quelled by comparison.

"We have Stroud and we saved Matthews Grimes. You can let this one go now."

"Kate, it's more than that." He considered her with earnest. "I've let myself feel things that someone in my position shouldn't feel. I've been too involved in this investigation and I overlooked the total picture, focusing on the one thing that mattered to me."

"You're not..."

"No, wait. I don't just mean that. I won't put you in that position again. I won't jeopardize all we've both worked so hard to achieve. It doesn't matter what I feel or how much this damn job gets to me." He paused to study her again. "You have a brilliant career ahead of you and I'm not the only one who sees that. Campbell sees that, he just doesn't like to admit it."

They both smiled.

His words, although indirect, pointed to the elephant in the room and both were reluctant to articulate the truth of his feelings. Whether real or emotionally tied to his state of mind, neither seemed quite sure. Kate opted to believe the latter. She knew he did too.

"I just wanted to say that I'm sorry if I caused you any confusion or made you question your purpose here in any way. That wasn't my intent and I was most definitely not myself. I appreciate that you recognize that."

"We're a team; the three of us. And I'm concerned about you because it seemed like it used to be so easy for you."

"Easy?"

She nodded. "Easy for you not to let your personal feelings play a role in your job. But things seemed to change after I got here; after Quantico."

"I suppose they did."

Why did you and Georgia break up?" she asked.

"You know why."

"Yeah, but that was a symptom, though, wasn't it?"

"Maybe." He turned away from her. Perhaps so she

wouldn't see the truth in his eyes. "I guess we didn't love each other as much as we thought we did."

"I just want us to be okay, Nick. I finally feel like my life is whole again. I have a great job and amazing friends. I wouldn't want to do anything to jeopardize that. Like you said, we've worked so hard to get here."

"Yes, we have. I just need to find my bearings again and I will." He reached for her hand. "Forgive me, Kate."

"There's nothing to forgive."

"I'd better get back. Dwight's going to wonder what we're doing in here." He pushed off the bed. "Goodnight."

She followed him to the door and locked it behind him. Kate closed her eyes, and a stray tear trailed along her cheek. The idea that she might have hurt him was painful in its own right, but it would be too hard to leave him. She loved him, even if it wasn't in a way that he might want right now. And, given time, his feelings would change. His heart was broken by what Georgia did and now from this. In time, he would heal and all of this would be forgotten.

Nick opened the door to his room to find Dwight sitting up in bed, waiting for him as though he were his father.

"Everything all right?"

"Fine. Didn't mean for you to stay up, Dad." Nick dropped his trousers and slung them over the chair next to his double bed. Once his shirt was off, he slid under the covers. "You should get some sleep."

But when Dwight didn't turn off the light, Nick rolled over to face him. "What?"

"Maybe you should take a break from this."

"What do you mean?"

"Kate and I can handle the rest. We've done it before."

"Without me, you mean. You've done it before—without me."

"I'm just saying that I think this investigation has thrown you for a loop. And nobody blames you, man. I mean, this was your friend's son, for Christ's sake."

"Why don't you say what you really mean, Dwight? This is about finding me drunk off my ass the other night."

"I'm worried about you. It just seems like when shit starts to go south, you run for a drink."

"What the hell are you talking about? I've always had a few drinks and it never bothered you before."

"You're right. But you've been different for a while—worse, I guess. Ever since..."

"Ever since Georgia left?" Nick tossed his legs over the bed and sat up. "You sure you're not just angling for a promotion? I mean you're due, right? You want my job, Dwight?"

"Goddammit, Nick, no, okay? I don't want your fucking job. Something's changed in you, man, and it scares me, all right?"

"Why don't you just spit it out, then? Tell me what this is really about."

Dwight's face appeared as though ready to lambaste his boss, the Senior Special Agent. But instead, his shoulders dropped and he resigned himself. "I just want you to get over whatever the hell this is so we don't fuck up anymore and let people like Lyle Stroud slip out from beneath us." He switched off the light and turned away.

Nick sat on the edge of the bed in the dark, wanting to fight back, but he had no argument. There was no excuse for how this investigation lagged behind. He was the man in charge; had insisted upon it, and Dwight called him out. He could do nothing but accept the frank criticism. Nick quietly crawled back under the covers and didn't utter a word.

Stroud stood in the middle of his cell, showered, clean-shaven, and appearing to be anything but the monster he was.

"Time to go home. Move closer and turn around with your hands behind your back." Officer Jackson approached the cell with handcuffs ready.

With a smile that revealed near-perfect teeth thanks to a great prison dental plan, Stroud complied with the orders and turned his back, placing his hands through the iron bars.

The officer secured the cuffs on his wrists and tightened them enough to make Stroud wince. "You must be looking forward to seeing some of your old buddies again." He tugged on the cuffs for good measure.

Once they were locked in place, Stroud turned to face Jackson. "Doesn't matter much to me. I did what I came to do."

"Murder some children?" The officer's lips curled with anger. "You won't last long in there."

Stroud smiled as Jackson led him out through the rear entrance where a helicopter waited to transport him.

Nick stood outside next to the chopper, the early morning

rays reflecting off his sunglasses, obscuring the lethal stare of his eyes that was aimed directly at Stroud. He stood firm with his arms folded and legs shoulder-width apart. His partners were already inside, but both had their sights glued on their colleague.

"Good morning, Agent Scarborough. I'm doing fine, thanks for asking. Still have a little headache though." He lowered his head to be sure Nick could see the wound he'd left. "I'm sure they'll patch me up when I get back. Just hope you don't get into any trouble for this."

"Just get in." Nick grabbed his arm and turned to Jackson. "Thank you. I got it from here. Everything signed?"

"Yes, sir. He's all yours." Jackson slapped Stroud firmly on the back.

Nick got Stroud inside and secured him to his seat. He sat opposite the other agents, leaving one seat next to his and that was where Nick would be.

With the door shut, the chopper fired up and readied for departure. The pilots looked toward the rear and Nick nodded that they were ready.

Kate stared at Stroud with steely eyes as though she herself might launch toward him and save everyone the trouble.

"You trying to scare me, little lady?" Stroud asked. "Or is it that you're just attracted to me and can't keep your eyes averted? Why don't you come on over and give me a little treat?" He pushed his hips toward her.

Nick hurled his elbow and landed it square against Stroud's chest, knocking the wind out of him. "Shut the fuck up, or I'll throw you out of this God damn helicopter."

When Stroud regained his breath, he turned to Nick. "Did I

hit a sore spot, agent?" He coughed again. "Didn't realize she was your girl. My bad."

"I read your file," Kate began with an inexorable stare. "Those boys must've fucked you up pretty good." She watched as Stroud's face turned dark. He wasn't going to get away with trying to intimidate her. "Is that why you did it?"

"Did what, agent?"

Kate smiled. "What a weak, pathetic man you are. They're going to have all kinds of fun with you after you're locked up again. You won't be asking for a treat then. Oh no. You'll be the one giving them." She refused to let go of his gaze. "Might've been better for you to take a bullet rather than face what comes next."

Nick regarded her with what appeared to be admiration. "Did she hit a sore spot?" He nudged Stroud and grinned at Kate.

Word had already reached the media before they returned to the Fairfax precinct with the man in question. Lyle Stroud's prison mugshot was showing up on news feeds across America with the headline "Ex-con and child predator-turned killer, captured!" A few reporters waited for their arrival to catch a glimpse of the man who'd murdered two children along with members of his own family and held two others captive.

The chopper landed in the back parking lot to avoid the growing chaos.

Once the pilot shut it down, Nick opened the door. "Let's get him inside."

Kate stepped out first while Dwight helped to unshackle Stroud from the seat and the two carefully lowered him to the ground.

"Nice one, Agent Reid," Dwight said as they both stepped away from the helicopter.

"How do I look, agent?" Stroud turned his cheek toward Dwight. "Got the press waiting to see me and I want to be sure I look good. Mind you, the injury might raise a few questions about your technique.

"You look like a God damn peach; don't you worry about it." Dwight yanked on his arm as they made their way toward the station entrance.

Stroud looked over his shoulder at Kate, leering again, attempting to rattle her. But she refused to allow him to elicit a reaction. Instead, she attended to Nick, whose expression revealed no relief at their accomplishment.

"I know you wanted this to end differently, but that's not who you are, Nick."

He stopped cold and square in front of her. "I know exactly who I am and what I'm capable of. My judgment was clouded and now this man won't get what he deserves."

She dropped the conversation and they entered the building only steps behind Dwight and Lyle Stroud, who was about to be tossed into an interrogation room to wait for a court-appointed lawyer. And so it would begin, the grueling task of juries and trials and convictions, and he would go back to prison to live out his life while the children whose lives he took would never get real justice.

As they entered the corridor, Kate spotted Jake Talbot. "I thought he went home."

"He must've heard the news. I'd better nip this in the bud." Nick picked up his stride to get out in front of Dwight and the man who killed Jake's son. "Jake." He wrapped his arm around his friend's shoulder and ushered him away. "What are you doing here? You should go home, man. You don't want to be here right now."

"Is that him? The man who killed my son?" His cheeks flushed with a rising anger. "Why didn't you kill that son of a bitch when you had the chance?"

Nick felt Jake's body tremble and saw his fists clench. In only seconds, Lyle Stroud would cross Jake's path, steps away, but easily within eyeshot of him. He would have to restrain him because he already felt Jake pushing back, waiting for the moment to lunge. "Come on, buddy. Come outside with me for a minute."

"No. I want to look him in the eyes."

"It won't do any good. He doesn't care about what he did."

"Then I'll make him care." Jake wrestled away from Nick and pushed toward Stroud. He reached beneath his shirt.

Nick's eyes widened when he saw what was in Jake's hand. "No!" He ran toward them.

Dwight's head spun toward Nick as he cried out, still maintaining his grip on Stroud.

"You killed my son!" Jake plunged a knife into Stroud's gut and stared him down.

Stroud's face masked in shock as he looked down at the knife sticking out of him. His knees buckled and he fell to the floor.

Jake lost his balance fell on top of him and began pummeling his face. "You killed my boy!"

Nick spotted several officers drawing their weapons. "Stop! Don't shoot!" He stood over Jake and pulled him up with his hands still swinging. "Goddammit, Jake!"

"Son of a bitch!" Dwight began to drag Stroud out from beneath the man who would see him dead.

Nick managed to pull him off and yanked him backward, dragging his heels on the ground.

The grief-stricken man sobbed while Nick sat him down on a nearby bench toward the lobby entrance. Flashes of light flooded the room from the media outside, who had to have seen the commotion.

"We need an ambulance now!" Dwight knelt over Stroud, who'd begun to spill blood from his mouth. The knife was lodged at an upward angle from the middle of his abdomen to near the sternum. Dwight wrapped his hand around the handle of the knife.

"Wait! Don't pull it." Kate squatted next to him. "He'll bleed out. Ambulance is on the way. We'll have to keep him calm." She looked around for a jacket or sweater or something to put under his head. A nearby chair with a sweater hung over the back would do. "Here." She rolled it up. "Let's get this underneath his head."

Stroud began to cough and appeared to struggle to breathe.

"Jesus. He's not going to make it." Dwight peered over the desks to eye Nick and Jake, ensuring the man wouldn't make another run for it. Although most of the officers standing around were palming their holstered guns.

Nick viewed Detective Mason's approach and tightened his grip on Jake's arm. He was already shaking his head at her as if to imply she couldn't do what he knew she was going to do.

"Jake, I'm afraid you're going to have to come with me. I'm so sorry." She retrieved a set of cuffs.

"Wait. Just hang on a minute." Nick knew the law and knew there was no other way but was trying to buy them some time. "Christ, Jake. I can't help you now." Nick's eyes glistened as he tried to comprehend what the hell had just happened.

Mason lifted his arm to help get him to his feet and turned him around, wrapping his arms behind his back. "I'm so very sorry." Her eyes revealed regret as she looked at Nick.

Jake held Nick's gaze. "Tell Rachel I took care of him."

They heard the approaching ambulance sirens and Mason began, "I hope to God that bastard lives."

Several officers were assisting Dwight and Kate to stabilize Stroud, but he was going downhill fast.

"I hear the ambulance. We need to keep him alive." Kate knew the stakes. They all did and so helping this monster to live was the only choice.

Stroud's eyes met with Kate's and he managed to find the strength to raise his lips into a faint smile, as though this was the best possible revenge he could ask for.

At that moment, all she wanted to do was push the knife deeper into his gut and watch the light fade from his eyes. This man deserved to die for what he did, but that would mean Jake Talbot would spend the rest of his life in prison. And a family that had already suffered would suffer yet again.

Another burst of chaos erupted when the EMTs rushed through the entrance. Shouts from reporters sounded in the distance as they made their way inside.

"Over there!" Nick rose from the bench, taking his eyes away from Mason and leading his friend toward the booking area. "He's over there." He followed the paramedics and for the first time, saw the damage that Jake had done.

Stroud was a robust man, but now his gut swelled as though he was a six-month pregnant woman.

"He's bleeding internally." One of the EMTs squatted. "Please step back."

Dwight and Kate moved away to allow the men to do their jobs.

"Sir? Sir, can you hear me?" He flashed a penlight into his eyes.

The other began taking his vitals. "Radial pulse is weak. We need to get him into the truck." He reached for the backboard and the two began to carefully slide it beneath Stroud. "Watch the knife."

They stood up to lift him and haul him outside.

"Will he survive?" Nick followed them out while they carried him to the ambulance with reporters beginning to swarm around them.

"We'll do our best, sir." The EMT closed the door after his co-worker jumped in to begin working on Stroud. He climbed into the driver's seat and pulled away, lights blazing and sirens sounding.

Nick watched them leave as the reporters, who'd grown in numbers, began to throw questions at him. He could only stand there in shock.

Dwight rushed out and came to the rescue, taking hold of Nick's arm. "A statement will be made shortly," he said to the press while pulling his friend back inside.

Mason approached them as they walked through the lobby toward Kate. "We're processing him. He'll need to stay until we can get him in front of a judge to request a bond. He's refusing to make a call to his wife. You want me to handle that?"

"No. I'll call her."

"You sure, man? I can make the call," Dwight said.

"It has to be me. I have to be the one to tell her that her husband is going to jail for attempted murder."

"I think the DA will opt for the lesser felony assault charge. And I doubt there's a jury on this planet who would convict him." Mason seemed to want to comfort him, but that was an impossible task right now.

"I hope you're right, detective. They better keep that son of a bitch alive." Dwight looked on through to the crowd outside. "Where's the chief? We should make a statement before those guys get out of hand."

"I'll go get him." Mason turned to leave.

Nick rubbed his eyes as he stared at the phone, finger, ready to press the green call button. "Dammit, Jake," he whispered before glancing at Dwight again. "I should've done it. I should've killed him when I had the chance, just like Jake said."

"That's not how this works. None of us knew he had a weapon. None of us thought he was capable of doing it."

"We're all capable. It just depends on how desperate we are." Nick finally pressed the button and turned away.

Dwight took his cue to leave him to make a call he wouldn't wish upon his worst enemy and began to make his way toward Kate again.

She held the sweater in her hand and began to place it on a nearby chair. "I doubt she'll want to wear that again." She cast a glance at Nick. "How's he doing?"

"Not good. We're going to have to stick to him like glue today—and tonight."

"Are we heading back to the office?"

Dwight checked the time. "We'd better so we can start getting the paperwork in the system. I'll call Campbell. I'm sure he already knows what happened."

"I doubt he knows the worst of it."

"Maybe not. Listen, the chief's going to make a statement. I'll stand by him. Nick shouldn't be in front of the cameras right now. Why don't you stick close to him until we're through and then we'll head out?"

"Okay." Kate rested her hand on Dwight's shoulder. "I sure as hell didn't expect things to go this way."

"None of us did." Dwight continued toward the chief's office.

Kate was left alone to try to comfort a man who was already on the brink and no doubt would take the blame for this too. On her approach, he remained with his back turned, still on the phone. She stepped back and waited, overhearing some of the conversation.

"You can't blame yourself, Rachel. Jake was fueled by rage and I should've been the one to stop him; get him to see reason." He paused. "We won't know until I get the call from the hospital."

Kate continued to listen.

"You want me to come by?" He pushed his hand through his hair, a nervous tick that seemed to worsen recently. "Okay, then. It's probably best if you and Scott stay with your parents for a few days. But just know that Lyle Stroud won't hurt anyone else ever again."

Kate closed her eyes and her heart broke at the sound of his trembling voice, on the verge of a meltdown.

"I'll let you know his condition as soon as I hear, I promise. I'll talk to you soon, Rachel." He ended the call and turned to see Kate. "She blames herself. Can you believe that? Says she knew where he was going and didn't try to stop him." He covered his eyes with his hand, trying to shield their growing redness from her view.

Kate moved closer and reached for his hand, gently pulling it away from his face. "This isn't anyone's fault. Not yours and not Jake's. Certainly not his wife's either. Lyle Stroud will survive and justice will be served. If anything, Jake won't serve for long. And it's something you need to remember to tell yourself."

Nick inhaled a deep breath and rubbed his hair again. "We need to get the hell out of here and back to WFO. Where's Dwight?"

"He and the chief are getting ready to make a statement."

"I should..."

Kate stopped him. "Let him do this."

"Yeah—okay."

Within minutes, Dwight walked past the two of them and nodded before heading outside with the chief to face the swelling masses. Lights came on, brightening the already day-lit skies, and shined on the two men who stood at the ready.

The chief began. "At 10:00 yesterday evening, the fugitive, Lyle Stroud, was captured inside the home of an intended victim in the suburbs of Baltimore. The FBI assisted Baltimore PD officers as well as our own, in the tracking down and capturing of this man who, as you know, was wanted in connection with the deaths of several others in the past few weeks."

A reporter shouted, "Is it true he was targeting kids he'd found online?"

"Sir, if you'll let me finish, please. As you may already know, Stroud was brought here at approximately 7:30 this morning where he was subsequently attacked and is now in critical condition at the hospital."

"Will he live?" another reporter shouted. "Who attacked him?"

Dwight stepped beside the chief. "We are not releasing any details of the assault at this time." He nodded to the chief.

"A very bad man is off the streets and is no longer a threat to this community or any other. Further information will be made available as we receive it. Thank you." The chief turned to Dwight. "I appreciate you standing by me. These guys can get pretty brutal sometimes."

"Like sharks after chum." Dwight smiled.

When the agents arrived back at the WFO, the elevator doors parted and revealed an empty office, dark and quiet.

"Guess no one else works on a Saturday," Dwight joked.

Agent Vasquez emerged from the hall. "You're back. Good."

"What are you still doing here?" Kate asked as she approached.

"I wanted to come in and tell you guys that you did a great job last night. And I know it wasn't easy."

"You played a big part in this too, so thank you for your help." Kate smiled. "I assume Campbell's gone?"

"Nope. He's in his office, waiting for you guys."

"Guess we'd better get back there," Dwight replied and started down the corridor.

They arrived at Campbell's office. His door was open and he sat behind his desk, looking more tired than they did.

He glanced away from his monitor. "Welcome back. Come on in. Take a seat. I'm sorry about what happened this morning, Scarborough."

"Me too, sir."

"For what it's worth, your efforts didn't go unnoticed. I got a call shortly after Stroud was apprehended. Lasseter has had nothing but good things to say about you and your team, SSA Scarborough. As the field coordinator for NCAVC, I expect he'll authorize any expenditure you might need."

"Thank you, sir. I'll be sure and reach out to him later and give him a full briefing," Nick replied.

"You don't seem pleased by the news."

"I'm sorry. The team did do an incredible job and is worthy of the praise. But you'll have to forgive me. I have more pressing issues."

"Of course, I understand. And to that end, I'm sure you're all exhausted. I know I am and I've only been sitting at my desk, fielding calls." Campbell began to rise. "You should all go home and get some rest. The paperwork can wait until Monday. Give yourselves some time to recoup." He moved from behind his desk and patted Nick on the shoulder. "Good work."

"Goodbye, sir," Kate said as he walked past them. She turned to the others. "So, we'll get started?" They weren't going to go home, not yet. Things needed to be done and no matter what the boss said, he wasn't the one to have to do it.

Several hours passed and it was approaching the evening. Kate walked to Nick's office and noticed he was still buried in files. "Hey. You mind if I head out of here?"

He looked up from his desk and laced his fingers behind his head. "No. In fact, we should all get out of here. I think I've had enough of these bullshit reports."

"Good. I'll see if Dwight wants to head out too, then." But before she could leave, he appeared behind her.

"What's that?"

"You ready to take off?"

"I think so, yeah." He turned his attention to Nick. "Why don't we hang out at your place? Sit on the boat for a while with subs and beer and then I can crash with you tonight?"

"I know what you're thinking, but I'll be fine. I appreciate you wanting to look out for me. Both of you." Nick's cell phone began to ring. "I won't do anything stupid." He answered the call. "Scarborough." He was silent and eventually raised his eyes toward his colleagues. "Thank you for letting me know." Nick ended the call and stared at his phone.

"What is it?" Dwight asked.

"Stroud's dead. Died about twenty minutes ago."

"Oh, God."

24

A **chill fell** upon Kate's shoulders as this new reality took hold. Stroud was dead and she could have wished for nothing better than for that man to die. But what it would do to the Talbots would be devastating.

"I need to go back to the station and talk to Jake." Nick's face turned pale as he spoke.

"Not yet. Let the man hold on to some hope for a while longer," Dwight replied. "This can wait until morning."

"He's right, Nick. You're in no state to see him and he deserves a few hours of respite."

"Respite from what, Kate?" He looked up toward the ceiling. "Maybe you're right. Maybe it's best to destroy his world after he's had a chance to think about what he's done for a while longer."

"That's not what I mean. I just think you need some time to process this. We all do. Gain some perspective and figure out a way to help him. Detective Mason was right about one thing, getting a conviction from a jury on something like this? It'll be damn near impossible."

"Why don't I come over and hang out with you?" Dwight said. "You don't need to be alone right now."

A brief nod from Nick and it was settled. The three headed toward the elevator and Kate looked back.

"You coming, Vasquez?"

"Right behind you."

The parking garage was nearly empty, lights above sporadically shining on the oil-stained concrete below. Their footsteps echoed as they continued along the third level where their staff was assigned to park.

Kate's old Nissan was parked three spaces down from Nick's giant Lexus SUV and Dwight parked his Infinity next to her. Vasquez drove a mid-size Honda sedan and it quickly became obvious the hierarchy of the team.

"You'll keep an eye on him?" Kate asked.

"I will." Dwight turned his attention to Nick, who'd approached his car. "He'll be better after some rest."

"Okay. Call me if you need anything." Kate pressed the keyless entry remote and the lights on her car flashed, and a faint beep sounded. "I'll see you guys later." She slid inside and started the engine.

Kate arrived home and the sun was already low in the sky. The day was almost over and her eyes were heavy. She noted a few missed calls and texts from Mike. He was obviously concerned about her safety and she opted to text him back. But she was much too tired to speak to him.

I'm home and safe. Exhausted. Talk tomorrow. She pressed the send button and headed straight for her bedroom. She secured her weapon and shed the clothes she'd been wearing for the past three days, opting for a t-shirt, and crawled under her covers at six o'clock in the evening.

With eyes closed, her mind repeated the events of the day. So much had happened so quickly and it was hard to believe it was finally over. The hardest part was always remembering the ones they couldn't save. Colton Talbot, Emily Aldrich, and even Stroud's grandmother and sister. It was understandable why Nick had begun to feel defeated like he simply had nothing left to give. His exponential decline in recent months was probably due to the many personal blows he'd suffered and it would be up to her and Dwight to help him through this because Kate simply couldn't imagine doing this job without Nick by her side. He'd groomed her. He'd supported her and she needed him.

The question still hung in the air, though. Would it completely alter their relationship or would he really be able to move beyond it as he said? She believed he was merely longing for a relationship to succeed. Nick had never been married or even engaged. And Georgia seemed to have been the closest person to putting all of that within his reach. She betrayed him and now he was looking for a substitute. Yes, that made sense. Kate was the only other woman in his life and so he projected his feelings onto her.

This was what she needed to convince herself of because anything else would mean she would have to hurt him. And, she had Mike—a man for whom she cared greatly.

It was too much to think of right now. She inhaled a deep breath and released it to bring calm to her wandering thoughts.

"This is a sofa bed if you're okay with that." Nick began to toss away the cushions and move the coffee table and grabbed hold of the bed frame, yanking it out. "It's not much, but I don't often get house guests, unless it's the female kind, and they end up in my bed anyway." Nick smiled half-heartedly at his poor attempt at humor.

"Well, I'm glad to see your wit hasn't abandoned you." Dwight approached him. "Let me give you a hand. And yeah, this is fine."

They'd spent the evening on the boat but used the time to decompress and watch whatever weekend sport was on the television. It was something they both needed, but the time had come to address the real problem, at least, as far as Dwight was concerned.

"I'll put some fresh towels in the bathroom. I think we both could use a shower in the morning." Nick headed down the hallway and opened the linen closet door, retrieving a fluffy towel that the maid had placed inside. He walked into the hall bathroom and set it on the edge of the counter, next to the sink. He caught sight of his appearance, something that seemed to have escaped him for the past forty-eight hours. They were right to be worried about him. He did look like hell. Scruffy, blackened circles under his eyes.

The future was uncertain now. He'd planned out so many

things and each time, they seemed to fall apart. A dear friend was about to face prosecution for a murder that anyone else in his shoes would have committed. A woman whom he had the utmost respect for now likely questioned his motives and, by default, their friendship. There was no question in his mind that all of this was of his own doing. Even Jake. He should've been prepared. He should've known the man would be unstable. Who wouldn't be?

"Nick, you okay in there?" Dwight's voice carried down the hall.

"Fine." He made his way back to the living room. "Okay. Is there anything you need? Water or food or a drink?" He raised his hand. "I'm kidding about the drink, don't worry."

"I've been wanting to ask you something," Dwight began. "You want to sit outside for a minute? I guess I wouldn't mind some water before signing off."

"Sure. Go on out. I'll get the water."

A moment later, Nick stepped through the opened sliding glass door to find Dwight with his feet up on the lounger and arms folded across his thick but solid stomach.

"Here you go." Nick handed him the water and sat down on the lounger next to him. "What's on your mind?" He opened up his own bottle and downed half of it in one go.

"The other night—when you were..."

"Drunk?"

"Yeah... Did something happen between you and Kate? When I got back to the room with your coffee, she looked like a deer in headlights. Did you two have words or something?"

Nick turned his sights to the bay and watched his boat bobbing in the water. "No, nothing like that."

"Then what? Nick, come on. It's me. What's going on with you two?"

"I just felt bad for dragging you guys down with me and I apologized to her, that's all. I might've gotten a little emotional about it, but it was just the booze talking. I don't think she'd ever seen me that upset before."

Dwight continued to examine him for signs of untruths. Finally, after what felt like a much too-long silence, he started, "Well, we're both worried about you and now with what's going to happen to Jake, we're concerned about you turning to something that won't do you or anyone else any good."

"I know that, man, and I appreciate it. I do. I'm just going through some shit right now. A come to Jesus situation, if you will."

"Okay. If you're sure that's all it is. I mean, it's a big deal, I know, but I just need to be sure our team is going to stick together. With Kate coming off probation soon and this thing she's got going on with Burgess, well, I guess it seems like it wouldn't take much for us to implode, you know? And I'd hate for that to happen. I've come to think of you two as family."

Nick smiled. "Thanks, man. Same here. I just need to get my head out of my ass and straighten out. I will, though, I promise." He turned again to the bay one last time. "We'd better get some sleep."

Kate appeared from around the corner, towel drying her hair and wearing a long T-shirt. She still hadn't gotten used to the blonde and would make it a priority to get to her stylist soon to return to her natural brunette unless she was looking to put a shock into Mike when he came up next weekend.

The time was coming up on 5:30 and she would need to leave soon to make it to WFO by 6:30. It was Sunday, but they wouldn't be taking a day off, not after capturing Stroud. After a quick check of the news, she switched on the TV. Her jaw dropped as she read the headline beneath the picture of Lyle Stroud. "Child killer dead."

"Oh shit. Oh shit. How the hell?" She knew how reporters worked and how they wouldn't stop until they got their story. And so they did. Broadcasting all over the state and Rachel Talbot was probably watching. "Damn it!" Kate picked up her cell. "Nick, it's me. Did you see the news?"

"Yes. I'm heading out the door now. I'm going straight to Jake's house. Dwight's going into the office."

"I can meet you over there." She waited for a reply, but none came. "Nick, let me go there with you, okay? You're going to need backup. You're too close to this and perspective is what Rachel needs right now."

He seemed to consider her proposal. "Fine. I'll text you the address. See you in a few."

Kate tossed her phone to the couch and returned to the bathroom to quickly dry her hair and get the hell over to Rachel Talbot's. This news was supposed to come via Nick or Detective Mason, not the goddam press. She was going to be devastated.

Minutes later, Kate locked up and hopped in her car, speeding out of the driveway and heading to the address Nick sent her. Her phone rang and the caller ID showed that it was Mike.

"Hey, hon."

"It's not too early, is it? I really wanted to hear your voice and make sure you were hanging in there."

"I'm already out the door, actually, but, I'm fine. Really. I'm heading over to Rachel Talbot's place. The media released the news of Stroud's death and she's probably beside herself right now. Nick and I are meeting over there to help her through this."

"Oh jeez. I'm sorry to hear that. When it rains it pours, doesn't it?"

"Yeah. How about I call you when I'm heading back to the office? You going in today?"

"Just for a while. Call me on my cell when you can. Bye, Kate."

"Bye." Kate continued along the highway and was maybe twenty minutes from the Talbot home. She hoped Nick wouldn't beat her there, but that was unlikely. He'd left before she did.

On her arrival, she spotted Nick's SUV in the Talbot driveway. She parked along the front of the house and quickly made her way to the door. She raised her hand to knock but heard elevated voices inside. Well, one raised voice and it was undeniably that of Rachel Talbot. She knocked loudly and waited.

Seconds later, the door opened to reveal Rachel's swollen eyes and tear-stained cheeks.

"Mrs. Talbot? I'm Agent Reid. I work with Nick Scarborough. Is he inside?"

Rachel moved away, holding the door open for Kate but not saying a word.

Kate entered the home, peering around the corner to the

right, and there he was, looking as though he'd been punished by the headmistress at a boarding school for boys. "Agent Scarborough?"

He acknowledged her arrival.

Kate entered the room, waiting for Rachel's return. "Mrs. Talbot, I can't imagine what you must be feeling right now..."

"No, you can't, Agent Reid, so any words you have to offer will fall on deaf ears, I assure you. And Nick over there, he promised to keep me informed as to what was going on with that monster and he couldn't even do that much. So forgive me if I don't have much faith in you or the FBI right now."

"Mrs. Talbot, this news was not to be released until later today at the assurance of the District Attorney."

"Well, that didn't work out now, did it?"

"Reid, just stop," Nick interjected. "Rachel has every right to be angry. We didn't —I didn't do my job. Stroud should have never made it out of that boy's house alive. Rachel's just calling me out for my mistake."

"Mrs. Talbot, we are confident the DA will not charge Jake with murder. And even if he did, no judge or jury would convict him. That's what we've been discussing." Kate turned briefly to Nick. "We will do everything in our power to get Jake back home to you and your son."

"And what about my dead son? What about Colton? They won't even release his body to me so I can put him to rest."

"We'll work on that too; I swear to you. This isn't over. Agent Scarborough, Agent Jameson, and I will find a resolution to this."

Nick stood up and walked toward Rachel. He was inches from her, looking into her eyes and finally wrapping his arms around her shoulders. "Rachel, I'm so sorry this has happened. We'll do all we can to minimize the damage this will do to Jake. You have to believe me. He's my friend. You're my friend."

Rachel began to sob with her head buried against his chest. She raised her forearms and made fists and began to pound against him. Not to cause him pain, but to release hers.

"Do you have anyone who can stay with you today? At least until we can get Jake out on bond?" Kate asked. "For his sake, you should stay here with your son."

Rachel pulled away and wiped her tears. "You think they'll still let him out on bail?"

"That's what we're going to work toward."

"My mother is here. She's upstairs with Scott."

"Good. We should get down to the station and make sure we're there to hear Jake's official charges. We'll meet with him and his attorney to discuss what the options are."

"I will call you when I know something, Rachel," Nick replied. "But if we're going to act, then it has to be now."

"Okay." She walked toward the front door. "Please, let me know as soon as you find out anything. I'm counting on you, Nick."

Kate began to walk toward her car and Nick followed.

"We need to get him out of there, Kate. I have no idea what Mason's planning on doing or the D.A. This isn't our area of expertise."

"I know, but we'll figure out something. We can't let Stroud harm this family anymore than he already has." She unlocked her car.

Nick jumped into his SUV and pressed the call button. "We're going to head down to the station to see Detective

Mason. You want to meet us there?" He was silent while it sounded as though Dwight was typing away, probably dealing with the mounds of paperwork that accompanied multiple jurisdictional cases.

"I'll hang back. Between coordinating with Baltimore PD and gathering the statements, I'm going to be at this all day. You two go. Sort this thing out and get Jake Talbot back home where he belongs."

25

Apparently, the reporters hadn't taken the night off and were now in even greater numbers as they huddled outside of the station. The agents arrived via the rear entrance and made their way through the building to find Detective Mason waiting in the lobby along with the district attorney. She turned her attention to them as they approached.

"Good morning."

An unusual expression on her face caught Kate's eye. It was as though she already knew something and they weren't going to like it.

"I don't know how good it is," Nick said. "I suppose that depends on how this discussion turns out." He offered his hand to the D.A. "I'm Special Agent Scarborough."

"Agent Reid." Kate greeted the middle-aged, tall,and slender man with a firm handshake.

"Pleasure to meet you both. I'm District Attorney Robert Olmstead. Shall we get started?" He turned to the detective.

"Yes. Follow me." Mason led the way to the conference room that had been used as the makeshift command center only a day ago. She closed the door. "Please, have a seat."

"First of all, Agent Scarborough, the work you and your team did, including Detective Mason's team, was above exemplary. You saved that boy's life."

"Thank you, Mr. Olmstead, but I'd like to just jump right in. A dear friend of mine is facing serious charges. Not to mention that he lost his youngest son at the hands of Lyle Stroud."

"Of course." Olmstead turned to Mason. "Has Mr. Talbot spoken with his attorney yet?"

"No. He's due in at ten a.m., after our meeting here. I'm hoping to be able to offer him a deal and I believe the agents would like to ensure the same."

"Our office is willing to work something out. None of us want to see this man who has already suffered so much serve out a murder sentence for taking the life of a wanted child serial killer."

"Then what do you propose?" Scarborough asked.

"If acceptable to Mr. Talbot and his attorney, our plan is to offer him the lesser charge of voluntary manslaughter."

"What kind of sentence are we looking at?" Kate asked.

"The circumstances here would merit leniency by a judge and jury. Sentences range from one to ten years, however, in this case, they would have the discretion to impose a sentence of less than one year. They might also impose the Class 5 felony fine of $2,500, but I highly doubt that."

"So he could serve less than a year in prison?" Nick asked. "What about getting his records sealed so he wouldn't have to worry about future employment?"

"I'm afraid Virginia wouldn't allow that under these circumstances. And in fact, it is rarely allowed and only if the person was wrongfully convicted." Olmstead appeared to study each of them. "This is the best-case scenario for Mr. Talbot."

Nick turned to Mason. "Can I see him before his attorney arrives?"

"We can't discuss this with him until his lawyer is present. You understand?"

"Got it. I just need to see him."

Mason stood up. "Okay then. Mr. Olmstead, are we finished here?"

"I think so. I just wanted to let the FBI know where we stand on things. I've got a few things to do before the meeting with Mr. Talbot. Is there an office I can use in the meantime?"

"Certainly. I'll point you in the right direction." She turned to Nick. "Agent Scarborough, if you'll follow me, I'll take you back there."

"Would you like to see him, Kate?" Nick asked.

"No, actually. I think I'll wait for you out here."

"Okay. I won't be long." He followed Mason out of the room.

Kate remained in the conference room while the D.A. and the others got on with business. She wasn't sure exactly why she didn't want to see Jake Talbot. Maybe she felt it was best to let Nick deal with his friend alone. He didn't need her to be there and in fact, it might just make it awkward for Jake to express his feelings. And she could only imagine they were overwhelming for him right now anyway. In truth, Kate had felt the need to offer support to Nick, but he seemed to be handling things just fine. He always did when people were looking.

She was pleased that Nick seemed relieved by the D.A.'s offer. Although it wouldn't be as slam-dunk as she expected. The problem now was whether would Jake be allowed bail or would he be required to remain in jail until his trial? That could take months. Then again, it would be counted as time-served. But she'd wanted him to have a chance to be with his family right now. Rachel would be forced to come to terms with the death of her son all on her own. And Kate wouldn't wish that on anyone, for it was something she'd sentenced herself to some time ago.

The time had passed quickly and Nick returned to the conference room. "You ready to go?"

Kate was brought back into the moment. "That's it? What happened?"

"I told him about Stroud. He was understandably upset, but —and I know I wasn't supposed to mention this—I told him what we discussed with the D.A. and he seemed relieved."

"Why wouldn't you be allowed to tell him?" Kate stood up and began to gather her things.

"Because his lawyer wasn't there to 'advise him.'" Nick's use of air quotes was rare. "You know how all this legal bullshit goes."

"That I do." She walked toward him. "Better get back to the office and give Dwight a hand."

"Actually, you go on ahead. I need a minute to speak with the detective."

Kate felt that there had been something between the two of

them and his wanting to hang back seemed to prove it. Maybe it was just her, but the way Mason responded to Nick was that of a woman who'd slept with him. She'd seen it before. "Sure. I'll see you later."

Kate walked outside and stopped for a moment. She turned back and noticed that Detective Mason was standing in the lobby now with Nick and he had his hand on her arm. She observed the two of them and recognized the look in Mason's eyes. "I was right." Kate smiled and continued toward her car.

Mike stood on the front porch with flowers in hand shaded beneath a blazing mid-day sun and knocked on the door. Kate answered with mild surprise. "Wow, thank you." She took them from his hand and stepped aside. "Come in. I've been looking forward to this all week. I'll go put these in some water."

Mike removed his weekender bag and tossed it on the couch. "How's Jake Talbot doing?"

"Considering the circumstances, pretty well, I guess. He was arraigned on Monday and entered a plea of No Contest. According to the D.A., he'll remain on house arrest until his trial."

"Wow. That's pretty lenient, considering the crime." Mike walked into the kitchen where Kate was placing the flowers in a vase. "I don't think I've ever heard of that for a murder charge."

"It's voluntary manslaughter and both the judge and prosecutor have no desire to provoke a negative public response from this. Jake killed a murderer and a molester who should never have been released from prison to begin with. No one wants to keep a man like that behind bars until his trial."

He opened the refrigerator and grabbed a couple of beers. "I suppose the political ramifications of that alone are worth avoiding." He opened them up and handed one to Kate as she turned away from the sink.

"Thanks. These flowers are beautiful. You're very thoughtful." She reached around his neck and kissed his lips.

"I'm glad this case is over, though. I was really missing you."

"Me too. Let's go sit down." She took hold of his hand and led him to the sofa.

"Listen, now that this is over and you've had a few days to get back to normal, I was hoping we could finish our conversation we had last week. You know, the whole moving house thing?"

She hadn't thought about it much if she was being honest. Lives had been at stake and her closest friend was suffering, so it hadn't seemed a priority. But she didn't want to dismiss his feelings. He deserved to know where they were headed. Even if it hadn't been on her agenda for tonight and certainly not within minutes of his arrival.

"Well, you know, my lease will be up soon and of course, I'll be off probation in the coming months, so I'm feeling pretty confident that I'll be staying at WFO for a while."

Mike nodded.

"I guess the real question is, would you be happy living here, in D.C?"

"I told you before that I have no problems moving here. I can get work; I'm not worried about that. I mean, I'm kinda well known now, thanks to the Blackwater case. So, I've proven I can work with the big boys."

"Oh, you mean like me?" She laughed.

"Yeah. Just like you." He reached for her hand. "I know we haven't been together that long, but I knew from the moment I met you. The moment I saw you standing on the slippery banks of that river, drenched from the rain and still trying to find clues. I knew then I wanted to be with you. That you were someone special."

He was laying it on pretty thick and doing a good job of buttering her up. Kate adored the attention. It was so very welcome. And he would understand when she had to work late or didn't come home at all because of a case.

But moving from this house and buying something, presumably with him, meant a level of commitment she wasn't sure she was ready for. She looked at the picture of her and Marshall that still sat on the side table and wondered if he was bothered by it. Bothered by the constant reminder that there had been a man in her life who had meant everything to her. And there was still the one thing she'd never mentioned to him before. The thing she'd never mentioned to anyone, except Marshall. And if she was going to make him move up here, then he had a right to know what his future would hold.

"You're very special to me too, Mike." A deep breath preceded the words she needed to get out. "But you need to know something about me."

"Whatever it is, it won't change how I feel about you."

"Just wait, because this is important. We talked about how I came to know Nick and about my former life in San Diego."

"And about what happened; yes, we did."

"Well, there's one thing I left out and it was only because it's incredibly personal for me and it isn't easy to talk about."

"I'm listening."

"Mike, when I was abducted by Hendrickson the first time when I was six, he did assault me."

He nodded and his lips tightened as though pained.

"And the result of that. Well, let me start by telling you that I was pregnant several months before Marshall died. But I lost the baby."

"Oh God. I'm so sorry."

"The reason I lost the baby was because I suffered irreparable damage as a result of that assault. I never knew because I'd always been on birth control and never even tried to get pregnant. But accidents happen as they say, and well, I got pregnant. And I was happy and Marshall was happy.

"But then, very early on, the pregnancy had to be terminated. It was ectopic as a result of the damage suffered during the assault." She paused. "I guess what I'm trying to say is that, according to the doctors, it's highly unlikely I'll be able to get pregnant, at least via the old-fashioned way."

"Okay. I'm not seeing a problem here. I mean, and this would obviously be down the road if we were to consider a child, but there are fertility specialists who offer services for things like this, right?"

"There are, yes. But there are no guarantees and it's incredibly expensive."

"Kate, I appreciate how hard it must have been for you to come to terms with this, honestly. But, for me, it's a non-starter. I want you. And if down the road we want a child, we'll find a way to have one." He caught her gaze for a moment. "Any other excuses you can think of?"

Kate smiled.

"I'm only joking. I know that wasn't easy for you to tell me and I appreciate you wanting to be sure that *I'm* sure about this. I am, though, Kate. I really am and I hope you are too."

He appeared so hopeful, eyes bright with a future he envisioned with her. It could be good. Hell, it could be great. "Well then, I guess we should start looking for a place."

Mike's eyes lit up even more and his smile nearly blinded her. He pulled her close. "I can't tell you how happy I am to hear you say that." He leaned back but was still inches from her face. "I know I can make you happy."

A tender kiss followed and Kate was happy. She'd leaped at an opportunity that she never believed would come again. The time had come to finally put away the ring and although she no longer wore it around her neck, it was always in her bedside table. Now it would be returned to the box that contained a few remaining mementos of a time long since passed.

The two rose from the sofa and began to walk toward the bedroom. Mike closed the door with his hand above her head as she stood against it. He leaned into her and pressed his lips against hers once again, only this time with more vigor.

Kate wanted to let the moment sweep her away and so she tried hard to keep the thoughts from forming. The ones that so often seeded doubt and fear of what might happen should she let her heart belong to another again.

He took her to the bed and laid her down. His love for her was unmistakable and perhaps in that moment had grown even stronger as they now would face a future together. But the memories came back regardless of how hard she tried to stop them. However, they were different this time. They were not of a former life with her one great love. They were of a time when a confession arose that Kate had not imagined. And the one behind that confession, whose eyes now burned in her mind, was forefront of this new dilemma.

He was a man she knew well and yet a man she didn't know at all. A man who led a secret life of personal demons and heavy drink. Yet this was also a man whose support she needed.

And as Kate peered into the eyes of the man with her now, his loving and passionate eyes devoured hers as he unbuttoned her shirt. This man was her future and the other? He couldn't decide her fate. She couldn't let him.

Kate would resolve herself to the idea that Nick had no true feelings of that kind for her and that it had all been a rebound from a woman he did truly love. Because if it were any different, that could mean the end of their friendship. And she wasn't going to let that happen either.

26

Saturday morning and Kate still felt like it was Friday night. Sleep came in fits and waves and when she did sleep, dreams of a future with Mike and a new house and all that came along with that overwhelmed her. Now it was six a.m. and she stared at the ceiling as the sun's light filtered through the curtains in her bedroom. She turned toward Mike, who was still sound asleep, and decided to get up because lying here any longer would make her crazy.

Her feet swung gently from the bed and rested on the floor, which had grown warmer in recent days. She no longer felt the need to wear slippers. With tired legs, she made her way into the hall and toward the kitchen to make a pot of coffee. Although slightly cooler in this part of the house, which didn't have many east-facing windows, she still felt comfortable in her t-shirt and shorts as she reached for the Folgers.

Kate stared at the pot as it brewed, thinking about where they would live and if they would buy a house together. It seemed like a huge step after only six months. But what was the point of renting another house? She might as well stay here if that was the case. She could tell, though, that Mike wanted a fresh start. A place that would be a clean slate for both of them. And why not?

After the final beep, signaling the pot was ready, Kate poured herself a cup. Cream and sugar as always. She sat at the small breakfast table in the haze of the morning glow. This time was always looming just around the corner and so to have to make this decision was inevitable. Kind of like the decision to get rid of her old Nissan and get something newer.

The problem was that there had already been so many things in her life that she'd given up, most of which were involuntary. And this sort of felt the same, although she knew Mike would understand if she changed her mind. He was insisting she take a step in a direction she knew she should take, but it was like a child learning to ride a bike for the first time. Scared shitless, but forced to pedal on their own when their parents let go. That was how Kate felt now.

The decision to move to Virginia had been an easy one because she wanted to leave behind a painful past. She wanted to run away. And now she was here and happy and this time, she didn't want to run.

Kate heard Mike's footsteps pad along the hall.

"Good morning. You're up early." He leaned in to kiss her cheek and then headed toward the kitchen for coffee.

"Morning. I had a hard time sleeping and thought I'd just get up."

"I figured that was the case." He held his mug and joined her at the table. "You're having second thoughts."

"No—that's not it." It was. "I just feel like it's taken a long time for me to feel settled again."

"And now I want you to change things up." He put the mug to his lips. "I'll tell you what, I think I know that you'd feel better making this decision after discussing it with your best friend."

"Who's that?"

"Nick. I know how close you two are and it doesn't bother me. Everyone needs a good friend, Kate, and while I hope one day you'll consider me your best friend, I am a realistic person. You've known him for a long time. He's helped you through a lot of pain. I wouldn't dare disrespect that friendship by being jealous of it."

Kate smiled at him, knowing he was a good man. "I don't need Nick's approval." She didn't, but the idea of a final confirmation that he was, in fact, hiding nothing from her—maybe it was what she needed to make an ultimate decision. She was a strong woman and this idea seemed to go against that belief, but it just might release her of the uncertainty she felt. She began to feel irritated with Nick, wishing he'd never said anything at all.

"Just go talk to him. You'll feel better. And hey, I know the guy likes me so, I'm thinking he'll give you the thumbs up." Mike set his cup down. "I'll tell you what. I've got a little bit of work that I could take care of. I brought my laptop. How about I get that out of the way while you take some time to yourself to see Nick or just to be alone; either way is fine by me. Then, when you come back, we can decide which way to go."

Kate furrowed her brow in amazement. "You'd really be okay with that?"

"Of course I would. It's a beautiful day. I'll set up outside on the front porch, soak up a bit of sun, and get a few things in order on my end. Later, we'll go out for lunch or do whatever you'd like to do. Does that sound okay?"

"It sounds perfect. Just like you." Kate rose from her chair and kissed his coffee-stained lips. "Thank you."

SHE DIDN'T CALL or text him. Instead, Kate showed up in the lobby, certain he would be home, praying he wouldn't be hung over. She pressed the intercom buzzer to his apartment. His voice sounded a moment later.

"Yes?"

"Nick, it's Kate. Can I come up?"

Another buzz sounded and Kate heard the latch on the door release. She moved quickly to get inside. *Well, at least he's awake,* she thought, making her way onto the elevator. The doors parted on the 7th floor and Kate stepped into the hall and headed left toward his apartment. She admired the beauty of the building. Even in the corridors, it offered stunning, almost panoramic views of the bay. She could see Nick's boat off in the distance and wondered if they'd get a chance to get out on it this summer. He rarely took it out, mostly because there never seemed to be any time.

She raised her hand to knock, but he opened the door before she had a chance. "Morning, or is it afternoon yet?" She glanced at her wrist, though she wasn't wearing a watch.

"Still morning, I think." Nick stepped aside. "Come in. I'm surprised to see you. Isn't Mike in town?"

"Yes, but he's got some work to catch up on, so I thought I'd stop by." Kate turned as she entered the living room. "You don't mind, do you? Did I catch you at a bad time?"

"No. Not at all. Can I get you something to drink? Coffee or water; soda?"

"I'm fine, thanks."

Nick joined her in the living room. "Have a seat." He sat down on the chair next to her. "So what's this about?"

"Now that this case is over and we can catch our breaths again, Mike and I discussed getting a place together."

"In Florida?" His expression revealed surprise, or maybe it was horror.

"No. No. Here, but just getting out of the rental and into something more suitable for both of us."

"I see. That's a big step."

"I know." Her face screwed up as if experiencing mild discomfort.

"So what's the problem? How can I help?"

Kate observed his body language and he appeared very closed off; almost standoffish. His words were abrupt, bordering on curt. He was pushing her away right before her eyes. And therein lay the problem.

"Listen, now that you've had a few days to get through some of the bullshit we've been dealing with and what you've gone through with your friend, I wanted to ask you...what you said before..."

He stopped her dead in her tracks. "I told you, I was drunk and in a bad way, you know that. I didn't mean anything by it and the last thing I'd ever want is for you to feel uncomfortable around me." His tone suddenly softened.

Kate studied his eyes. Nick had never lied to her. He'd

always been upfront about everything so why would he lie now? He was good at hiding his feelings; very good. But after all that she'd been through, no way would he lie to her. "So, you'd be okay if Mike and I moved forward with our relationship?"

"Why wouldn't I be, Kate? I want you to be happy. Your happiness is all I've ever wanted."

"What about your happiness, Nick? We've known each other for a long time. Georgia made you happy, I could see that. But you don't look happy anymore."

"Like I told you before, I should've been able to save Colton and I didn't. Now his father is facing at least a year in prison for killing a man who the state would have spent ten years feeding and clothing before they eventually did the same thing. Spending tens of thousands on appeals. Frankly, Jake did this state a favor."

He was deflecting.

"You've been through a lot this past year. You had to fight for your job a while back, you broke up with your girlfriend, and now this. I suppose that would make anyone unhappy. But somehow, knowing who you are and what you're capable of handling, forgive me, but I think there could be more. And I can't move forward with certainty unless I know if there is."

Nick rose from the chair. "So you're putting this on me? Your decision to move in with Mike somehow boils down to me?" He walked toward the kitchen and opened the fridge to retrieve a bottle of water.

"This isn't on you and that's not what I mean." She stood up and joined him as he remained in the kitchen. "There've been times when I've wondered why you've helped me so much. Getting into the academy, getting through the academy, even being assigned to WFO. All of those things happened because of you."

"That's not true. You passed the training, not me." He tossed back a gulp of water.

"I suppose I did, but you certainly aided in that effort."

"I've helped you because I felt responsible."

"Responsible for what?"

"Marshall."

"What are you talking about? Edward Shalot was responsible for Marshall's death. And that had nothing to do with you. Look, I'm the one who called you, remember? When all of that started? How could you possibly take the blame for that?"

"Because I should've convinced you in the beginning. The very beginning as we drove to the Davies' home to return the necklace. I asked you then, but I didn't push."

"I remember. I wasn't ready then, you know that. I loved Marshall and making that sort of change so soon after all that I'd been through. It just wasn't even a remote possibility that I could've handled then."

"And after he died," Nick began. "I convinced you to start fresh. To come here and work with me. And you did."

"And it was the best decision I could've made. I've started fresh and that has everything to do with you. You had the faith in me and it made me believe in myself."

She turned away, unprepared to have this conversation. Years had passed and neither had really ever talked about how they came to be here, in this moment. Kate walked toward the balcony and stared through the glass doors at the calm waters of the bay. With her back still turned, she continued, "Even if you had convinced me then, I would've had to leave Marshall."

"And he'd still be alive," Nick said.

Kate lowered her head and closed her eyes. "Now you see? You aren't the one to blame for what happened to Marshall." She turned to face him again. "I am."

Nick moved quickly toward her and embraced her with his whole body. And for the first time in many months, she cried for Marshall.

"I'm sorry. I didn't think—none of this was supposed to happen this way, Kate. And now I feel lost." He released his hold. "I used to know exactly where I was going, what I wanted to accomplish, and just exactly how to accomplish it. But these past few years, since you've been such an important part of my life, it's thrown me."

Kate wiped her eyes. "Why? How? You've always been such a strong leader and mentor to me. You've helped me to find that—gift, as you like to call it. You don't seem thrown to me."

"That's because I work incredibly hard at not showing it. I thought I'd shielded it from Georgia too, but she saw through me."

"What do you mean?" They stood inches apart, but Kate pushed back, fearing another revelation.

Nick must've felt her trepidation and moved away in response. "When we were in Florida, toward the end before the Durham standoff, Georgia and I had a fight."

"I remember something happened."

"She said some things that, at the time, I refused to believe. But afterward, on further reflection, I'd come to realize she was right. And that was the reason she did what she did."

"You mean cheat on you? She did that of her own volition and there's no way in hell I'll let you take the blame for that."

"That's not what I mean exactly. I know that was her decision and hers alone. What I mean to say is that she asked when I would realize that I..." He trailed off and closed his eyes.

"What? Nick, what is it, please? I have to know." And she did. Making a decision like this, to move in with Mike when she thought that Nick... well, that he might have feelings for her. She wasn't sure why, but she knew it would change things.

"I can't, Kate." He moved further away. "I just can't."

"Why?"

He turned back. "Because I know that I'm the only one and I don't want to hear you say it."

Kate's eyes welled as she turned away for a moment. He admitted it without saying the words. "I can't let myself go through what I went through with Marshall, Nick. You of all people know how much I loved him and how much I relied on him. To the extent that I started to feel encapsulated. I feel like a terrible person just admitting that to you now. But before he died, I'd begun to feel stifled beneath his wing. And it wasn't his fault—not really. I allowed myself to do that. It's the one thing I've never admitted to anyone—ever, until now."

"You think I would ever stop you from doing anything you wanted? Have I ever given you that impression?"

"No, you haven't. But I can't risk even the remote possibility. And I can't risk that kind of heartbreak again. I won't survive it."

"Do you have feelings for me, Kate?" He stepped closer to her again. His eyes, haunting in their expression.

She looked away. "I don't know—I don't think I'm capable of those kinds of feelings anymore."

"So what about Mike? Do you love him?"

"In the only way that I can love any man, I think; yes, I do."

His eyes finally revealed his surrender. "Then you should take that next step with him."

Kate turned back. "You think he and I should move in together?"

"I think you should do what makes you happy. I would never put you in a position to feel anything but happiness, Kate."

A sudden wave of relief passed through her. "What about us? Are we going to be okay? I don't want this to change our friendship. I need your friendship, Nick, I swear I do."

"I would never abandon you. I will always be here whenever you need me. Please believe that."

Kate smiled. "I do. I believe you." She moved closer and wrapped her arms around him. "Thank you." She kissed his cheek.

Releasing from the embrace, Kate stepped away. "I'd better get going." She reached for her purse. "You'll be okay?"

"Me? I'll be fine. I'll see you on Monday."

"See you on Monday." Kate walked out, ignoring that he'd tried so hard to hide the truth. She finally learned how to read him and her heart sank.

Nick locked the door and turned toward the empty living room. His face was pained, his eyes resembled that of a wounded animal. For a split second, he felt euphoric, waiting for her to reveal her feelings for him, but in the end, she couldn't. And he understood, but it hurt just the same. He gave her his blessing to move forward with Mike Burgess, deputy cop from a hick town in Florida. Soon to be working for Metro police, he suspected. And she would be lost to him forever.

Perhaps that was the way it needed to be. After all, look at what it had done to his relationship with Georgia. One of the best profilers in the BAU and she'd transferred offices because of their split. He couldn't bear it if something like that happened with Kate. And so, at least he could still be friends with her.

Friends, he thought. Nick smiled and walked toward the kitchen and grabbed a bottle of Jack Daniels.

KATE OPENED the front door and noticed Mike sitting at the kitchen table, laptop open and a few files spread out in front of him. "I'm back."

"Just in time. I'm finishing up now, then I'm all yours." He shut the lid of his laptop. "It was a little too warm outside. So, did everything go all right?"

Kate sat down next to him. "I had a good talk. Got a lot of things off my chest about this case, about, well about a lot of things."

"Good. I'm glad to hear that."

She could see the apprehension in his eyes, waiting for that shoe to drop he was sure she held behind her back. Kate reached for his hand as it rested on the table. "Mike, I don't think we should move in together."

There it was. His face dropped and his chest appeared to raise higher with each breath more rapid than the last. "Okay. Care to elaborate?"

"I'm just not ready. I tried to be, I really did, and I'm so very sorry to hurt you this way. It wasn't what I wanted."

His eyes turned cold. "You and Nick must've had quite the conversation."

"This has nothing to do with him. I woke up feeling this way and I just came to terms with some things that I'd kept hidden from myself. That's all. I should never have agreed in the first place and for that, I am truly sorry."

"So you just want to keep things the way they are right now? Just seeing each other on the odd weekend and having a little fun?"

"I realize that wouldn't be fair to you, Mike. You've been so good to me. So understanding and so kind."

"I feel a 'but' coming on."

"But I can't ask you to wait because I don't know how long that wait will be before I'm ready."

"You're breaking up with me? If you need time, Kate, I can give you time. I'm sorry I brought this up at all. I should've respected what you've been through and I pushed you. I'm the one who's sorry."

"Stop. Please."

"Do you have a thing for Nick? Please, be honest with me. You owe me that much. Is that what's brought all this on?"

Kate didn't know how to answer. Were there feelings in there somewhere? Buried deep where she kept all her true feelings, in a place where no one could expose them or use them against her? "It's complicated."

Mike revealed a closed-lip, tight smile. "Well, that says it all." He stood up to gather his things.

"What are you doing?"

"Leaving; what else?"

"You don't have to go now. Your flight's not until tomorrow."

"I think staying here would just add salt to the wound, don't you?" He walked toward the bedroom.

Kate sat at the table, confused as a fresh uncertainty about her future reared its ugly head. This wasn't what she wanted. She did care for Mike a great deal, but it had become obvious he wanted much more than she could give. And perhaps there was more to it than that. But that was something she wasn't ready to address; now or even in the future.

Mike returned with his bag over his shoulder. "I'll catch an earlier flight." He grabbed his laptop bag. "I kind of wish I hadn't sent you off this morning. Things might've been different."

Kate stood up and opened her mouth.

"I'm just kidding. This would've happened sooner or later. I guess I should be grateful it happened before I quit my job." He walked toward the door.

"Wait." Kate caught up with him. "I do care for you and I'm so sorry things turned out this way." She kissed his lips but felt nothing from him in return.

"Goodbye, Kate. You take care of yourself now." Mike opened the door and walked out.

Kate watched him get into the car and drive away. She closed the door and peered around the room. "What the hell am I supposed to do now?"

THE END

ABOUT THE AUTHOR

Robin Mahle has published more than 30 crime fiction novels, many, of which, topped the Amazon charts in the US, Canada, and the UK. And most recently, she has delved into the world of psychological thrillers.

Also a screenwriter, she has adapted some of her works into teleplays, which have gone on to place in film festivals nationwide.

From detectives to federal agents, and from killers to corruption, her page-turning tales grab hold and refuse to let go. Throw in tense action and thrilling twists, and it becomes clear why her readers come back for more.

Robin lives in Coastal Virginia with her husband and two children.

If you enjoyed Ms. Mahle's work, please share your experience by leaving a review on Amazon

ALSO BY ROBIN MAHLE

The Kate Reid FBI Thriller Series (17 books)

The Chef (stand-alone psych thriller)

The Man in My Attic (stand-alone psych thriller)

The Compound (standalone psych thriller)

The Remy Fontaine Fugitive Hunter Thrillers (4 books)

The Det. Rebecca Ellis Thrillers (5 books)

The Allison Hart PI Thrillers (5 Books)

The Lacy Merrick Thrillers (4 books)

**Visit robinmahle.com to join Robin's newsletter and stay up to date on all her latest releases, contests and much more!

www.ingramcontent.com/pod-product-compliance
Lightning Source LLC
Chambersburg PA
CBHW060531180626
46817CB00002B/522

* 9 7 8 0 9 9 6 6 8 3 0 3 6 *